SUN TRAP

'Intense and immersive. Reeled me in
and kept me hooked till the bitter end.'

ROBERT RUTHERFORD

'Perfect for balmy summer days
and chilling by the pool. Great escapist fun.'

SAM HOLLAND

'You will literally not know who to believe.
A page-turner from opening scene to showdown.'

JO FURNISS

'Wolf transports us into the mysterious and compelling
lives of Hollywood's stars where nothing is as it seems...
A high-octane dice with death that I could not put down!'

HEATHER CRITCHLOW

'A glamorous, gripping tale of sun, sand
and deadly sabotage.'

S.E. LYNES

'I devoured this! Insanely gripping, hard recommend.'

ANGELA CLARKE

'A delicious joy to read...
the shock of the reveal was just gasp-worthy.'

ALSO BY RACHEL WOLF

Five Nights

SUN TRAP

RACHEL WOLF

HEAD
of ZEUS

An Aries Book

First published in the UK in 2025 by Head of Zeus,
part of Bloomsbury Publishing Plc

9 7 5 3 1 2 4 6 8

A catalogue record for this book is available from the British Library.

ISBN (PB): 9781035913725
ISBN (E): 9781035913718

Cover design: Jessie Price | Head of Zeus

Typeset by Siliconchips Services Ltd UK

Printed and bound in Great Britain by
CPI Group (UK) Ltd, Croydon, CR0 4YY

Bloomsbury Publishing Plc
50 Bedford Square, London, WC1B 3DP, UK
Bloomsbury Publishing Ireland Limited,
29 Earlsfort Terrace, Dublin 2, D02 AY28, Ireland

HEAD OF ZEUS LTD
5–8 Hardwick Street
London, EC1R 4RG

To find out more about our authors and books
visit www.headofzeus.com

For product safety related questions contact productsafety@bloomsbury.com

For Emily

Prologue

The sand has turned everything orange. I blink but it doesn't shift. It's like the world has been coated with paint. It's in my mouth, my eyes. I force myself to concentrate on breathing. The air feels coarse and rough.

I half look back at him, but I can't...

He's dead. He must be dead.

Banging on the horn of the dune buggy again, I scream, 'Help! We're still here!'

They all left hours ago. And my phone is dead.

The wind howls like an animal. What kind of creatures haunt the desert at night? Snakes? I hate snakes. But that only matters if the storm slows, and it doesn't sound like it's going to any time soon. Buried alive in sand. Is that how it all stops?

All those dreams – big screens, movie premieres, big-dollar roles.

Does it all end in the desert, miles from anyone?

It's been three days since I got on the plane.

Four since I agreed to come.

It's cold now. All the heat has been sucked up. I'm sweating, but I shiver. Night arrives quickly here. From everything I've learnt about this place, this is hopeless.

But I can't give up.

'Help!' I bang again. I don't turn around and look at him.

All I've done, trying to save him. All in vain.

SUNDAY

DAY ONE

New York

1

The first time Phoebe suggests the swap I dismiss it out of hand. I don't even realise she means it. I laugh. Then I see her expression.

'Please, Ellie,' she says, her voice cracking a little. 'We'll swap places. You be me. I'll be you. It's the obvious answer. To what we both want.' She pauses. 'Well, what I need. I just can't...'

She doesn't finish. She picks up her drink – it's a minimum two-drink rule to sit at the table and we front loaded. She finishes it in one swallow and picks up the second.

The laughter around us is loud but I tune it out. She can't mean it? It's like someone's giving me a gift but chopping off their own arm to pass it over. The glow from the stage is bright and we're caught in the periphery of the halo. It's as close to the warmth of a New York stage as I've ever been. It's all I've ever wanted.

She wants me to take her role? Actual lines in a major Hollywood movie, directed by Freddie Asquith-Smith. I stare at her as the pull of the suggestion builds in strength. But no, the role is surely sealed. There's no way I could step in at this point. I don't even have an American accent.

Phoebe's caught in something. She looks like she's falling off a cliff.

'I love this table! These twins are here for it!' the comedian says, gesturing at us as Phoebe knocks back the second drink and the sweaty room roars; I wait a beat for the attention to shift away from us. The mention of twins often gets a second look. But we're not even related.

The first time I met Phoebe it was like looking in the mirror – almost. Enough to stop me in my tracks. They say everyone has a doppelganger. You never expect to meet yours. But here we are.

'Phoebe, you can't walk away from this role. That's the craziest thing I've ever heard!' I say, keeping my face neutral, but my tone is anything but. Something's going on with her. She's my friend, and I want to help her. She's been unwell for a few days and it's making her spiral. She's caught in some kind of rip tide. I need to stop her going under.

It's hard to speak to her at the table – I don't want to attract any more attention. We'll be kicked out if we talk through the show. Phoebe must be desperate to have raised this now. We're in a comedy club in Chelsea, New York. Front row and centre. Not the place to discuss life-changing plans.

Felix had given us two free tickets last minute, as he couldn't make it – the date of a lifetime had presented itself, he said. Felix has been the other part of our trio this summer. It's been just over four weeks since we met on the course, but I can't imagine my life without either of them now. My best friends.

What a summer it's been.

But Phoebe hasn't been the same this week. She's gone from the sunny, optimistic doppelganger I met four weeks ago to someone likely to fall down in a fit of tears, without any warning.

I'd discounted all the myths about doppelgangers when we'd met: ghostly, evil, demonic. But maybe there was some kind of bad luck that came with them after all. Felix had declared one night, soon after we'd all met, that one of us must be the evil twin. He'd gone as far as to pull me aside, promise me he'd keep an eye on Phoebe. But now it's her who's crumbling.

She'd be throwing away a life-changing job by doing this, swapping places with me. It's impossible to consider – but impossible not to think about, just for a second. Acting is all I've ever wanted to do.

'More drinks?' The waitress appears on our right and I nod. 'Same again.'

We both need them. Phoebe's falling apart, and I'm trying to put her back together. Trying not to get excited about this role of a lifetime that she's offering up.

I look at the stage. A woman in dungarees is killing it. She cracks a joke about teaching her kids the modern ABC. The crowd is laughing, full belly laughs. I catch the end of B, and she says, 'And C is for Consent. Say it with mommy.'

I laugh, and look at Phoebe; she smiles weakly.

The drinks arrive and we finish those and order more. By the time the last act is on stage the room has softened to a place without edges and we're so drunk the sting has gone out of the conversation. The question's forgotten. I hug Phoebe during the applause.

'Best night ever!'

'Yes,' she says, and whatever had set her off earlier seems forgotten. 'Ellie, *you* are the best! I can't believe how lucky I got when I met you!'

'BFFs,' I say, and we link arms as we stumble out into the hot, dark night of the New York streets. A grate smokes nearby and a rat runs across the pavement as we approach the Flatiron building. Someone sends a wolf whistle our way from a passing car, and despite it being close to midnight, the lights from the city are bright and I'm not ready to go to bed.

A tuk tuk passes us, singing about a New York State of Mind, and I remind myself I'm really here: The Big Apple, the city that never sleeps. So good they named it twice.

'Let's get more drinks!' I say, and I pull Phoebe to me as I wobble on my new shoes. She smells of the expensive perfume we'd spritzed ourselves with from the samples in Saks this afternoon, of deodorant, of the fancy dark ginger shampoo she'd promised her brother she wouldn't touch, and yet we'd both almost finished. She smells of tequila, of the moisturiser I'd loaned her, of sweat from the club, of this intense summer heat. She smells like the best four weeks of my life. Here. Now. It's due to end tomorrow and I can't face it. My heart literally breaks in two. A dagger, right through me.

'Tonight's on me,' I say, feeling like I could fly, as we head into the reception of a fancy hotel and we duck through a blue velvet curtain to a small cocktail bar with panelled walls and rude waiters, smartly dressed.

'We can't afford this!' she whispers and, already drunk, I stumble again and swallow a laugh as I grab her arm.

She starts giggling and I can't help it; my stomach cramps with the effort of not losing it and luckily the music in the bar turns up a notch otherwise we'd be in danger of being thrown out before we sit down.

The air-con is on high and we're dressed for the steamy streets. I shiver. Goosebumps rise up on my arms and legs. We're wearing almost identical dresses we'd picked up in a thrift store that afternoon. Hers is pale blue with mini daisies; mine is yellow. They're short and strappy, and we wear wedge heels from Target. What we don't own we imitate – four weeks of an acting class for out-of-work actors at a top New York school. It's a course you dream to get on. I still can't believe I made it – that I'm really here.

I sit up, feigning money and class. I glance around, checking out the bar and say, 'Top drawer,' in my best Upper East Side drawl.

Phoebe explodes in laughter, choking on the water the waiter had put down before us.

'Whadda you two, like twins or something?' A slurring man in a suit leans over. There are four of them at the table and I feel their eyes on my legs, on my chest. I'm not the most covered up.

C is for Consent, fuckers, I think, as Phoebe says, 'We're not looking for any attention.'

'Well you two got the genes. I mean, you are both—'

'Cut it out, Jack,' the friend to his left snaps. 'You're drunk and they've asked to be left alone.'

I look the friend up and down. Dark hair, expensive suit. *C is for Cute*, but I turn away from him. Tonight isn't about men. It's about us.

The four-week acting class is something I'd gone out on a limb to do. I'd arrived planning to stay at the nearest YHA after registering. I'd gone to the school straight from the plane. But I'd met Phoebe on the first day as we'd filled in forms, and she'd offered me the sofa in her tiny studio, loaned by her brother who was working away.

We'd been pulled together by looking almost identical. There'd been no choice. Once we met, it had been like a pact.

Phoebe had offered up her brother's apartment the first day I'd met her. 'I'm literally paying him just cents. We'll split it. More for food and drinks!'

We'd survived on bowls of beans and pasta, and there was free coffee in the common room. We'd bonded quickly. It wasn't just a physical likeness – we liked the same music, films, had the same sense of humour.

Our budget allowed for drinks, but I felt like blowing it all tonight. What were credit cards for? Phoebe had woken sobbing a few mornings ago and she just couldn't seem to get a handle on anything. She was days away from the job of her dreams. Is the pressure making her crack? I thought a celebratory night out could put her back in the zone and it seems to be working. The course is done. Certificates tomorrow and I'm due to start work in a diner.

With Phoebe off to shoot a few lines in her first film, I'd needed something to do. A diner off Broadway paid waiting-staff-wages to actors hoping for their first big break on stage. Phoebe and I could both sing. I'd auditioned for the job for waiting tables, and I'd get to perform with the others a few times a day. The idea was that someone would spot us. It had happened a few times. The diner was pretty famous. And pretty famous was what I hoped to be in a few years. It wasn't as good as Phoebe's Hollywood film. But it was a start.

And now she's suggesting we swap roles. She would wait tables and sing for supper, and I would go and film in Abu Dhabi, in a role people would kill for.

I want her to get it together. I need her to. She can't give this up.

We order, and then as though she can read my thoughts, her head droops and her shoulders sag as the waiter brings over the cocktails. Whatever is bothering her hits again.

'Phoebe, come on… You've dreamt of this – I mean, your first few lines in a major film! And acting with Hanneghan. He's movie-star royalty.' I push the cocktail towards her and take a gulp of mine while grabbing her hand. 'Don't lose it now, Pheebs, don't let it get to you!' I know her agent is on her back. He'd screamed at her yesterday when she'd called and said she felt sick. *If you're not on that fucking plane then don't call me again. Do you even know how embarrassing that would be for me? You're nothing yet.* She'd sobbed again when he'd hung up.

She shakes her head and her hand trembles in mine. 'I don't know what's wrong with me. I just feel so... so fucking fragile. If I get on the plane and fly there then fuck it up, my agent will drop me in a flash. And he'll do the same if I don't go at all... I know you said you don't want to, but please, take the role, do it for me. We look so similar, they'll never—'

I push my forehead with the heel of my other hand. 'I can't. I can't take your place. This is your role. You got it, not me.' It's not that I don't want it. I'd kill for it.

Her hand tightens on mine and she pulls me in, hugging me. Her voice is fierce in my ear. 'Ellie, please. I'll fall apart. I've never felt this much pressure. We look the same. Everyone says so. Pretend to be me. I can't lose this agent.' She pulls away, shakes her head, tears in her eyes. 'They're flying to Abu Dhabi on a private plane. The rest of the crew and cast are flying from LA, but there's an awards thing here, in New York, tonight, so it's just a small plane leaving tomorrow. I don't think they worry about advance passenger lists on those jets. You can travel on your passport and just give my name as your acting name. You'll look like the headshot they have of me. You can have the money, and you can get your name on the credits. When it's all done, I'll get my agent to change the name to yours. I'll say it's my new acting name or something. No one will care, as long as the paperwork is right and someone turns up who looks like me, and can act. And I've seen you act. You'll be amazing! Then I'll work out whatever the fuck is wrong with my head, and when the pay comes, I'll send it to you. It's two weeks. I *can't* piss off my agent. I need to turn up for this. Someone they think is me, needs to turn up for this. I've signed the contract. You just need to do the scenes. I mean, whoever thought I'd find my doppelganger?'

I take a breath.

11

My last-ditch attempt to sway her. 'I don't have an American accent.'

'You can do one. You'll just work hard at it. For two weeks you can hold it down.' She looks desperate and I can feel myself relenting. But it's terrifying.

'What if they find out?' I whisper this bit, because it scares me, the whole thing.

'They won't.' She leans in. 'Please, Ellie. For me.'

This is when I steal from her, cheat her out of everything she's worked for.

I say, 'Half of it – you keep the other half. You landed the role.' I can't believe I'm saying it. I can't believe I'm agreeing. 'Just give me half of the money. If it means that much to you, I can't say no.'

Her arms tighten again round me and she swallows a sob.

'One thousand dollars.' The man at the next table takes a seat.

'What?' I say, sitting up. I don't let go of Phoebe's hand.

'One thousand dollars.' He puts down an unopened bottle of Laurent-Perrier. 'Here, I've bought this. The waiter's bringing glasses. One thousand dollars on the table now, if you'll kiss. For thirty seconds. One thousand dollars for a bit of tongue.'

For someone talking of tongues he's practically panting. I stare at Phoebe. Then I stand.

'C is for Cunt,' I say as loudly and as clearly as I can, wobbling again on my wedges, my voice scratchy with the tequila. One strap of my dress has fallen down on a shoulder and I pull it up, feeling the man's eyes on me like I'm made of fucking chocolate. I lean in, and raise my voice. 'Now fuck the fuck off! Before I call the police.'

Before he has time to react, his friend stands between us, the cute one. 'Keep the champagne, your bill is paid for the night. I'm sorry, ladies. I'll get him home. Have a good evening.'

As they leave, all the eyes in the bar follow them. One woman much older than us, who I'd written off as priggish, claps silently in our direction.

The waiter puts down two crystal champagne glasses and I sit back down as he opens the bottle with a flourish. 'Your bill has been paid, and there's extra on there. The kitchen closes in half an hour. May I suggest some dessert?'

Phoebe looks as though she's bathed in relief, like she's still swimming in it. The heaviness around her eyes, which she'd carried these last few days, is gone.

She lifts her glass and smiles. 'To new beginnings, *Phoebe Thomas*! Congratulations on your new role. The birth of a superstar.' She holds out a champagne glass and I pick up mine.

'Are you sure?' I whisper, though no one has a clue what we're talking about. The mere idea of pretending to be her, and daring to undertake a role in a film ... but to *be* in a film! 'Are you really sure?'

'Ellie, you're literally saving my life. And my career.'

'To the future, then.' I clink.

Hanneghan. I'll get to act alongside Hanneghan. Lights spark up in my future like a landing strip. I've arrived. I've navigated this far and soon I get to breathe out.

A spark of fear lights up too. This could all go badly, badly wrong.

MONDAY

DAY TWO

2

I head out to get coffee in the thin heat of the early morning New York streets. The light hasn't thickened yet and I can still take an easy breath. It helps me to work out what's going on. Where my head is.

Phoebe's still asleep. I woke up wired, packed for the flight. Questions had come at me in the dark: am I committing fraud? Am I liable for something? If I wreck this, do I wreck my career? And what about Phoebe's?

The private plane leaves for Abu Dhabi in a few hours. Then two weeks of filming in the desert. Acting with Hanneghan. I still can't believe that. The first time I saw him act my life pivoted. My dream was born. This is huge for me.

So I'm going to pretend to be Phoebe.

And Phoebe will pretend to be me.

She's going to rock up at the diner near Broadway as Ellie Miller and sing her way through the next few weeks. You never know. She might be picked up by a talent scout. I'd been hoping to.

It's just gone 7.30 a.m. and already the streets are busy. Coffee shops open early here and so I head towards Battery Park.

'It's Ellie, right?' The man behind the counter gives me a bright smile. He picks up a coffee cup and writes my name on it. 'Oat milk cappuccino, two?'

'Just one this morning.' Phoebe will still be in the land of nod. 'Thanks.'

'I appreciate you!'

I smile at him, still unused to the energy of the US.

Sitting outside, I text mum. I'll miss not getting back to London. Having said that, I know she'll enjoy having the flat to herself for a few more weeks. It's just her and me so she'll still have the run of the place.

Something's come up, quite sudden. A few lines in a movie. They're filming in the Middle East, and I'll be heading out soon. Can't wait to tell you everything! xxx

I can't tell her I'm taking Phoebe's part, but I know she'll be pleased about the job. I hesitate before I press send, watching seagulls dive and rise again, the Hudson's colour deepening under the strengthening sun.

If I tell her there's any risk involved, she'll immediately start talking about therapy. She thinks I've never really got over losing Dad, that all my decisions, that she deems crazy, are driven by it. If I have to listen to the counselling lecture one more time I might explode. The freshness of the morning has dulled my fear from last night. Maybe this will work out.

I press send, then quickly tap out another:

Love you xxx

It's just me, the coffee cup and the Hudson, which opens up to the ocean, then the rest of the world. When I'd first said yes, I'd been terrified. Now excitement has crept in.

What can go wrong?

The private airport sits outside the city, and when I pull up the sun is beating down without mercy. The smooth surface of the runway ripples under a mirage of water. My confidence of a few hours ago is drying up. I check my make-up. I'd applied it carefully, and I touch the mascara wand to my lashes one more time.

Heat can change everything, even what you think you see.

'Here you go, ma'am.'

The driver opens the door, and I can barely speak a thanks. My first go in my new accent. Like a reality check, the plane sits in front of me – it gleams white, but is a fraction of the size of the planes I'm used to flying in. I realise that my role starts now, amongst a group of famous faces. With Hanneghan. I'm terrified.

I'd felt the nerves crashing in on the way here so I'd chickened out and swallowed a calming pill. I've had panic attacks before when it's all felt too much. I don't want to freak out on the plane.

I can't believe this is my life. Phoebe had walked me down the stairs to meet the car and say goodbye this morning, full of last-minute instructions. 'Right, you've got the cast list, you've got the scripts. They keep sending new versions – I can't believe all the last-minute changes. Check your email, I gave the new email address – your email – to my agent.'

I'd made her promise to see a doctor and she'd just nodded and thanked me for doing this.

'Don't worry,' I'd said reflexively, but I was scared to death. I still am.

Phoebe had run through the cast as though we hadn't spent all the time since the cocktail bar going over and over the details. 'Pablo Lastra, from the indie film, is playing Cara's husband.

And also Elijah Hanneghan playing Cara's on screen lover – proof older men only get more attractive.'

Elijah Hanneghan. My stomach had flipped.

The car beeping its horn had stopped her.

'Oh my god, Phoebe, I'm going to miss you!'

'You too, Ellie. I love you.'

In the small terminal building, my passport gets a quick glance and someone with a clipboard, frowns. 'We don't have an Ellie Miller down.'

'I'm Phoebe Thomas.' My mouth is dry. It feels like such a loud and obvious lie. 'But Phoebe Thomas is my acting name, and the name I go by now. My legal name is on my passport. I thought my agent had let you know.'

She looks at me, then scans a sheet with headshots and names. I see Phoebe's headshot on there, and I hold my breath.

'Yes, here you are. No problem. Go on ahead, Phoebe.' She nods behind her, doling out a quick smile.

I follow her nod, my heart racing, and I thank God for the ease that comes with not flying commercial.

I message Phoebe:

Almost on board! No issues yet… xxx

Someone in a suit nods at me, scans my passport and takes my suitcase. 'Flight time is about thirteen hours. We're due to leave here at noon, and we'll land in Abu Dhabi at nine a.m. local time. Head out of these doors and up the steps. Someone will help you outside.'

'Thank you.' I smile at the suited attendant.

Back in the sun, I shade my face with my hand and put on sunglasses. It's only a short walk to the plane where another attendant waits outside.

Ten steps and there's no going back.

I've decided that if someone studied Phoebe's audition tape closely, I have no chance. But we're similar enough to pass as the person in the polaroid taken when her costume was agreed. Freddie, the director, met Phoebe after the audition, but how closely will he remember someone who he saw over six months ago? I have to pray the answer is not too much. Not so much I can't slip into her role, usurp her part without suspicion. A thief. Isn't that what history has painted doppelgangers to be? Malevolent – a sign of madness. Something to be frightened of.

I'm frightened right now.

Here I go.

'Hey, Phoebe?'

I pause on the hot asphalt.

'It is Phoebe? I saw your photo on the cast sheet. Josh. Your husband.' The man smiles and holds out his hand. He has black hair and is very tall. Blue eyes – they flash as he lowers his sunglasses to say hello. Good manners. Movie-star good looks. The hint of a southern accent. Texan? I imagine him on a horse. His tan is deep.

'Hi,' I say, knowing this is it. Where it starts.

I break out the biggest smile I have, tossing my hair a little to show off – there's nothing like assuming a confidence I don't have for convincing myself I'm not afraid. You dress for the job you want.

'How are you feeling? This flight will be interesting. And when I say interesting, I mean I'm scared shitless.' Josh slides his sunglasses back on and slips into stride alongside me as we head towards the gleaming plane. 'I checked out your IMBD. We're both rookies. Got it all to prove.'

'You ever been on one of these?' I say.

'Nope. You?'

'That would also be a no. You met any of the cast?'

He laughs. 'Not this lot. I reckon I've been within three feet of major talent, but only as an extra. You don't look directly at the sun, you know that. I'm guessing you've cut your teeth waiting round in the wings, hoping for the call? Three weeks on a set last year for me and I didn't even make the finished film.'

I decide I like Josh. We're almost at the plane and I offer up my planned backstory. 'I've done some theatre in England and countless extra roles, too. This is my first big film.' It's a relief that I'm holding down Phoebe's accent well. I've had enough practice. We pull to a pause as we near the steps. 'You ready for this, hubby?'

He smiles, and tips slightly forward in a bow. 'After you.'

There's a shout of greeting behind me, not aimed at us.

Josh sees me looking over my shoulder, and says quietly, 'Cara Strauss. Leading lady. Remember, don't stare directly at the sun. Smile, nod, small talk. Make like they're plain old everyday colleagues.'

I resist looking over my shoulder again as I walk up the steps. Cara's calling loudly, 'Lukas, darling, how good to see you!'

I peek as I'm at the door. She's smaller and thinner than I remember. I guess that's what the screen does – amplifies everything. She wears some kind of silk pyjama suit, with bare arms, and her blonde hair is lifted high on her head, sunglasses bedded in the mass of curls, which looks effortless and probably took a professional to arrange. She's eye-catching even now – slight, like she might blow away, but with an aura that's magnetic.

She calls the name Lukas again. I scan to see who it is and do a doubletake, my stomach tightening. Wearing a beanie and headphones, and huge Nike Jordan trousers with a loose t-shirt is Lukas O'Connor. He's recently left a boyband and is number one in the charts right now with his first solo single. He's on the front cover of any magazine going. He's also leading the charge as a mental-health guru – speaking out about the difficulties of the pressure of the spotlight.

'That's Lukas O'Connor!' I hiss at Josh as I get on the plane. 'Did you know he was coming?'

'Last-minute casting. But major coup, right?' Josh grins. 'They were worried they wouldn't get the young audience, but they'll pretty much get anyone under the age of twenty-five – and my mom – with him as a debuting star. Makes sense.'

On the plane a woman called Kidz ticks my name off a list. She has short, spiked hair dyed a pale silver grey, and an undercut on the left side. She wears a crop t-shirt and faded jeans with expensive trainers. She looks a couple of years older than me.

'I'm the AD. Make yourself at home.' She speaks quickly, and sounds like a New Yorker.

Assistant directors are usually waving at me amongst a crowd of extras – telling us when we're needed, which direction to go. I swallow hard and force myself to behave calmly as I pass Kidz, heading towards the small table we're shown to, with two plush seats either side, fairly near the front. The air on the plane is cooled and scented – fresh flowers and fancy hand gel.

An air steward says, 'Champagne?' She holds a tray with real glasses, cut like crystal, and I take it with a smile of thanks and peer round the cabin.

I'm quickly through most of the glass to cope with my rising anxiety.

I try to work out who is already on the plane, as Josh whispers the gossip he's heard about the married director and producer not getting on. We can see them through the window, chatting to Cara and Lukas on the tarmac.

'You must have heard,' he says. 'Freddie and Marianne – you know they're both working on this. Director and producer.

Rumours are their marriage isn't the best at the moment, despite the photos. I read something in an indie press magazine.'

Outside, Freddie laughs, throwing his head back. He's tall and blond. Marianne is smiling. She's the daughter of another famous director, a legend in the industry. Oscar winning, notoriously private – until she married Freddie, anyway. She's slight, but eye-catching. She has a regal posture.

Pablo Lastra sits closest to us on the plane, about ten feet behind us. He looks as though he's asleep, his head leant back and his legs up and crossed on the chair in front of him. He wears dark glasses so I can't see his eyes. Originally from Venezuela, he's relatively new to big roles. He's younger than Cara – maybe thirty, or just under. He was spotted in an indie pic that made it to Sundance, then began an affair with an older star, and moved to Hollywood. They're not together anymore. Once he was established, they broke up pretty quickly.

'Here's another car,' I say, as I watch it pull up outside. My glass is topped up so quickly I don't notice until its full.

Josh peers through the window to look, still talking. His slight drawl is easy on the ear. 'I was an extra in the latest Spielberg. If you freeze frame and zoom in you can definitely see me. Star quality. But I'm a charity worker in New York when I'm not trying to make it big.'

'Teacher, at a comprehensive,' I say, distracted by who might be in the car. 'Well, a temp at the moment.'

I curse, realising I'd forgotten my backstory. I'd remembered to speak in my American accent, but Phoebe doesn't work in London. She's not a teacher and they don't say *comprehensive* in the US. I pull myself up and widen the story. 'My mom's from England, so I spend a lot of time there. She's over in London right now, so I've worked there a bit.'

Josh looks surprised. 'I'm from Surrey originally. Moved to the States with my dad when I was ten.' He grins. 'I can do a great home counties. Who do you reckon that is?'

I miss the opening of the car door as I hear Lukas being greeted at the plane entrance.

'You're a fan?' Josh lowers his voice. 'I can't bear his music. But tell no one.'

I tap my nose. 'What is said between us newly-weds is sealed in silence.'

As Lukas passes us, I can't help myself. 'Hey, Lukas, I'm Phoebe.' I wave.

He offers me a nod, sage and wise, though he's only twenty-one. I've got a good three years on him. ''K,' he says. Then he pulls his headphones on, tugging his beanie down.

'Friendly,' Josh says. 'You seen the full list? Crazy that Cara's character is having an affair with Elijah Hanneghan. They were married for what, eight years? Couldn't get closer to real life! I was on a charity visit once with them. She was the face of the charity back then – he was a nightmare.'

'Elijah Hanneghan, a nightmare? No! I don't believe it.' I've watched every single one of his films. He must be nearly thirty years older than me. I've idolised him for as long as I can remember.

'I'll tell you about it sometime. It was basically a lot of...' He mimes taking a drink, quickly with a glance around him. 'But now, shhh,' Josh holds up his finger to his lips. 'Not so loud. We've got to play it cool.'

'Totally get it,' I say.

'Not sure if he's here yet. The awards dinner they were at finished really late last night.'

I take another sip of champagne.

Josh continues, his voice a bit distant. 'Did you see the press coverage of it? Freddie and Marianne got some huge award. That's why there are only nine of us on the plane today. They took the stars to the dinner with them for some PR and it must have been a late one. Too fancy for you and me. Even the assistants to the talent aren't on this plane. Only one AD. Everyone else is on the LA plane: the line producer, location manager, local wrangler, camera crew, sparks, grips, make-up and hair, wardrobe, art department. You name it. But they might beat us to the hotel. I think they're trying to look as eco as possible by letting us fly with the A-listers out of New York. Cara's hot on the environment.'

Josh is still talking, but his voice seems to be blurring. No, that doesn't make sense. Not blurring, just a bit…

The cabin spins a little. I clutch the arm of my leather seat.

'You OK?' Josh's voice sounds like it comes from a long way off.

Then it hits me.

'I took…' I try to remember the name of the pills. They were pink. *Shit*. Was I not supposed to drink?

'Are you okay? Here, Phoebe, just lie back. Is your seat belt on?'

I grasp the buckle of the belt, and hang on to it. I can't keep my eyes open. It's the strangest feeling. The sound of my heartbeat is loud in my head. This not the start I was planning on.

'The champagne. Knocked me out,' I say.

'Don't worry, I'll keep an eye on you. Husband's honour.'

But I only catch the end, as time does a strange thing. I flip into a long beautiful blackness, serene and calm. And it's like I've always been here. Utterly lost to the world.

I stay like that for a while. Until the shouting starts.

3

A crash, a bang of something falling. I wake to noise and feel like I'm underwater, sinking. My stomach keeps dropping as though I'm on a rollercoaster and I feel sick.

'We're going to die!'

'Shut up! You think that's helping?'

I've no idea how long I've been asleep. I'm forced back in my seat for a second, as though we're rising, then I'm thrown forward again.

What's going on? I look at my watch. I've slept for eight hours. *What?* My mouth is dry and my tongue sticks to its roof, wedged against the back of my front teeth.

The hum of the plane is loud. Voices are loud. I try to listen.

'Will you shut the fuck up!' The shouting comes from behind me.

'I will not! How dare you speak to me like—'

But whatever the voice was going to say is lost as I hear a scream and my stomach drops away again. Is it just the pills and the champagne? I fall forward, thrown hard in my seat and a wave of motion sickness washes through me.

'I've got you,' says Josh. His voice is tense.

I manage to open my eyes. 'What's going on?' My tongue is thick and it hurts when I speak.

'We're flying through a storm. It's a bit messy.'

'Tell them to land! Land now!' a woman screams.

'I said, just shut up! They're doing all they can!' A man this time. Pablo? A Spanish lilt through the chaos.

'Take it easy,' someone says. And I know that voice. I'd know that voice anywhere. Hanneghan is on board. I must have been passed out when he arrived.

Something hits my foot, a champagne glass rolling down the aisle as the plane drops again. My stomach churns. I'm going to be sick.

'Just hang on,' Josh says, sounding equally terrified, pushing me back into my seat. One of my hands still grasps the seatbelt, but he takes the other. 'Squeeze it if you're scared.' His grip is tight.

I open my eyes again. The blue of his is bright. I lock on to them.

With the drugs and champagne, I don't feel a sharp fear. A dull ache of dread instead competes with nausea. I don't know which one will win. *Why did I come?*

'We're all going to die!' someone shouts, and screams follow.

I grip Josh's hand tightly. I close my eyes.

My head spins, and when the plane drops the next time, I can't help it, I taste a burst of bile. I mime at my mouth – lips clamped – and Josh grabs a paper bag from the table.

I hold the bag with both hands and bury my head in it. Luckily, the plane stays relatively still as I do, and when I'm done, I wrap the top and grab my seatbelt again.

'Is it over?' I manage, my head aching and my throat hoarse.

Josh gives a tight shake of his head, and I push myself back against the chair.

'I'm going to sue!' A woman again. It must be Cara.

I close my eyes. My stomach is still swirling.

I deserve this. I shouldn't even be here.

This was a mistake. I hear Felix's words in my head about doppelgangers – bad luck, a dark omen. Maybe I've brought this on myself by agreeing to switch places.

I'm going to be sick again, and I hold my head up higher, eyes closed, trying to find a sense of balance.

Slowly, the plane feels as though it levels out. It doesn't drop as violently, and the noise on the plane settles too. People are quiet. There's a stillness in the aftermath of the storm, and the skies outside become blue again – I hadn't realised how dark it had been – and the lighting on the plane softens to natural daylight.

'Thank you,' I say to Josh, my voice shaky. I feel awful. I still feel sick and my clothes stick to my skin.

Freddie Asquith-Smith – there's no mistaking him – calls out, 'It's all done. You can all relax now. There'll be drinks. We all survived, so we can all move on.' It's short and not so sweet. Definitely an instruction for us all to calm down. But even his voice sounds tight and tense.

At some point, the seatbelt light goes off, and the attendants come round with hot towels, drinks and snacks.

'Peanuts?' Josh asks.

The attendant shakes her head. 'We have a nut allergy on the plane, so no nuts today. But anything else, do say.' Her tone is relaxed. It's like nothing ever happened.

One attendant takes the bag from me discreetly, which I still clutch. 'Would you like to freshen up? There's a bathroom at the back of the plane. Just head through the curtain at the rear for more privacy. There's perfume and a few other toiletries in there.' She's kind and I want to cry with gratitude.

'Go,' Josh says. 'I'll save you some food.'

As people recover, the passengers stir with the aftermath of the storm. Questions for the flight's attendants: *What was that? Will it happen again? Why can't we just land? Is it really over now?*

Moving among them, smiling brightly, the flight attendants hand out drinks and snacks, smoothing over the upset. I hear some replies as I try to ready myself to stand. *Just a storm. All perfectly normal. We've passed through it now. Can I get you something else to drink?*

I stand up and grab the seat. Someone behind me – I think it's Cara but my head is so foggy from nausea and sleep that I can't make anything out – is crying and telling someone down the phone that they love them. *I almost died!*

Kidz is making the rounds with the flight attendants, checking on everyone, but she's as white as a sheet and there are faint mascara streaks on her cheeks. It's clear she's been crying. I squeeze past her on the way to the bathroom and she smiles at me. I deliberately try to not look at Hanneghan. This isn't how I want him to see me.

My balance is all out. Nausea churns my stomach, and I don't look at the other passengers as I make my way to the back. I save my star-spotting for later, and I stumble against a chair as I pass Lukas O'Connor.

'K?' he says, looking up. His beanie is still on, and his dark hair pokes out from the edges. He has a tiny tattoo under his right eye which says *Believe*.

All I can do is nod, and I make my way to the back of the plane, through a curtain into a small private space. I lock myself into the toilet, all gold and marble, and I splash water on my face, using a clean towel to freshen up.

I look at my reflection. My carefully applied make-up has slid off. My hair is damp from sweat and water, so I tie it back, up and off my face.

I look very much like Ellie, and not much at all like Phoebe. The carefully applied lipstick, the eyeliner, has all slipped away.

There's an array of small, travel-sized lipsticks and make-up in a basket to one side. I grab a few, and break open the packaging, painting in my face. Then I tip my head upside down, and spray on some hair products – it finds its wave and bounce again as I look back in the mirror.

Finally, I feel ready to open the door, but the world spins a little – nausea, the drugs from earlier, the champagne.

I take one step, but I instantly feel dizzy. I see an unoccupied chair nearby, so I crawl away from the toilet and try to reach it. It's still between the loo and the curtain divider. I make it almost to the chair, but my head aches so much, I give up and crawl to the side of the plane, behind the chair, propping myself up, knees against my chest, and resting my head back against the cabin wall, which hums softly with the vibration of gentle flight.

I'm hidden by the chair, when I hear a voice.

'But are we alone?'

I tense and open my eyes, but I can't see anything.

'Didn't that girl come up here earlier?' A different voice this time. Softer and more hushed. A woman? They're speaking in an intense whisper. There's too much background noise to make out who it is.

'There's no one here – she must have gone back to her seat.' This voice is definitely male, but again I can't hear it clearly. They're obviously trying not to be overheard.

My head spins again, the dizziness coming back in a wave. I pull my knees in tight and hug them.

This is when I hear it. Or think I hear it.

'What are you doing anyway, dragging me here? We don't want to be seen whispering together!' The male voice.

'I can't do it. I couldn't wait another minute to tell you. Not after that! It's a warning – it's the universe sending a warning. It's off, OK? Enough. I can't,' they say. I'm sure it's a woman. It comes through the fog of nausea and I have no idea who it is. I'm so disorientated. For all I know I'm passed out on the floor, dreaming.

'For fuck's sake, you can't back out now.' The male voice is angry – still hushed but short and curt.

'That storm was a sign! Mock me, but the universe is saying no. What will happen if we go ahead? I can't—' Whoever the woman is sounds terrified.

'I knew it – I knew you'd say something like this. But it's too late. We've agreed. In the desert. Where no one will find him.' The voice is hissing, quick and harsh. Quiet.

What the fuck? Whatever this is, they mustn't see me. They are clearly trying not to be overheard.

'Are you sure you can go through with it? Now we're almost there, it seems so real. When it was just an idea, it felt more...' The voice trails off. Then is interrupted.

'He has to go. We've talked and talked about this. If you back out then I'll have to as well, and where does that leave us?' The voices are short with each other, close to each other.

I try to remember the last script Phoebe had given me. Are these lines from the film? It sounds like some kind of rehearsal. They speak in whispers, which sound more intense with each word.

There's a long pause now. I hold my breath.

The male voice speaks first. 'So, you're on board.'

'OK.' Uncertain. The female voice – but who is it?

She carries on. 'I'll go through with it, but I wish we didn't have to. That he hadn't joined the cast. If they'd just kept it as it was, then none of this would—'

The male voice is rough. 'We've got no choice. A couple of days, and then that's it. We kill him, and if we do it right, they'll never find the body.'

The first voice catches at this point. A sob. I daren't move, but my senses are on red alert. I listen as well as I can. I shake my head, pinch myself to check I'm really awake.

'OK. Then we're agreed.' This is the man speaking.

'I can't do it without you.' Another sob.

'Forty-eight hours. No turning back.'

I try to peer forward, to see past the chair, but the effort of forcing myself to move even the smallest amount sends a wave of dizziness from my toes upwards, and I feel a retch coming on.

'No backing out now. There's too much at stake. Let's go. We don't want to be missed.' A hint of menace darkens his tone. I hold my breath.

And then they're gone.

The nausea I'd been battling makes my head spin. I pitch forward, everything dizzy and black.

I wait until it passes, and an attendant finally comes in, followed by Josh.

'Oh my god, look at you!' He kneels down.

The attendant brings water.

Josh helps me back up. Thank God for him. I've only known him hours, but he's been amazing.

There are a few more attendants around when I come out, one is nearby talking to Lukas, discussing food.

By the time we move to the front of the plane, to our seats, enough to-ing and fro-ing has been going on that I doubt anyone will notice me particularly or realise that I was sat in the back of the plane when that conversation took place.

And they can't realise I was.

I hope I was dreaming but it felt so real. And if it was, then I'm sat on a plane with two people who are planning murder.

4

The air is like hot soup as I walk down the steps of the aircraft under a blanket of blue sky to a flat private airfield and a sleek white building with a shimmering, undulating roof. Then, beyond a line of tall palm trees, lie miles and miles of sand so bright the sun bounces off the horizon back at me and I blink, struggling to adjust. The conversation I thought I'd heard swims around in my head, making the whole thing overwhelming. I still feel wobbly. My sense of reality completely off kilter.

The rest of the flight had been smooth. Josh had relaxed after the storm, chatting about his work as an extra, about the hotel we're heading to. I'd looked around the plane in disbelief. Could someone here really be plotting murder? I look at everyone with new eyes – not just Hollywood legends, but now people I can't take at face value. I daren't trust anyone. Perhaps not even Josh.

From my seat, once I felt a bit better, I'd tried to watch Hanneghan without staring. Silvery hair, tanned skin. Strong jaw. I feel like I know him. There's no way he'd be plotting murder. My life goals had crystallised while watching him on screen. It had been more than just fangirling. It had made me want to act. It had changed the course of my life. I'm his biggest fan, yes, but he's my biggest inspiration. I don't doubt him. I couldn't. And now fortune has brought us together.

Josh holds my arm, and Kidz walks in front of me in case I fall as we descend the steps. Freddie, the director, who fills me with terror, walks past muttering about insurance. He's one of the biggest names in Hollywood. I can't adjust to the fact he's so close. I can't look at him for too long.

Downwind, on this intense thick heat where scent sticks to the air like glue, he throws me a dark look. His thick bushy blond eyebrows are tight and frowning. He's broad – up close much broader than he seems in photos. And he moves quickly, like there is important business calling him. More important than me. He gets to the bottom of the steps before me and heads towards the line of waiting cars. He pulls out his phone and frowns,

His wife, Marianne, the producer, doles out a smile as she follows him.

Then Marianne – Marianne *Asquith* – pauses by me, patting me on the arm. 'Poor thing. That flight was chaos. I thought you held it together well, all things considered.' She smiles at me, and I realise I'm staring directly into the sun, as Josh would say. I need to speak. I need to get over being star struck. *Quickly*.

'Thank you. I'm sorry,' I manage, trying not to gawp.

She isn't done. She lifts her hand to my brow, in a motherly sweep, and says, 'You're cold. How can you be cold in these temperatures? You must get some rest. I won't let Freddie bully you into any of his hectic plans. Kidz, keep an eye on her, will you?' She is taller than Cara, with thick chestnut hair, and moves with a grace which seems to override Freddie's speed, making his blustery exit seem somehow ungainly and all the more hostile.

Kidz nods in response and I watch Marianne head down the last few steps to the airfield.

'How much did you have to drink?' Josh says, raising an eyebrow as we walk out onto the airfield. He looks worriedly after Freddie and Marianne, the concern I've already ruined my chance of stardom writ across his face.

It's 9 a.m. here, but on New York time it's 1 in the morning. I haven't turned my phone back on yet so as far as I'm concerned it's still last night. My body clock will be screwed for a few days. We've got a full day ahead of us here, but I could sleep forever.

The blacked-out cars wait on the hot tarmac, behind them a horizon of sand, soft and fluid like melted gold.

I try to explain. 'It was the pills. I had no idea they'd react with alcohol. Then that storm finished me off.' I cringe and see my imagined Hollywood glory vanishing fast. Have I let Phoebe down already?

What I've heard is luminous in my head. Trying to pull off being Phoebe and fly under the radar is hard enough. Now, I may have heard two people agree to murder someone.

What do I do? I can't start raising hell. No one would believe me, and if they look at me too hard, then they'll pack me off home and I'll be forever discredited. Phoebe's agent would be furious. There's too much at stake for it to unravel now.

That conversation – had it been real? Had I just been half conscious? Had it been a rehearsal?

Josh reassures me while keeping his nose slightly upwind. I must smell terrible. 'Don't worry – no one coped with the flight well. Just because you were the only one who threw up, your reputation isn't in tatters. You have a week to shower every day and be the cleanest of them all.' He grins.

'Budget's out of control, don't worry. They've got more on their minds than you,' Kidz says, following us. 'Everyone else knows. You deserve to be in the loop. We've been pulling long days and nights back in LA to get the script finalised. You might've heard that Hanneghan is a late addition to the cast. They had someone else for his part, but they were pulled off last minute – some kind of assault charge. I can't name names for legal reasons but when you see the headlines about a star who just couldn't keep his hands to himself, you'll know you had a lucky escape.' She rolls her eyes. 'Anyway, Hanneghan, you know what he's like, he only came on board after getting agreement to some script changes. It's giving them a right headache.'

I nod like I do know Hanneghan, and he's not just someone I've read about, dreamt about. But I'm distracted – she said he was a late addition to the cast. It feels significant to my dehydrated brain.

Josh says, 'So what, they're behind schedule?'

Kidz rolls her eyes again. 'Behind? Freddie? *Never.*' Then laughs.

Pablo is descending the steps from the plane. He wears air buds and has a cap pulled down over his head. He's like a slightly older Lukas from behind. 'It's a joke. A fucking joke,' he mutters as he walks passed. His accent singsongs his words, and he glances over at Hanneghan and Marianne, who stand by one of the large SUVs.

'Pablo's taken the brunt of the script changes,' Kidz says quietly by way of explanation.

We watch Pablo head across to speak to a driver standing by a long black car. I realise I recognise him. It's Hanneghan's bodyguard and driver. Of course he'd be here. He goes wherever Hanneghan goes.

Lukas goes over to them, too, knocking back water from a can, and passing a few more cans out. I pause for a second to wait for my head to stop spinning, watching the cars and the Hollywood legends mingling. Everyone is stretching out under the sun after the flight, taking their time before the long drive to the hotel.

Marianne is near a huge Land Rover Defender, where Cara drinks water. Hanneghan talks to Freddie near another.

'Pablo's been bumped. From romantic lead to second now Hanneghan's here. The previous actor wasn't going to play such a key role. But what with Cara and Hanneghan's past...' Kidz shrugs, pulling out her phone.

I love the fact Kidz thinks we deserve to be filled in on all the background. It makes me feel like I've really made it.

'Hey, Kidz. I want to talk to Hanneghan, so he'll come with us, someone else go with Augusto,' Freddie shouts.

Kidz waves in acknowledgement. 'You two will need to ride with him. You must know Augusto Dittus – Hanneghan's driver and bodyguard. He's infamous. Rumours of the lengths he'll go to in order to protect Hanneghan are legendary. Been with him since the thing in Venezuela. He's been over here for a few days' holiday in Dubai. If Hanneghan is going with Freddie and Marianne, then you two should go in his car.'

I look out to the driver that I recognised, still talking to Pablo and Lukas.

Kidz heads over towards Marianne. 'Anyway, catch you at the ranch. That's your car over there. The other plane should be landing in the city now.' She checks her phone again, the screen reflecting the sun in a flash and I blink – blinded for a moment. 'I'll feel useless until they're all here.' She swings her arms as she heads over to a huge van with blacked-out windows and a uniformed driver.

The heat beats down like it's trying to defeat me and my legs give way suddenly. I can't remember the last time I ate something. Thirst burns in my throat.

Josh pulls me up. 'No you don't.'

Kidz waves Lukas and Pablo towards another car. 'You two want to jump in that one?'

'We can take this?' Lukas says, gesturing to Hanneghan's car, long and sleek; more limo than SUV.

'I've given that to those two. May as well spread out,' Kidz calls, then climbs in the van. 'Three hours' drive.'

'Come on,' Josh tugs on my arm. 'You feeling better? We should get going.'

He's not really looking at me, instead staring out to the fancy car. I wait a second for the dizziness to pass. I see Augusto stood next to the door, staring blankly at us.

Josh and I've become faux friends quickly. The two lowest ranking actors on the trip, husband and wife on screen. I'm grateful to him for looking out for me, but what I heard on the plane means I need to question everything. It's made me rethink. How much I can really trust him? Or anyone?

For a second, I watch the disappearing cars, then we head to ours. Josh walks quickly, my hand on his arm. His shoulders are broad. He has a confidence about him. It could be fake. I can wear confidence like I wear clothes, it's part of the job.

What I heard on the plane. Was it him? Was it real? Did I dream it?

Are you fake, Josh? We're almost at the car when bile rises quickly and there's nothing I can do. I stand and hurl everything left inside me, on the exclusive private airfield. My head aches and I can't even stay quiet. I hate myself as I bend and retch.

Josh stays with me, and I feel his hand on my back. 'Seriously, Phoebe, you need to stop soon.'

I hear him gag. But he doesn't step away.

Finally, I stand. 'I'm done.' I only manage a croak.

'Come on, chunder chops. I need a shower, and you need dousing in detergent.'

Augusto is staring at me hard. Of course he doesn't want someone covered in puke in his car.

'You're not going to cause me any trouble, are you?' he says slowly, staring, a thick Spanish accent, and a stance like a bulldog.

Josh bristles beside me. 'I don't think you're supposed to talk to us like that.' He pulls off indignant and entitled very well.

I stare back at the driver. Augusto Dittus. He's been in so many photos with Hanneghan – his right-hand man. He gives me a level eye. My knees are weak, and I almost faint, right there and then.

But he opens the door. 'Please, make yourself at home.'

I climb into the car, feeling like a worn-out rag, and for lack of anything else, I wipe my hand across the back of my mouth. 'Some kind of a start to wedded bliss, no?' I say, then I pucker up at Josh. 'Fancy a kiss?'

He laughs and pulls away, sliding further from me on the fancy leather seats. 'I'd rather kiss a snotty frog. Here.' He pulls open the fridge and hands me bottles of cold water, which I hold against my chest and cheek, before drinking.

'This place is a like a palace. Drink up. Only a couple of hours to go.'

'The hotel is nice? What's it called?'

'The Najma. It means stars. All that's out there is sun, sky, stars and sand.'

As the car pulls away, I look out as far as I can. Sand stretches out, rolling up and down the horizon, with peaks of gold rising up to the sky so bright with sun I squint. There are more depths to the desert than I'd imagined. I'd pictured it like a beach, all level and even, but instead it's more like a landscape of dunes, with shadows and all the shades of pale to burnt gold. No shelter, no water. The odd burst of vegetation, but it's sparse and not green. Nothing for miles. Nowhere to hide.

What I'd heard on the plane rings in my head: *forty-eight hours and he dies.*

It must have been a script rehearsal, surely. I'll check the latest version when I get to the hotel. I can't be the one who starts making wild allegations of a planned murder that I can't prove is going to happen. I can't jeopardise this job.

I'm sure it's nothing. And I've got enough to be worrying about.

5

I pass out in the car into a sleep like I'm dead and wake with a mouth like sandpaper as the driver tells us we're fifteen minutes away.

'Is he slurring?' Josh whispers, pulling a face.

'Too many fights and blows to the head, I bet,' I say, then I mime a scowl and a fake punch. Augusto is known for his fists.

I check my watch. We'll be there before lunchtime, so I'll be able to grab another nap. It will be chaos once all the crew arrive. I imagine we'll be busy from the word go and I need to get myself camera ready. From the googling I'd done, I'm about to arrive at the hotel of my fucking dreams feeling the worst I've ever felt. The luggage went ahead of us, so there's nothing I've been able to do about it. Josh has tried dousing me with fruit juice to take away the smell, but it's intense, and my head aches. I message Phoebe again. I tell her about throwing up, but I play it for laughs – I don't want her to worry I'm spannering this. She's not sent a reply since before we set off, but I imagine she's asleep.

The air-con in the car is the only thing keeping me from flaking out again.

I stare at the back of Augusto's head, thinking about what I'd heard on the plane. If it is real – which I can't believe it is, but my

43

brain keeps returning to it – who are they talking about? Which 'him' is the target? I worry it could be Hanneghan. And I can't have that.

With every mile closer to the hotel that I get, I feel more and more like this trip is cursed. Oh God – why did I come?

Josh gestures to the road. 'Hey, you think—'

Whatever Josh had been about to say is drowned out by my scream, as I lean forward and point.

'Oh my god! Look out! A gazelle!'

I grasp at the seat belt clasp to hang on to, braced for impact.

The car swerves quickly, throwing us all to one side.

Josh yells, 'Shit!' as I close my eyes and hang on as hard as I can.

The car up ends on two wheels, and swings off the road into the desert. One minute we're in the air, and I feel it stutter in the sand, and then it falls flat, upside down, jerking me backwards. My shoulders sink into my neck, and my feet hit the back windscreen, then rebound, flying forward.

It's over in a second but also seems to happen in slow motion. Once everything's stopped moving, I lift my head a little, just to check I can, and I run a quick inventory on all my joints, lifting my fingers, turning my ankles. I'm intact.

I fumble, my neck aching, and I manage to release my seat belt with one shaking hand while I push against the roof of the car, now beneath my head, with the other. As the slackening of the belt drops me down, I take the weight on my hand and manage to lower my legs, like I'm landing a half handstand.

'Josh? You OK?'

'Ow, my arm. I think it's out. Shit.'

'Out? What do you mean?'

I hear a loud pop and he says, 'Fuck.'

'Oh my god, what was that?'

'It's OK. It's back in. It does that sometimes.' He sounds drained.

'Give me a second, I just need to get out of this…' I hear a click, as he releases his seatbelt and I rest on my knees as I watch him right himself carefully, swearing every few seconds.

There's a blast of dry heat, and I realise the air-con isn't working anymore. The engine must have stopped, and from the gusts of hot air, like from an oven door, I realise the windows must be out. Sand blows across my face. I cough.

I'm shaking; the speed of the event alone is a lot to deal with. I'd gone from waking dozily to full adrenaline and I veer from ice cold to overheated. Then everything is numb for a second.

'Listen, we need to get out. Is your door working?' Josh says.

I blink a few times, sand thick in my eyes, and then I try the door handle. From all the shattered glass, I can see the window has gone, but the door won't open. 'It's wedged in the sand,' I say. I push it and it slides an inch or two, but then no more.

'Hello? Augusto?' I shout at the driver. I can't make out much. I see two legs but there's no movement.

'He must be out cold,' I say, wriggling round. 'Hello? Augusto?'

'I can't find my phone. It's somewhere here.' Josh sweeps one arm around where the roof now lies beneath us, and I remember mine had been in my pocket. I pull it out, but there's no signal. It's also cracked down the front and the screen is blank. It won't light up.

'Mine isn't working. The car must have had Wi-Fi. It's stopped,' Josh says. 'Fuck, I hope they realise we're missing.'

It's getting hotter. I don't think I'd fully appreciated the intensity of the heat in the short distance between the plane and the car, but sweat now drips in my eyes. I've managed to right myself, but I feel the burning from the metal on the frame of the car.

'We've got to get out,' I say. 'We'll have to go through the windows. Look, there's so much broken glass. Is it better at your side?'

Josh shakes his head. He's paper white, holding his arm.

'OK, look, I'll kick out the rest of the glass, then I'll try to cover the worst of the edges with something.' I kick, and thank God I'm wearing thick wedges and not the flip flops I'd considered that morning. Once there's enough of a gap, I pull my jumper from over my head, and lay it along the bottom of the window. It was a favourite – an old cashmere one I'd brought for the plane, in case my dress wasn't warm enough for the air-con. I wince as I see some glass cut straight through it. I begin to crawl.

The sand is hot on my hands and it burns. I blink in the light, which bleaches everything I can see and frays the edges of the horizon, unpicking the normally solid ground.

I make it out completely, nicking my skin on shards of glass as I go, then turn to help Josh. He inches out, wincing.

Standing tall hurts. Everywhere has been jarred, but thankfully it all seems to be working. It's a relief to stand up away from the burning ground, and I feel a bubble rising in my throat. I think it's tears, but it comes out as a laugh. For a second, Josh looks at me as though I'm crazy, but then he slowly shakes his head, and laughs too.

'Fuck!' he says.

For a moment, relief makes us giddy.

'What is happening on this trip?' Josh says, catching his breath. 'We nearly die on a plane, now we almost die in a car.'

The relief recedes as I remember Augusto. There's been no sound coming from him at all, and I drop to my knees, pulling at the door. The front of the car sits slightly higher in the sand to the back, and I reach my hand in, trying to check his airway.

But—

The way his head buries into the airbag, and the angle of his neck...

'Josh, you need to help me,' I say, swallowing hard, and he must be able to tell from my tone, because he kneels next to me, without saying anything, and reaches out with both arms, despite how much it must cost him to use his shoulder. We work quickly, pulling the airbag away from his face. Just in case.

But when I see his eyes, unblinking in the bright light of the sun, I sit back on my heels.

'I spoke too soon about *almost* dying,' Josh says, quietly. He drops his head and whispers. 'Do you know any prayers?'

'I don't know which god he prays to,' I say. 'He's from Venezuela like Pablo, isn't he? Maybe Catholic. I can't believe it. I mean, it was so sudden. Did you see the gazelle?'

Josh looks up at me. 'I can't remember. It was such a blur. There's nothing out here so we must have missed it.'

We stand for a moment, looking down at the dead man. The heat sends sweat down my back, and the burn is quick and intense. It feels wrong to be worried about ourselves, but I start to feel dizzy again. I'm probably massively dehydrated.

Josh turns and looks down the road. 'Look, we need to get to the hotel. Hopefully they'll come looking for us, but we can't just stand out here in this heat. It must be close to 40 degrees Celsius. We'll cook here, and there's no shade.'

I scan the horizon; there's nothing for miles.

'Is that even the right way?' I ask, doubtfully, thinking of spinning off the road, and wondering how sure I can be that in the upside-down car I haven't lost my sense of direction. I wouldn't stake my life on knowing which way is forward and which is back.

'I think so,' Josh says, but his hand is back on his arm, and he doesn't sound sure. He stares at the road ahead, but then swings round and looks behind us. They're identical.

The bright sun is blinding. The desert blanches under its heat. Sand, dry everywhere. The skin on my arms is starting to burn.

We're both covered in scrapes and scratches. Smears of blood cover us and Josh's face is already flowering blue and purple in shades of early bruise.

I open my mouth to say something determined, but while I'm composing it, I hear the ring of a phone.

'Augusto! His phone!' I drop to my knees again, and follow the sound, trying my hardest not to look at the dead body. I find it, vibrating near the top of the seatbelt, and I press answer before it can ring off.

'Hello?' I say, trying not to shout or to panic.

The person on the other end of the phone says something in Spanish, and I say as clearly as possible. 'We've had an accident. The driver is…' I shake my head, take a breath. 'I think we're only fifteen minutes away from the hotel, but we don't know how to get to you, and we don't know—'

'Shit, Phoebe, Josh, is that you?' A woman's voice comes on the phone. 'We were starting to worry. Listen, don't move. We're sending a car. There's only one road so we can't miss you. Are you both OK? It's Marianne. We're coming to get you.'

TUESDAY

DAY THREE

6

It's Marianne who meets us at the tiny clinic, in the small village, when we enter with the ambulance crew.

'How are you?' she says, walking towards us quickly as we drink in the air-conditioning of the white room. Her voice is warm and rich. She places her hand beneath my elbow, as though holding me up. Looking to the paramedic, she asks, 'Do they not need wheelchairs?'

'They insisted they'd walk,' he says, and disappears off to speak to the doctor who hurries out of an office.

'My shoulder came out, but it's back in. Other than that, we're fine,' Josh says.

He looks exhausted and I need more water. But just being in the cool is a relief.

It clarifies everything around me. I'd felt so nauseous and out of it on the plane and in the car. The accident has thrown that into sharp relief. Adrenaline is like rocket fuel and I feel hyper aware of Marianne, of the brush with death. That someone has actually died. I'm also panicking that the doctor may have access to Phoebe's medical records rather than mine – is this something the film company will have pre-arranged? Will I have to lie?

'You go in first,' I say to Josh. The clinic is spit and polish. Marianne must see me looking round.

'It's a new clinic. It's run by the government but the hotel have donated to it too. All the scanning equipment you could need after a car accident. We'll get you checked properly. Kidz has taken care of the details.'

I see Kidz stood behind us. She looks shaken.

I half glance at Josh, who's lost all his colour. When Marianne speaks to someone at the clinic, I try to get a smile out of him. But he only half nods his head in reply. Maybe his shock at seeing Marianne herself come to greet us is part of it. It feels a very generous act. I guess that if someone was to be badly hurt out here, it wouldn't look great for the production. Maybe Marianne coming isn't entirely unselfish.

I look at her again, and she smiles. Blood and flesh, she's nothing like the stand-offish, aloof character often described in the media. I'd read up about everyone before I came and Phoebe had gone over and over what to expect. Everyone who had worked with Marianne had spoken highly of her, but she doesn't speak much to the press. The media don't respond well to figures who slight them. Freddie is the opposite. He has quite a quick-tempered reputation on film sets, but he's all charm for cameras at events.

'Here, come and sit while you wait.' She passes me a bottle of water and I sip it gratefully, following her to a row of chairs.

'I'm so sorry,' she says, again her voice warm as it quietly fills the room. I remember her accepting an award recently, and her tone is the same now. Always measured, graceful, like her clothes. She carries an air I wish I knew how to grasp.

She leans her head back and sighs. 'What a week!'

'Congratulations, by the way,' I say, thinking of the award.

'Oh yes – that was a good night. I wish it had set the tone for the next few days.' Her phone beeps, and she flinches. A frown crosses her face.

I try not to stare.

'Excuse me.' She stands to read the message and heads away towards the entrance door, and Kidz' face creases in concern. I realise from her flinch and Kidz' expression that something must be wrong.

Josh is still in with the doctor so the room is fairly empty. Marianne glances around then steps out of the clinic door.

'What's happened?' I whisper to Kidz.

She looks uncomfortable. 'I think there's been... well, there are rumours of some over-eager fan. Marianne's been pestered in LA. We're just hoping they haven't travelled out here.'

'What... like, a stalker?"

Kidz nods.

I'm shocked. My head fills with images of axe murderers and knives smuggled beneath tea towels.

Kidz bites her lip. 'These things happen.' But she doesn't elaborate, and Marianne comes back as the doctor calls my name. I glance at my phone – I'd asked Phoebe if she had any allergies, but no reply. I'll have to wing it.

I head into the consulting room thinking about stalkers, and thinking I mustn't answer questions too emphatically, in case the doctor is reading from Phoebe's history, about which I know nothing.

'How are you feeling?' The doctor flashes a light in my eye as I stare straight ahead.

'Much better. I ache, and I've got some scratches.'

'We can get these cleaned up. Does it hurt if I do this?' The doctor checks my head, my limbs, and then when a scan is done, holds out a pad.

'I'm going to give you some painkillers with anti-inflammatories.

Keep an eye on your vision. Any sickness, you need to let us know. Are you allergic to anything?'

My first pause. Then I shake my head. 'No, nothing.' I wait for a few counts, watching her carefully. But there's no expression of surprise. I begin to relax. This isn't a test. This is just a check.

'You were lucky,' the doctor says. 'Take things easy. Shock can come back and bite you. Be vigilant.'

Vigilant.

On this trip, which appears cursed from the outset, being vigilant is advice I plan to live by.

7

The hotel blends into the desert in stone the colour of sand, and a low-level spread of turrets and landscaped palm trees offer up a luxury oasis in the middle of nowhere. I stare at it all, numb.

I glance at my phone, which has come back to life, and switched to Abu Dhabi time. It's now officially tomorrow, and almost 1 p.m.; New York is a long way behind us.

My body aches as we're ushered into the main foyer where Marianne gestures to trays of water and Freddie hands me a whiskey in a weighted glass that promises liquid gold will take away the sting of the day so far. It's not how A&E would do it, but I don't refuse.

'Come, sit,' Marianne says, her voice deep and low, and I notice her elegant summer dress, which I'd been too distracted to take in at the clinic. There's something of Grace Kelly about her, with darker hair. Old Hollywood glamour and an aura of authority and money. She's throaty, like she's just finished a pack of cigarettes. Josh and I follow her lead and sink into the sofa with velvet cushions like clouds. There's a tray of nuts and dates nearby, and I take a handful. My empty stomach has started to protest loudly.

Marianne's been completely composed since the clinic – I'd

heard Kidz ask her about the call, and she'd said something along the lines of the police closing the case. Hopefully whatever it was is resolved.

The idea of a stalker is unnerving though, and I watch her carefully. This trip already seems so ill-fated. Whatever bad luck I'd brought with me has appeared to seep into this golden group, so seemingly a cut above. No one is immune to bad luck.

'Now, we need to make sure you're both OK. We've promised the clinic we'll keep an eye on you. We don't want to push you too much, given what's happened.' Marianne is again both regal and motherly.

I nod. 'I'm fine. A few cuts and bruises.'

Josh nods. He looks exhausted.

I drink the water I'm handed and I feel it flush into all the sand-dry hollows inside of me. 'I'm fine. Really.'

'The authorities have been called, to check the car and the accident scene. They'll be here soon.' Marianne looks about her, and Kidz nods at the side of the room.

'Don't worry,' Kidz says, seeing my face, and guessing I'm worried about what comes next. 'Augusto's family will be told. And poor Hanneghan. They've worked together for years. He's basically a bodyguard. With his level of fame, he's mobbed getting coffee so Augusto rarely leaves his side.'

I take another drink and realise I'm shivering. I'm so tired.

Freddie stands, tall and looming over us. His dark blond hair is ruffled, but if anything, he looks more attractive. 'We need to ask you not to post about this on social media. We don't want to hush this up, but it needs to come out in a controlled—'

Marianne shuts Freddie up with a look. 'I'm sure these two budding actors wouldn't in any way want to compromise the privacy of the family. We don't need to instruct them how to behave, Freddie. I'm sure they'll be discreet, and allow us to handle this sensitively.'

'What the fuck?' The shout is loud as Cara strides into the room. She's all bluster and noise, and she waves her arms, gesturing, almost stamping her feet. 'I hear someone's just *died* on the way here? What kind of shoot are you running? First the plane, now this!'

Freddie is by her side quickly. 'Cara, darling, it was an accident. There was nothing—'

Flat out ignoring Freddie, she spins to me and I don't hear the end of whatever Freddie was about to say. 'Are you OK? You look like shit.'

'I'm sure I do,' I say, measuredly. 'We had to crawl out of the car. It crashed in the desert.'

'Christ! This is ridiculous!'

'It was no one's fault,' Marianne says, folding her arms. 'And it didn't happen to you. So calm down.'

Freddie hurries over to get Cara a glass of champagne from the tray. 'Cara, darling. It's a shock for us all. Please, have a seat.'

A sycophant to the stars, it seems.

'Has anyone told Hanneghan yet?' I ask.

No one speaks.

'Really?' Marianne stands. 'I'll do it now. Freddie, is he in his room?'

Freddie nods, one hand on Cara who pulls away a little, and Marianne disappears.

My legs are wobbly now, and I don't trust myself to stand just yet. Josh is pale, and touches his shoulder gingerly as he gets up.

Kidz helps him, then turns to me. 'I'll take you both to your rooms.'

As we reach the lift, she says, 'How are you feeling?' She steps back and looks from Josh to me, a concerned expression on her face.

'We're the lucky ones,' I say, glancing at Josh. 'The driver, Augusto, he...' I stall, because I realise I'm going to cry. I'm surprised at myself. I wasn't expecting it, but I feel tears quickly spill onto my cheeks. I don't want to open my mouth and speak, do some kind of cry heave.

Kidz takes my arm, and we head into the lift. 'You must be in shock. You both need to rest.'

As the doors slide closed, I catch the sound of Freddie continuing to gush loudly over Cara. It's not what I want to hear. Marianne seems to deal with all the grown-up stuff and, so far, Freddie the 'great director' appears confined to flattering a select few. It doesn't make for the calmest of environments.

Once out of the lift, on the next floor, Kidz leads me to the biggest hotel suite I've ever seen.

'Marianne insisted on you both having great rooms. The only plus side to the accident!'

There's a lounge area, two bathrooms, a huge double bed and the view looks out over a huge pool, with hills of sand rising in the background. I'm starting to get used to seeing sand and sky for miles and miles. It's unsettling – amazing, but utterly disorientating and I feel lost. This hotel really is in the middle of nowhere. I'd give my right arm to head back home to Mum's flat right now. Everything hurts and I try to hold back tears until I'm alone. *What have I let myself in for?*

'It will get dark around seven-ish. The sun falls quickly out here. One minute it's light, then night lands. It can be colder then. Not at this time of year– it doesn't ever seem to get cold right now. Really, we should have come later in the year, but Freddie got the best deal in August. You know why? 'Cause we'll roast. Ain't that showbiz?' Kidz busies herself pouring me more water from the carafe. Her speech fires like bullets, upbeat, with the odd question that doesn't appear to require a response. 'We'd planned a sunset camel ride tonight, but you and Josh will need to rest. Marianne doesn't want you to push yourselves. It's for the big scene and Freddie wanted everyone to have experienced it first. But you can do it another time.'

I think about Phoebe. I need to do a good job here. 'No, I'll be OK to go. It sounds fun.' I'll make sure of it. I take the water from her with a thanks and open the doors to my balcony. I flash a smile and remember the affirmative American accent. 'Oh my god, this view!'

'I know, right? Honestly, I can tell Freddie you can't face the camel ride. You must just want to rest. Are you tired?' She sounds hesitant.

To do this properly, I have to go, I have to do everything the rest of the cast does. The black look Freddie gave me when he got off the plane had felt like a reprimand. He seems anxious, jumpy, always unsettled, almost angry. He won't want his plans changed.

I shake my head. 'No, I've already been in enough drama; I need to toe the line. This is my first real role and I've got to impress. I want to. I've never had a chance like this and I can't slack off.'

She nods, seeming to understand. 'Totally get it. I remember my first shoot and it was crazy. Look, I'll tell you this so you understand the tension in the crew right now. I've worked with Marianne and Freddie a few times before. This isn't for public gossip, but everyone knows and it's not fair you don't. You can keep it quiet?' She raises her eyebrows and I nod. Her voice has taken on a hushed tone and she glances round the already empty room.

'Things haven't been going too well for them. Their last film was panned. They'd put in some of their own money, and they lost like...' She gestures with her hands to something large and imaginary. 'They had to fight to get this one off the ground, but now they've lost their leading man, and with Hanneghan coming on board, there are new demands for script changes – with push back from Pablo. Marianne was always the money, coming from Hollywood royalty. Freddie's career only really took off when they married. It's a lot of pressure.' She shrugs and then flops in the huge bamboo sofas which sit on the balcony. 'I've said too much, probably, but basically what I'm saying is you need to be prepared for Freddie being a dick.'

I drink the water, considering how to answer as I look out at the sheer opulence of the hotel. I see someone in the pool, swimming quick lengths, up and down. It looks like Lukas.

I want to find out more but I instinctively know I need to reassure Kidz before I ask anything or she'll clam up. 'Don't worry, I'm the soul of discretion!' I say. 'I totally get the pressure you're under and I appreciate you including me in all this. To add to everything, I think Hanneghan and Cara used to be married, didn't they? That must be good for PR, them being in the film together now, but I imagine that could be tense,' I say, like I don't already know everything about Hanneghan. Kidz seems to be in a sharing mood. She doesn't know me, but as bruised and battered as I am right now, this must be her taking me under her wing. I push for as much information as I can get. If what I heard on the plane was real, and I wasn't just hallucinating in some semi-conscious state, then I need to get a handle on these people. And I want to learn as much as I can about Hanneghan while I have Kidz' ear.

'Yeah, like ages ago. It's apparently an amicable split, but Freddie had to run the new casting by her. She said it was fine. She knows the media attention they'll get by starring in this together. It's a publicity coup. It works in everyone's favour... as long as the film's *good*.'

I watch Lukas swim, and think again of the voices on the plane and the fact that Hanneghan could be the target. If Freddie and Marianne are having problems with Hanneghan, then they've got a motive to get rid of him – but does that damage the film or create even more publicity? And Cara – an ex-wife – well, she might have reason to want him dead. He's worth a lot more than her. If he died, she might still be entitled to a chunk of his fortune. He's never remarried.

I put my feet up on the table and try to rationalise the vague memory of those voices that I could well have dreamt with the likelihood anyone could actually want to *kill* someone out here, on the set of this multi-million-dollar movie.

'Keep your eyes open later, and give Freddie a wide berth,' Kidz says. 'It's supposed to be a fun ride tonight, but it feels... Someone's died, and tensions are already running high. They're probably crazy to go ahead. You could all do with a break. But I know Freddie and his scheduling, especially when so much is at stake. There's no slack in the timetable.' She pulls a face, pursing her lips and shaking her head quickly. 'That reminds me, the rest of the crew and cast should have arrived by now. They must be running late. I better chase it up. Odd I haven't heard anything.' She looks down at her phone, slipping back into professional mode. 'But even without them, Freddie loses it if the schedule changes. Short of an act of God, we'll be out on those camels tonight.'

I get a call an hour later, telling me the police have arrived. Two officers in green uniforms are sat in the luxurious side room I'm taken to. Dark hair and eyes, attractive but stern – they're both expressionless as I approach. But then one offers me a smile of encouragement, which helps me lower my shoulders and smile back. I realise how tightly I'd been holding myself. Is it good cop, bad cop?

I'm on edge. I can't let the police think I'm anyone other than I claim to be. I travelled on my real passport so there's no immediate danger of any identity questions. But if the film crew find out I'm not the person who auditioned then there might be all sorts of questions. I just don't want to be caught out in a lie. Not when someone's dead.

We sit at a small round table, and I sink into the velvet cushions, still struggling to relax properly. They run though introductions, the reasons they're here, and the smilier of the two does more to make me feel at home.

My American accent is sharp in my mouth, ready to come out clean and unwavering, yet I'm so nervous.

'In your own words, if you could just talk us through the accident. We'll take some notes, then you can sign the statement if you're happy.'

I nod, and tell them about the car, the gazelle. I tell them how we were spinning, and how Josh and I got out through the back windows. The heat of the desert comes back to me, and then when I get to the part where we realised what had happened to Augusto, I stop.

'You're doing very well,' the smiling officer says. 'In your own words.'

'He was dead,' I say. 'I knew straight away. His eyes were wide open.' There's a catch in my throat. There's a spin of the wheel and a toss of the dice to the whole thing. An accident. Fate had decided.

'You saw the gazelle?'

I think this through in my head. What I had seen, who had

said what. What I'd heard on the plane I *think* I'd heard. I'm not sure I trust my own brain for the whole of the journey. 'Augusto was the one who swerved the car. When I think back, I'm not sure what I saw. I was chatting to Josh – my colleague – in the back of the car. We were tired. The journey had been pretty rough, and I'd been quite sick. The whole thing seems a blur – not real at all. One minute we were talking, then we heard the shout, and then… bam. It could have been Josh who saw something. I honestly can't say for sure.'

'Gazelles are very common on that road,' the officer says. He has a goatee and has about ten years on me. 'They come out of nowhere. There really isn't anything to do. You were unlucky.'

They write more stuff down, and look at each other, then the tape they're running is stopped and I'm thanked and taken out of the room.

Leaning against a wall, I sag for a second with relief. That went as well as I could have hoped. No query about who I was. And no tricky questions.

Do I go back in there and tell them what I heard on the plane?

The problem is, I still don't really trust my dehydrated brain.

No. The last thing I need is more scrutiny from the police. Or from anyone.

I pass Josh on my way back to my room. He holds his shoulder carefully – it's in a sling now but he still looks pale.

'How are you coping?' I ask.

'So, so.' He smiles. 'What about you? Come across any more gazelles in the hotel?'

I pull a face, and hope this is the last time I have to talk about the accident. I don't want to think about it again. 'Looking forward to a desert ride,' I say, shifting the focus of the conversation.

'Of course – bring on the camels later. Just call me Desert

Dan. Let's hope that trip goes more smoothly than the last two. I'm putting in a nap first.'

I watch him walk away, and I feel sick. If what I heard on the plane was real, then there is more to come.

All I can do is hope things don't really happen in threes.

8

'Josh?' I knock again on his door. I check the room number that I'd got from reception.

I'd slept for a few hours, waking exhausted, and stepped on my balcony. The heat had been flattening. The camel trip isn't for a few hours. Kidz had said the rest of the cast and crew should have arrived by now.

We have an early dinner soon, so I'd gone looking for Josh's room – I'd rather head downstairs with him than alone. He's being so friendly, and I need that. I don't have the headspace to start questioning that friendliness.

There's still no answer. The hotel is huge and I wonder if I've ended up in the wrong corridor.

I'm just about to knock again when I look at the list of names and room numbers, and realise I've blurred the lines. I'm outside Freddie and Marianne's room, and I reel my hand back like it's been burned. Thank God they're out and didn't answer. I head towards the right number, and just as I'm almost at the end of the corridor, there's a noise, a door banging closed.

A flash of yellow. A cap? A scarf? Shit. Were they in the whole time and just ignoring me? I wonder if that's worse than me banging needlessly on their door and them opening it.

I check my phone and it seems to be working, but the screen is broken. I give it a shake. Still nothing from Phoebe. I'm starting to worry.

'Phoebe?' Josh opens the door in joggers and a grey t-shirt.

He looks heavy-eyed and his hair is sleep mussed. The blue of his eyes stands out even more now he is wan and drawn.

'How are you feeling?' I ask.

'OK – the shoulder is fine, and the doctor gave me some pretty strong painkillers. I've been unconscious for a few hours.'

'Me too. I wanted to see how you are. I don't want to have to take you back to hospital.'

He gives me a funny look, then smiles. 'Come in? I have coffee. I needed something to wake me up.'

His room is gorgeous – a huge reception lounge area like mine, but the colours are all blues and golds. I sit at a low sofa, by a coffee table, where a tall brass pot is surrounded by small brass cups.

'How was the interview?'

'The police thing was easy – easy in the sense that I couldn't really piece together what happened,' he says, sitting down and pouring me a drink.

'It was just so sudden; I found it difficult to clearly say what happened,' I reply. The memory of the heat in the car and the sand in my mouth makes me shudder. 'Is your shoulder really OK?'

'Yes, it just aches. Christ, it's such a blur.'

The shaded light, which hangs like velvet in the room, makes the whole accident feel a world away now and I don't want to look back at it. I deflect instead.

'I can't really remember. I suppose it still feels… raw.'

'Of course,' he says. He smiles, clearly trying to lift the tone.

'Now, wifey, I hear we're due to head out and have supper desert style. There's a run through of the scene too, I think.'

'I'm so nervous—' I begin, then my phone beeps. A message from Felix. *Can you call me?* I can answer him later. Phoebe and I haven't told him what we've done, and it will be hard to lie to Felix.

'Important?' Josh asks, pouring me another drink.

'Friends checking in,' I say, thinking of Phoebe. If Felix's messages are getting through, why aren't hers? I've been checking constantly. I've sent her about a dozen messages since we arrived and had nothing back.

I would swap places with her right now, working in the diner, instead of in this heady place. Back in New York, we'd be out for cocktails, the three of us, or drinking cheap wine on the sofa, watching old movies.

The hotel phone rings, and Josh picks it up.

I watch his face change.

'What is it?' I whisper.

He holds up a finger as he finishes.

'They want us downstairs, now. Apparently, there's a change to the schedule. Something about the other plane. The one from LA with all the crew and cast.'

'What's happened?' I stand slowly, going easy on my shaken limbs. Everything's starting to hurt.

'I don't know. But it didn't sound great. You OK to head down?'

Surely nothing else has gone wrong?

9

Freddie looks thunderous at the side of the room. A drinks tray is circulated by a staff member, along with canapes, and everyone has changed. It's almost 5 p.m. and we're due to have dinner at some point, but this impromptu meeting has been well catered for by the hotel.

I remember Kidz saying the camel ride was booked for 7 p.m., once the sun and the temperature were going down, and – more crucially – once everyone else had arrived. But there's no sign of them.

Marianne clears her throat. Her chestnut hair is swept up into some kind of complicated French plait, and her poise demands our attention. She commands an authority I wish I possessed.

Everyone else is already here. Lukas sits on a low sofa with a drink, and Hanneghan is next to him. I make sure I don't stare, though I couldn't be more aware of him if he was on fire. I wonder about asking him how he is – he must have been so close to Augusto. In fact, I'm surprised he's here at all. But maybe no one wants to disappoint Freddie or Marianne. He looks fairly composed. Not grief-stricken. Just quiet. But then I guess he's not a leading actor for nothing.

'The storm we flew through,' she starts, and I remember the

screams, how sick I'd been. 'Well, it didn't just affect us. We passed through before it took full hold and were lucky. But it became worse faster than predicted, and we'd probably have been diverted if they'd thought...' She stops, and glances at Freddie. 'Well, they were encouraged to get here quickly, and they flew through it. The plane coming from LA took a direct lightning hit.'

'No!' Cara's hand shoots to her mouth.

Unrest darts round the room. I think of a plane full of people in the sky. I feel sick.

Marianne holds out her hands, calming everyone. 'They're fine. Everyone is fine. That's obviously our main concern.' She looks again at Freddie, who has the grace to nod in agreement.

She carries on. 'But they had to make an emergency landing, and getting another plane organised, from where they are, is going to take a day. A few need to be checked for shock. They won't arrive until maybe the day after tomorrow.'

I remember what Kidz had been saying about the schedule and I understand Freddie's muttering to Kidz, who is making notes. I guess as the only AD here she will have her work cut out for her.

'What does that mean for us?' Cara asks, crossing her legs and looking from Marianne to Freddie, tossing her blonde hair, which lies in curled waves down her back. 'We were due to start filming tomorrow.'

'I'm sorry,' Marianne says. 'Until the crew and cast have arrived, I couldn't say. But it's likely that filming might take a little longer than we initially expected.'

I don't know how to feel. I have no objection to staying in this gorgeous hotel for longer than planned. But can I keep up the act for a longer period of time?

Cara rolls her eyes. 'I have another awards dinner soon, in LA this time, and I don't want to miss it. It's happening a few days after we were due to get back.'

Freddie is all sweetness and honey. 'Don't worry, Cara, I'm sure we can make it work.'

Marianne looks round the room, and smiles, her voice even and warm, her tone understanding but upbeat. 'We haven't had the easiest start to filming out here. We will all miss Augusto, and I realise it's a lot to cope with. However, we need to remember why we're here. To make a little bit of magic. To offer up something that allows others to leave their worlds and join us, just for a couple of hours. It's what we do. What we've always wanted to do, and we're in the privileged position of being able to create and entertain. We need to remember this. Whether we are missing our friends who are delayed, or missing our friend to whom we've have had to say goodbye.' She looks at Hanneghan at this point. 'We must remember that at the end of this, as hard as it has been, we will create something special. Something to capture the imagination.' She smiles at the room, then glances to a waiting attendant.

'Dinner now,' Marianne says, with an air of finality, as Cara looks as though she's about to say something else. 'Come. The camel ride is still going ahead, if everyone is happy. We'll leave a little later than planned. As we're filming the desert scene in a few days, it will be good for you all to get a feel for it out there. We need to use these extra few days to orientate ourselves in this heat and location. It won't be easy filming here, so it's a good idea to take this time to prepare.' She finishes with a look at Cara. 'The more comfortable we are, the easier filming will be, which means fewer hold ups.'

A waiter, carrying the tray of canapes, gestures for us to follow, and we head out of the lounge through another door. It leads into a large and airy dining room, with a wall of huge windows, the glass broken into squares by black frames, and thick drapes that fall in swathes either side. Purple and silver cushions are plumped out on each chair, and huge chandeliers lower down from high ceilings over each table. The dark wooden floors in the centre of the room gleam, and the edges of the room's floors are pale marble. The room is as sumptuous as the food.

I look out though the windows, and the sky is still bright blue, though I can see the sun lowering. The edges of the hotel building fade out into the sand behind, rising in peaks.

There's a table laid out for all nine of us.

This is going to be hard. This is the first time I'll be under everyone's scrutiny at once, trapped around a dinner table. I'll have to talk to them and maintain Phoebe's accent. With Josh, I've found it easy. He's put me at ease. But here, my acting skills are on full display in front of everyone. My body still aches from the accident and the nap I had hasn't quite given me the time I needed to recover from the last twenty-four hours.

My head also starts to spin when I realise how close Hanneghan will be to me. He sits across from me, a bit to the left. I'm opposite Pablo.

Pablo is busy on his phone for a few minutes, and I listen to Josh and Lukas talking either side of me. A waiter arrives and I hear Pablo ask about nuts. It must have been him with the allergy the flight attendants were talking about earlier.

Nerves swallow me and I daren't open my mouth to speak. I take a breath and try to focus. I can do this.

Josh is asking Lukas about the TED talk he gave the other week.

'Just keeping it real – being true to yourself, always speaking and living your own truth. Eating right, exercise. This world is all the better for us being our authentic selves, you know?' Lukas talks easily as Josh nods.

I'm so aware of Hanneghan, I feel my skin prickle, conscious of each turn of his head, his hand as he lifts his glass. I'm building myself up, just about to ask him how he's doing since he heard about the accident, when Pablo tackles it from a different angle.

'Augusto's death hasn't been released to the press yet. Nada, anywhere,' Pablo says, putting his phone down. He lifts a glass of water and drinks it straight down.

If I wait to start speaking my nerves will break. I steel myself and say, 'Freddie wants a social-media blackout. I guess until PR land with the plane. And his family will need to be told first.'

'Sorry, I was talking more to myself there.' He looks at Hanneghan, then to Freddie and Marianne. 'What a day. The crash, then this lightning strike.' He looks back to Hanneghan, before he seems to shift focus slightly, frowning. 'The delay will end up costing a fortune, we'll be rushed for time. How much of a chance I will have to discuss my role is…' He waves two hands, as though weighing air.

'Well, I suppose at least no one on the plane was hurt,' I say.

'It must have been terrible in the car this afternoon – what happened exactly? How did it crash?' He rests his chin on his fist, as he leans on the table, his dark eyes now intent on me. I should have kept my mouth shut. I feel Josh turn at the question. Lukas and Cara also look. I suppose everyone loves gory details.

'It was such a blur,' I manage to say, feeling uncomfortable. 'Crazy, right?' I look to Josh.

'It was confusing,' Josh says. 'One minute I'm showing Phoebe the hotel on my phone, then there was this gazelle.' He shakes his head. 'The next thing I knew we were spinning, crashing in the sand.'

'Did you hit it?' Pablo asks.

Josh looks at me. 'I don't know – did we?'

I shake my head. 'Either hit one, or swerved to avoid one.' I look at Hanneghan now. 'I'm sorry about your driver. He was with you a long time, wasn't he?'

Hanneghan blows air through his lips in a half sigh, half disbelief. 'Almost eleven years since *Tourist*, the film in Venezuela. Your first film, I think, Pablo? I honestly can't believe it. I saw him at the airport, then the next thing I know, he's dead.'

My stomach churns at the memory.

'I've heard some rumours about him. Not all good,' Pablo says, pouring more wine.

'He wasn't everyone's cup of tea, but he was very loyal to me. I owe him a lot,' Hanneghan replies.

Then, as he stares at his glass, not looking at anyone else, Pablo says, 'He was a cop in Venezuela, wasn't he, before you met him?'

I shoot a look at Hanneghan, who presses his lips together tightly.

'He was,' Hanneghan says, short and brisk. 'I was mobbed and he came to my rescue on the shoot down there. I was lucky he was just outside the set that day. As I say, I owe – sorry, owed – him a great deal. He's been my bodyguard and driver ever since. But I don't think today is the day for gossip, do you? The man is dead.'

Pablo opens his mouth to say something else, and I'm not sure it is going to be an apology, but either by luck or design, Marianne, at the head of the table, raises her glass. 'To those we've lost.'

Everyone around the table follows.

In the silence which then falls, Marianne begins telling us about the camel ride under the stars, the outdoor rugs that will be laid out, the wine, the magic of the evening ahead of us.

Slowly people turn to her and the conversation takes a different path.

But I keep my gaze on Hanneghan, who is still not smiling, looking down at his plate, then at his phone briefly. He then stares at Pablo, who refuses to look back.

10

'This is your camel; she's called Amina,' Kidz says, reading from a list. 'And meet Hassan. He'll lead Amina for you.'

'Salam, Hassan,' I say. I stroke Amina's neck as she lowers her head and blows hot air out of her nostrils onto my face.

'She likes you, no?' Hassan says.

'I hope so,' I say, smiling at them both.

It's a little after 7 p.m. and we stand outside of the hotel, where the desert begins to open into the wide darkening emptiness we're surrounded by.

Freddie is already up on his camel, and he waves his hand out into the unfamiliar landscape like some kind of Arabian guide. 'OK, we'll ride for about forty minutes, and then we'll stop where the picnic and tents are set up. This is the ride we'll be filming when the rest of the crew arrive so it's important you stay in the moment. Marianne, Kidz and I will scope out for shot locations, and all you have to do is enjoy this!'

I glance around at the group. There are some interesting outfit choices. Desert chic is clearly a thing. Pablo is busy taking a selfie wearing some kind of headscarf, which he definitely pulls off. Lukas is wearing a leather headband and some kind of baggy leather trousers. Cara looks breathtaking. She wears a light green safari suit with her shirt tied up in a knot at her waist. Her hair sits in a messy yet perfect bun, and a white scarf is tied around her neck. She goes to talk to Lukas, and I see Hanneghan looking over at her. Of course he does. How could anyone take their eyes off her? There's a moment when she glances up and holds his gaze. They both stand still, in freeze frame. Then her hand goes to her throat, and she drags her eyes back to Lukas; Hanneghan still looking, still watching her.

Hanneghan.

The fact he's actually here, and so close I could touch him, is the stuff of years of fantasy. And I actually spoke to him at dinner. I still can't get over it. Getting drunk on the plane, then arriving at the hotel covered in scratches and blood – I haven't made the kind of first impression I was intending on anyone here. But especially him. He wears a white shirt, and his silver hair contrasts with the darker stubble on his cheeks. He's tanned, just a shade lighter than his eyes.

'You ready for this?' Josh speaks from behind me, and I hear the smile in his voice before I turn around.

'Yep, all saddled up and ready to ride!' I say. 'I didn't get the memo about the desert dress code.'

'Yee-ha!' He taps a kind of Indiana Jones-style hat he wears. 'I'm a dick, right?' He laughs, then glances left and right, speaking quietly with a gleam in his eye. 'Insta ready, baby.' He pulls a face at some of the outfits.

'Your shoulder's still OK?' I ask. I know I ache from head to toe. In many ways, this all feels unreal. Being out here – barely any time since New York, the comedy club. Phoebe still hasn't messaged and if it wasn't for Josh keeping me grounded, I would run home. So far this trip is part dream, part nightmare.

He nods. 'And you? Coping after earlier?'

'I think so.' I stroke Amina. 'Looking forward to some more

desert adventures. No point half doing something. Ready for the ride, hubby?' Dress for success. I throw in a confident, upbeat tone. No need to let anyone see me wallowing.

'You betcha.' He taps his hat again. 'I'll be right behind you – any problems with your camel just holla!'

He steps backwards as Freddie calls for everyone to mount up. Kidz waves at me from further down the line. She's on some kind of electric dune buggy. I can see an expensive-looking camera strapped on carefully. She's changed into shorts and a white ripped t-shirt.

'See you there!' she calls. 'Didn't really fancy the camel ride. These are apparently quiet, so shouldn't frighten them!'

Marianne is gracefully mounting a camel which sits on the sand, and Freddie calls to Cara. 'Cara, darling, are you comfortable?'

I look over again at Hanneghan. Regal against the royal blue sky in a pale cream shirt and linen trousers. I daren't go over, but as Amina lowers down for me to mount, I notice something fall from Hanneghan's pocket. Not realising, he leans forward to pick up the reins before climbing onto his camel.

'Hanneghan, you dropped something!' I call out, pleased that the sky is darker and no one can see how red my face is as I say it. It feels like fire. I run over, and pick up his phone. 'Here we go.'

He takes it from me, dusting it off. 'Thanks. I wouldn't want to lose that. Phoebe, isn't it?'

'Yes,' I say, my voice a squeak. I force myself to speak clearly, keep my accent steady and convincing. I decide to pick up the chat from dinner. 'I'm so sorry again about Augusto. This can't have been top of your list of things to do tonight.'

Around us I hear the group preparing. The saddle leather creaks; there's laughter. Freddie is calling to Cara again.

I can't turn from Hanneghan's face. In the evening light, the shadows on his cheekbones are deeper than they seem on film. In interviews he seems self-assured, slick. Tonight, he is quiet. He says, after a moment, 'Were you the one with him when he died?'

I nod. I don't want to seem like a kid instead of the confident actress I'm trying to project. 'It was all very sudden. We had no idea what was happening. I don't think he suffered at all.'

His eyes, which had looked out into the desert when I'd spoken, now focus on me, and he offers a half smile. 'Thank you. He's been with me a long time. Him leaving so quickly, it's… a lot. He didn't really have any family. He pinned himself to me. That's a lot of loyalty.'

Freddie shouts, sounding impatient, 'Time to leave! The cars are picking us up about ten and I want to be in my bed before midnight. I'm exhausted and we're up early tomorrow. Let's get a move on! Come on, look at Cara, she's already set off!'

Hanneghan turns to mount his camel, and I drag my feet backwards towards Amina. It's hard to turn my face. I still find myself watching him, staring at him, as Josh calls, 'You're going to miss the group!'

I realise almost everyone else is already moving. Josh has waited for me, astride his camel. He laughs at me as a I mount Amina. 'Starstruck?'

'Don't!' I say, shaking my head in shame. 'What did you say earlier? Don't stare directly at the sun. I think I've embarrassed myself enough for the first twenty-four hours.'

'Come on, let's stir up this desert and catch up,' he says.

I apologise to Hassan for keeping him waiting, and we set off. Amina strides quickly in a loping style to catch up with the rest of the camels.

Hanneghan has caught up to the back of the party, near Cara's camel. She must have asked her handler to wait for him.

She leans to the right, towards him, and then says something. It's the first time I've seen her speak to him. Maybe she caught some of my fangirling and it's annoyed her. She looks back to me. I can't hear what she says, and I can't really see her face. But she waves her hand in my direction, and then says something to her handler and kicks her camel, who half leaps away from Hanneghan, sand rising up like a cloud of dust against the background of sky and stars.

11

It's haunting out here. The air is warm, and the smell is different to anything I've known. Partly leather from the saddles, partly the animals. There's magic in the desert at twilight: a hint of danger, the promise of romance. I can't believe I'm here at all. This is not some busy tourist excursion with a coach waiting for us. This is five-star elegance and a life I've not lived before. It's transcendent. It's nearly all my dreams come true. I almost forget to worry about anything. I almost forget my ambition, Phoebe, Hanneghan, everything. Almost.

After we'd all set off, the camels were looped together on a long rope, which slid through the bridle of each, the front camel in the line acting as a guide. There are two of these lines. Hassan leads me, and Josh is second. Lukas had been attached afterwards, followed by Marianne. Freddie and Cara are at the front of the first line, and Freddie's voice floats back to me on the still air.

His fawning of Cara has crossed the line from irritating to nauseating. I noticed that Marianne's tone had been sharp with Cara earlier, after the accident. Freddie paying Cara that much attention must bother her. I'd think there was something going on but Cara can't seem to stand him. I suppose keeping the talent happy is part of the job, but Freddie has been quite distant with Hanneghan. Lukas is a huge name, but this is his first film. He might pull in the younger crowd, but it's Cara and Hanneghan on the ticket. Freddie would do well to keep Hanneghan happy too.

I remember an article I read about rumours that their marriage was in trouble and feel instantly defensive of Marianne. She's had so much going on, even a stalker to contend with.

As the camels tread the sand, and we wind our way into the dark, my legs start to ache. I'm not used to sitting like this and it's not the kind of thing I would have picked to do after a car accident. I'm pleased when Freddie calls out that it's only another five minutes.

The route has been fairly straight, but it has involved climbing and descending peaks, sand rising and falling as though it's been groomed – the patterns in the dark orange raked into long lines. It's like magic. Like a thousand snakes have slithered through and left tracks, neat and even.

Hanneghan continues to be quiet. I search for him through the dark blue light as we arrive at the picnic spot, amongst the figures dismounting in the deep sand. There are huge oil lamps laid out around rugs, and low wooden chairs with deep red blankets have been set around a huge array of food. More food than we can possibly eat. I'd expected dessert and wine, but this looks almost like a three-course meal. A big metal fire pit is lit to the side, offering a burst of red against the darkening sky.

'Going overboard with the food! But I suppose it's so hot during the day,' I say.

'They do cater well out here,' Kidz says, walking over to me. 'By the way, this is the location for the confrontation scene when Cara and Hanneghan are found by Pablo with you and Josh as background characters. I think Freddie is going to go over it in a minute with everyone.'

'Great. Can't wait!' And I can't. Finally, a chance to actually act. To do what I'm good at. In front of Hanneghan.

We sit on the backless wooden chairs, covered with dark red blankets with intricate stitching, and Josh flops on the one next to me. He winces as he lands on the low seat, and touches his shoulder, gingerly.

'Was the camel a bit much?' I ask.

'Let's just say I can feel it,' he says. 'Are we allowed to drink on these painkillers?'

I pass him a brass cup of wine which has been laid out next to our plates. 'I think your shoulder is asking for some.'

I glance round the group. Pablo is stood apart, fiddling with a camera and looking through a lens with Kidz. Cara arranges herself on one of the low seats, and Hanneghan positions himself next to her, which I find interesting.

The amber lighting softens the lines on Hanneghan's face, making him look like the young star I remember from my teenage years. I'd rented film after film, just before our local Blockbusters had closed down. Friday nights were Hanneghan film nights. All my friends knew they'd be required to come with me to see any new release featuring him, over and over again. Mum hated it. She'd got to the point where she'd banned any more posters of him going up in my room. She put all the copies of his films in a cabinet in the living room so she didn't have to see them, day in and day out. *Hanneghan overload*, she'd called it.

Cara catches me staring, and she leans to Hanneghan and whispers something. He looks over and I glance down at the food quickly, my cheeks burning. I see the expression on Cara's face though. I've been discovered.

It seems my interest has sparked Cara into talking to Hanneghan. Maybe someone else looking longingly at him has ruffled her a little.

There's a fine line between respect and adoration when hanging around stars. This level of fame is a game changer – you're never one of the ordinary people again. And everyone knows it. I can't get a name for myself as some kind of soppy super fan.

The colours of the night have darkened from blues to a near velvet black now. There had been fire in the sky earlier, and the almost blackness is just as impressive.

Freddie claps his hands as everyone picks at the food. 'OK! Let's go over the scene. It's a flashback, to when the affair was discovered with disastrous consequences. It drove Cara's character into a spiral of anxiety and chaos. Although it will only feature briefly in the film, which, as you all know, is mostly set in New York, this is central to the plot. We'll have some food and wine, then we'll do a read through. It's important you experience all of this!' He waves his hand, and we all follow his gesture: the near velvet sky, stars like jewels, and the night, which we wear like musk on our skin.

'It doesn't hurt to get a head start. Phoebe and Josh, you are the other members of the party. Your presence forces the other characters to keep their arguments hidden. The characters have been on a sunset camel trek and they camp in the desert overnight. During dinner, Cara and Hanneghan sneak out to Hanneghan's tent, where they make love. Pablo – Cara's husband – is drunk and asleep by the fire. Wandering into the wrong tent, Phoebe is witness to their affair, and when she returns to the fire, she is conflicted. Should she tell Pablo? When Pablo stands to retire to bed, Phoebe calls out a goodbye to him so loudly it signals to Cara he is returning. Pablo realises something is going on, and he runs to their tent, to find Cara and Hanneghan naked, hurriedly dressing. This scene is all about a love Cara has spent years repressing. Repressed desire and the desire for revenge lies at the heart of this film. I need you all to soak up the magic of this scene – the danger and the passion of the desert, the sun, the isolation. It is against this background that Cara's passion for Hanneghan reawakens. It lies at the very heart of the film, as we return to Cara and Pablo years later, trying to rebuild their relationship.'

When he finishes, there is silence. Why did he refer to the characters by the actors' names? It's pretty close to the bone. Did he *need* to refer to Cara's passion for Hanneghan? It's not like the split and the heartbreak hadn't been plastered all over the media for the world to see.

It has a very powerful effect on the group. Their faces, half-lit by the oil lamps, are all shadows and darkness, and each one is blank.

For a second, no one speaks. Then Cara, out of nowhere, stands, half sobs, and runs off into the night.

'You really are a piece of shit,' Hanneghan says, staring at Freddie. 'It's all a game to you, isn't it? Stirring it all up for as much media exposure as possible.' Then he lifts a brass cup, filled with wine, and hurls it at Freddie before he stands and walks away.

The cup sails up and over Freddie's head, but not without raining wine over his face.

I gasp, and I notice Josh's eyes darting from Freddie to Marianne. No one else speaks, the air is tight with tension, until Marianne finally climbs up, shrugging her shoulders, her voice tired and weary. 'Freddie, what the fuck.' Then she follows Cara, out into the black of the waiting desert.

No one moves. Freddie sits like stone, then carefully wipes his face with a napkin. Pablo, who hasn't said much until now, speaks in a low voice. 'Why am I drunk in this scene? I wasn't in the latest version of the script I read. And this argument – this was supposed to be a romantic getaway, and Cara's character's affair was supposed to be a betrayal of me. Am I now the oaf in the script? Am I the ridiculous husband figure who gets in the way of true love?'

The silence feels loaded. With tensions running so high, I see Freddie considering his answer, and I realise Pablo is right. I remember Kidz had said Hanneghan had insisted on script changes. Was he becoming the romantic lead? Before, Pablo had been described as a wounded romantic. Now he seems more desperate, cuckolded, like a pantomime husband.

He sits quietly, staring at Freddie, waiting for an answer. When Freddie says nothing, still focused on wiping the wine from his face and refusing to look anyone in the eye, Pablo rises, and moves over to the table where the remainder of the wine is laid out. He opens another bottle and strides off into the dark, still holding the camera from earlier.

Finally, Freddie moves. Saying nothing, he walks away – looking as though he needs a drink. It allows me to exhale and stretch my legs. I look at Josh, whose face is full of shock.

'What now?' I whisper.

12

Needing to escape the tension of the picnic rug framed like a stage by the lamps, I head out into the shadows of the desert. Not too far because I don't want to get lost, but the tension has formed a break in the evening and I wonder if I might use it to find Hanneghan. I guess we're still going to run lines once everyone has calmed down, so I may as well get a head start. And I've been dreaming of acting with Hanneghan for years. I'm not ready to let Hollywood-size egos derail this. I have no idea if this behaviour is to be expected on a film set.

My heart beats a little faster, imagining rehearsing an actual script with the man I have dreamt about for so long.

Instead, though, I bump into Pablo. I almost trip over him as he sits in the sand, drinking from the bottle.

'Are you all right?' I ask, stepping backwards to see him better. He barely looks at me. He's hunched over the bottle he holds, looking more morose than I'd imagine a successful Hollywood star would ever feel.

He shrugs. 'Now they bring *him* in, I've been relegated.' He spits in the sand. 'Fuck. I'll still get paid the same, but the attention, the PR, the buzz – that won't belong to me... You will learn. It's never enough. Freddie will bend any which fucking way for him. For the media. For the attention. With Cara and Hanneghan on screen together, for the first time since they split, we all know what it will do for the audience figures. And that is why we're here, yes? For the money. Not for the art.' He spits in the sand again.

'You mean he'll bend for Hanneghan?'

'Who else! Your part has been cut too. Freddie probably hasn't shown you the last rewrite, but I insisted on seeing it. You had a scene camel-riding out to this spot with the actor who was playing Hanneghan's role previously. I was riding with Cara, and although she still had the affair, we had a big argument. It was a great scene. Now you and I ride together on the camels, and while I'm distracted, Cara and Hanneghan flirt – all sexual tension. My dramatic row is gone. Our lines have been slashed. Your husband's – Josh's – role barely has any lines now.'

'But… I still get to…' I'm not really sure what to say. The script Phoebe had given me outlined Josh and I as honeymooners at the hotel, there to offset the drama of Cara's affair. While small parts, we both had lines and a few scenes, some with Hanneghan. The desert shoot was a flashback in the overall film, but significant. 'I mean, I'm still *in* it?'

He seems to ignore my question, much more focused on his own situation. 'With Hanneghan demanding screen stealing moments, they've taken screen time from me. It makes my blood boil. I could tear Freddie limb from limb. Fuck!' Turning his head, he picks up his bottle of wine and strides away. I have a searing impression of his charisma on screen setting moments alight.

The air twists. The heat, for a second, disappears.

All this anger.

I wonder if it's true that I will lose lines. I suppose I just have to hope that I get to act at all.

Has Pablo gone to look for Freddie? Should I do something? Was he the one on the plane talking about a murder?

The longer I'm around these people the more I'm beginning to believe I did hear something on the plane. Yet there can't be more drama to this group, can there? Surely they're at peak dramatic behaviour as it stands.

Pablo is an outline in the dark, near the electric dune buggy. He's talking to someone although I can't make out who. But if I really *did* hear something, is Pablo talking to the other person from the plane?

I feel weak with stress.

The camels nearby stamp on the sand. The rattle of their lead reins ring in the night.

I wish Phoebe was here so I could talk this out. I look around for Josh. I need a friendly face. I gravitate towards Hassan and the other guides as they pile up buckets. I'm nervous. What I heard on the plane felt so unreal before, I'd written it off in my head. It feels very real now.

'Are we heading back?' I ask Hassan. The night isn't going as planned and maybe it wouldn't hurt to get back to the hotel.

'We take the camels back now. We just give them something to eat.'

I glance back at the fire pit, oil lamps and picnic rugs. They're about thirty feet away. Freddie holds a script in his hand. He looks ready to start running lines, finally. I check my watch. It's almost 8.30 p.m.; I guess we'll have to stay here.

Shadows shift across the sand and I look nervously at the camels.

'How will we get back, if you're going?'

'Cars will arrive. Ten o'clock.' Hassan smiles. 'We ride the camels back now.'

I glance at my watch. That gives us some time for a drink and then an hour or so to run the lines a few times. I'm exhausted. I wish I'd listened to Kidz and just stayed at the hotel.

I give Amina a stroke as Hassan asks her to sit. He climbs up and I feel a wave of foreboding.

'Thank you, Hassan,' I say, giving Amina a final pat. She grunts as she walks away, leading the others.

I can taste dread.

13

head back to the picnic rug, ringed by the light of the oil lamps. Josh looks exhausted. He sits near the fire pit and his head keeps tipping forward in sleepy nods, then he jolts awake, before tipping forward again.

Freddie mutters something over the script, then says, 'Where is everyone? We'll need to do the run through to make sure this evening isn't a complete waste.'

'I don't know about everyone, but I was just talking to Pablo.' I don't say he's drunk and angry. I wonder if Freddie was just trying to wind everyone up to get them in character.

'Kidz!' Freddie roars. 'She's got the latest scripts,' he says to me. 'For fuck's sake.' He looks at his phone, which I don't understand because there's no signal out here. 'They've all fucked off somewhere. What a waste of time. We need to do this reading.'

I can make out Kidz, talking to Lukas, looking at the camera shots they've taken as they make their way back to the chairs.

'We can start now,' Kidz says. 'I found Cara and she's refusing to move. Marianne is going to sit with her. But Josh, Lukas and Phoebe can do theirs. I'll fill in the missing roles.'

'I'll join,' Hanneghan says, coming to sit down from behind me.

I feel a jolt of joy. I'm about to read lines with Hanneghan. The terror leaves me for a moment. Excitement takes over. After all, Hanneghan is here. Lukas. I'd seen Pablo. Whoever I'd heard on the plane had mentioned a man dying. But no one's dead and hopefully it will stay that way. I'm back to thinking I must have made it up.

Now that there's something to do, there's a bit more focus. The tension seems to dissipate slightly.

'Here we go.' Kidz hands out scripts and in the lamplight, we begin a read through of the scene, which involves the group of us taking this camel ride out in the desert, where we'll camp overnight. We then spend the next two days in the desert. 'Luckily, we'll actually be sleeping at the hotel when filming it.'

I scan it. My part is similar, but Pablo's has been cut down. He was right.

'Most of it is shot at twilight or at night,' Freddie says. 'It's why we're filming in August. Good rates but it doesn't affect us really. Can we go again from where we mount the camels? You've just done it, so think through the pace of the conversation. The movement of the camels will lend itself to the rhythm of the scene.'

Hanneghan starts reading and I look at his profile by oil lamp. It's unreal. All the times I've dreamt of meeting him. The inspiration he's been for me. Now I'm here, and he doesn't disappoint in person. He's magnetic.

'Here, Phoebe, let's read that part again,' Hanneghan says. 'Your character is quite bubbly. Let me try again and change tone, so I can match you. It will offset the drama of the affair.' He glances at Freddie who nods in earnest, and I'm relieved to see they can work together.

A few of the others disappear off as we prepare to read through it again. I guess to get more food or drink.

'We're just married,' I read. 'We got married in Alabama.'

'Great accent,' Freddie says. 'You handle deep South well.'

I breathe a sigh of relief. Having to switch between two accents is hard. I'd been sure that if anyone was going to spot me faking it then this would be the moment.

Hanneghan pulls a face in response to my line. 'Marriage is like a—' He breaks off. 'I think we need a different line here, Freddie. There needs to be a lighter moment.'

Freddie nods again. We run through the section a few more times.

We arrive at the part where Pablo finds Cara and Hanneghan.

'Let's take a break,' Freddie says. 'You've done well. Phoebe – great job.'

I want to burst.

He looks at his watch. 'Time's flown. It hasn't all gone as planned but we made it work. The cars should be here any minute. Can you check, Kidz?'

The others are drifting back as we're finishing up.

But Freddie's voice is cut off as, from nowhere, a scream flies out in the dark. Fear grips my stomach and I jump up. 'What's that?'

Hanneghan is on his feet now too. 'Stay here. I'll go look.' He jogs past the fire pit and out beyond the lamps.

Freddie, looking at his phone, raises his head. 'What now?'

Kidz looks worried as she watches Hanneghan leave. 'I wonder what that was. We need to get back. Fuck, no signal.' She holds the phone aloft. Then shakes her head. 'Nothing. I hope everyone's OK.' She looks out into the dark, touching her stomach like she's feeling unwell.

Freddie grunts at his phone.

I look around. No Marianne, Cara or Pablo. I imagine Pablo is sat in the dark, fairly close by, drinking himself into a stupor. But I haven't seen Cara or Marianne for a while.

I'm nervous. The voices on the plane rush back at me.

Again, a wail. Louder this time.

'What *is* that?!' Kidz says.

Freddie stands up. 'Cara?!'

'Shall we help? Phoebe, Josh? Come on.' Lukas looks at us and then starts to jog. 'We'll follow Hanneghan.'

Josh and I scramble to follow him.

'I'll sort the cars,' Kidz says.

I check my phone as I jog. It's almost 10.30 p.m. – the screen lights up but there's still no signal, still no messages from Phoebe.

As we leave, I hear Kidz and Freddie argue.

'If something else has gone wrong, we'll need the cars quickly. You're the bloody AD. Didn't you speak to Marianne? She said she'd confirmed them.' Freddie sounds angry – but anxious too.

The scream sounds again. Louder this time.

'Marianne! Cara!' Josh shouts.

We stop, looking left then right.

Nothing.

'Shall we head out further?' Josh sounds doubtful.

'We'll have to,' Lukas says.

We're on the outskirts of the camp and it's impossible to see far at all. The dark of night is impenetrable. Thinking of the scream, I follow Lukas, with Josh next to me. It's not cold, but I carry an oil lamp and the small circle of light we move in is disorientating – the sand is uneven beneath our feet.

The light makes it impossible to see far. I blink, trying to make my eyes adjust.

'Where are they?' Josh says. 'What do we do?'

'Go that way, I'll go this,' Lukas says, and runs off further away into the dark. He's swallowed up quickly.

'Cara!' I call. 'I don't understand why they would have gone so far.'

What I heard on the plane rings louder in my ears. I need to say something.

'Josh, you know earlier, on the plane—'

'Hello?' A voice to the left, still in the dark.

'Hanneghan!' I shout. I'd know his voice anywhere.

'Over here!' Josh calls.

We stand and wait. I hang the oil lamp I brought along in the direction of his voice. Slipping into focus, his frame appears – first as a shadow, then whole.

'Help!' The shout out in the dark is louder again. There's no time to talk to Hanneghan.

'It's Cara!' Hanneghan starts to sprint towards the voice.

'*Help!*' We hear her again. Her cry is shrill and scared. Hanneghan extends his stride and I fall as I chase him. Josh offers his hand and pulls me up, and as I follow the dust of Hanneghan's tracks, I hear the scream again, piercing, filled with horror – the echoes of alarm must ripple across the sand for miles. I swallow fright like a gulp of water.

Hanneghan shouts, 'Jesus Christ, Cara, are you OK?'

I open my mouth to ask a question, but before I can speak, I see her, her shape, loose and soft in the dark. Cara. The pale scarf she was wearing has unravelled and falls behind her like the hood of a ghost, and her hands are pressed to her mouth. The scream is a whimper now, leaking out between her fingers.

And I follow her gaze, to the floor of the desert. Hanneghan bends down, reaching slowly.

Before us all, lies Marianne. Her head is flat in the sand, but tilted downwards. She looks like a dropped doll. One leg is splayed to the left, knee falling outwards. One hand lies across the sand.

I look back to her head. I search for clues as to why she looks like this. What has happened?

'Marianne?' Hanneghan speaks softly, and he turns her face upwards.

'I don't think she's breathing!'

'Check her airways,' I say, dropping to my knees in the sand. I feel for a pulse.

Hanneghan pulls something out of her mouth as I hold her wrist. Nothing.

'I think she choked. There was food in her mouth.' Hanneghan lifts her head and breathes into her mouth, pinching her nose.

'Let me help,' I say. I link my fingers and press down hard on her chest. I push, rhythmically, like I was trained to do on some first aid course, and Josh shouts for help.

Between us, Hanneghan and I work on Marianne, until I sense, rather than see, more of the group behind us. At some point, someone puts a hand on my shoulder.

'Her eyes are just open,' Cara says, softly. 'She's not blinking. She's not doing anything.'

'I think she's gone, Phoebe.' This is Josh.

'Is Freddie here?' I ask.

Josh shakes his head.

I look at Hanneghan, who nods. 'I think we should stop.'

I sit back on my heels. Two dead in one day. It can't be. *What is happening?*

He goes as though to lift her head, to see if she wakes, but instead, he gently closes her eyes. Her French plait is frayed and loose. The lipstick on her mouth, smeared.

Her body lies still in the light of the lamp, and a hush falls.

'She's dead.' Hanneghan turns and looks to Cara, me, then Josh. 'How is she dead?'

Specks of light flash in the dark as a collective shiver runs through the group and they turn on their phone torches. It offers little consolation against the night. A vigil.

Cara surprises me. She unwinds the white scarf she'd retied around her neck, lifting it and letting it float out as wide as it will go, then lays it over Marianne's body, as softly as a kiss.

WEDNESDAY

DAY FOUR

14

'Kidz, are they lights? Is it the hotel?'

The desert rolls up and down. I was sure we'd gone wrong, but this last curve and descent on a desert peak feels very familiar. My arms ache from hanging on to Kidz. It must be 2 a.m. now. We're exhausted. I feel dizzy, and Kidz had stopped the buggy once to throw up – grief on the desert floor.

The aftermath was terrible – Cara crying, Hanneghan still and shocked. And Freddie… Out and out panic in the blackness. Terror had gripped us all. For a few moments I'd tensed – waiting for an attacker to spring at us. But there was no one. Just us. And it was clear that she'd choked, out in the dark, with no one around to help her. A tragic accident.

We waited and waited until it was clear the cars weren't coming. That's when we spotted the dune buggy still parked by the picnic rug – apparently it was going to be driven back by someone from the hotel when the cars arrived. Kidz had suggested she ride it back. But she didn't want to go alone. Her hands had shaken as she'd talked – we were all shaking.

I offered to go with her. I didn't want to spend another minute out in the desert.

Finally, we see the hotel.

Kidz swings the buggy left and slowly the lights grow brighter. I cling on with the last of my strength as we ride into the hotel grounds. The security guards on the gate run towards us, shouting, and I stumble as I clamber off.

There is controlled chaos as we enter the hotel. The staff move faster, people appear from nowhere. Flurry and busyness.

My whole body aches. I shake from having gripped on for so long. The relief of arriving must hit Kidz, who wipes tears from her eyes as she collapses onto a sofa.

I can't talk about Marianne's death. I leave it to Kidz. But she doesn't start with that. Instead, she begins with the cars that didn't arrive.

The manager hurries out. It's the same one I met earlier. His friendly calm is ruffled.

'But the cars were cancelled?' He runs his fingers through his hair.

There are calls to bring food, instructions to investigate.

Then he sits with us. 'We were told before you set off, that no cars were needed until six a.m., because you wanted to do some night filming. That's why we added extra food for the picnic.'

All the food. That makes more sense now.

'What?' Kidz is almost shouting, exhausted and incredulous. 'Why would we leave ourselves stranded out there over night? So much has already gone wrong! One of us died yesterday! Of course we wouldn't want to stay out all night!'

Kidz still hasn't mentioned Marianne. I look at her. I wonder if saying it will make it real.

'Well, it's warm enough, and some of our guests do like to camp out there. You are film people! The normal rules are different.' He moves to the reception desk and dials a number, managing to stay calm; we sit shivering in the gilded reception room, from exhaustion more than anything. Around us the décor is for the rich and elite. Pale tiles, a fountain in the centre of the room, jars of dates and nuts. How could this happen in the seat of such luxury?

'The storm, the crash, now Marianne,' I say to Kidz. 'What's happening?' I try to hold it together, but I can't help thinking this is my fault. That we're cursed because of me. The curse of the doppelganger. We've messed with something dark and now we're all paying the price.

Kidz barely speaks. She looks broken.

Then I remember. 'The stalker!' Why hadn't I thought of it. 'Do you think they followed us out?' I grab Kidz's arm. 'Tell the police when they come. Tell them someone had been following her in LA.'

'That's finished with.' Kidz is short with me. She doesn't really look at me as she says, 'The call yesterday was to say there's nothing behind it. It was just a fan. No threats were made.'

'But you need to tell them! Freddie will know all about it.' I sink against the chair and rest my head back. Everything spins. I still can't really believe it. Marianne dead. Augusto dead. All that's happened.

'Cars are on their way. We'll get them back as quickly as we can.' The manager waves his hands again, and bronze trays arrive with hot tea. I grab mine, needing to wash away the mouthfuls of sand I'd swallowed on the journey here.

'Have you looked into who cancelled the cars?' Kidz moves away from me to the reception desk and places her hands flat on the counter. I hold my tea still, waiting for the answer.

The manager opens his mouth then closes it, then finally he looks at us warily. 'The message came from Mrs Marianne Asquith. She called from her room.'

'Fuck,' I say. I stand from the sofa and head over to them.

Kidz looks back at me. 'Can that be right?'

'Did she give her name?' I ask. 'You might know which room the call came from, but did you recognise her voice? Did she say who she was?'

The manager, already flustered, waves his hands a little more, rebutting any expected accusation. 'Well, I took the call. It came from her room, and she just said she wanted to change the pick-up time to six a.m.; they had some filming to do. I suggested additional food, and she said that would be fine. She said they needed to do rehearsals out there. And she requested privacy once you'd arrived. No staff.'

Earlier, I'd passed Freddie and Marianne's room. I'd seen someone coming out of it, but I can't remember who it was. I try to focus on a face. They'd been wearing something yellow – a cap?

I try to think, but I'm so tired.

Kidz looks back to me and I nod. We need to tell them.

She says, 'Well, there's something you should know. One of our party...' She breaks off at this. Marianne's body, under Cara's scarf, empty eyes looking up into the heavens. I realise she just can't say it. She's known Marianne far longer than I have. I put my hand on hers.

'Marianne Asquith is now dead,' I say. 'You need to report it to the police, and if they say it's OK, bring back the body. But you will need to speak to the police, please. Now.'

15

'Hunak!' The night manager flaps his hands and barks out orders. He is busy on the phone, speaking to the police, to doctors. I don't understand what he's saying but every now and again he updates Kidz and me with details and questions: *the police will take over at the scene and look after the body. Is anyone else hurt?*

I wait with Kidz in a lounge area, where there are trays of snacks and tea laid out. Staff are poised in the wings, waiting for instructions. It's less than an hour since we arrived, but well into the night.

'Here,' I say to Kidz, who looks as fragile as I feel. 'Drink this tea.' I pass her a cup and we huddle into the velvet sofa.

The cars are quick with the others, and I've managed a five-minute shower and a change into clean shorts and t-shirt by the time they arrive. I needed to get rid of the sand. A wave of shock had hit me as the water pummelled down, and I'd bent over, my hands on my knees, and sobbed. For the second time today, my throat burns and my head aches.

And I'm still shivering.

Marianne is dead. This trip is now a nightmare.

There is noise outside the lounge as the cars return.

Lukas enters with Freddie leaning on his arm. The others follow quietly, looking shell-shocked.

'Freddie, I'm so sorry,' I say, leaping up and gesturing to a chair. For want of something to do I reach for a cup of tea for him, but Kidz is already there, saying, 'Here, Freddie.' She holds it, waiting for him to sit as he leans on Lukas.

I'm surprised by the expression on her face. There's a tenderness there I wouldn't have expected, given the way he speaks to her. But then I suppose she has worked with him for a while. And maybe it's more for Marianne than Freddie.

Lukas lowers him onto the sofa and the manager waves his hands. Another tray of sweet treats is brought over.

'Sugar is good for shock,' he says.

'Yes,' Hanneghan says, sat with his arm around Cara on a nearby sofa. 'And Cara you must have some too.'

Josh and Pablo sit on another sofa and look on as Cara's hand trembles when she takes the tea, which she doesn't drink.

Freddie glances at the manager, then at me. Then to Hanneghan. He seems dazed.

'Go on,' Lukas says. 'Drink up.'

'I'm so sorry, Mr Asquith-Smith,' the hotel manager says, bowing slightly. I admire the tone he takes – he is courteous, sympathetic, but also pragmatic. 'The police will want to speak to you soon. They've said they'd like to speak to you and the first two people to find Ms Asquith to begin with. They won't be here immediately. For now I have suggested you all rest. The police have said they will take it from here. We will leave them to do their job.'

'I want to sit with her.' Freddie's gaze catches me again in his sweep round the room. His eyes are red and the skin beneath looks bruised. He sounds angry. His tone is quick, full of distrust. He looks behind me, at everyone else. 'It all happened so quickly. I want to see her and know she's safe. I do not want to wait until tomorrow. She's all alone. She's just lying there, all alone!'

He looks at Kidz. 'I didn't want to leave her. They made me. They said a member of staff would wait with her, so I left her there. I've left her out on that sand, with no one she knows.'

Then Freddie's head falls to his knees and he howls. He's in the grip of something and I have no idea what to do. Lukas places his hand on his arm. 'Freddie, I'm so sorry.'

The rip of grief makes him seem much smaller and older.

I wish I had never got on the plane; never decided to do this. I wish I had stayed in my room earlier, to rest, like Kidz had suggested.

The manager speaks, and I'm relieved he sounds so clear-headed. The rest of us are floundering. 'There is nothing you can do, sir. It is best we leave it all to the police. They will tell you when you can see your wife. I will take care of the details. I would suggest going to your room.'

Freddie stands, obviously trying to take control of himself. 'I need to sit with her.' He takes a deep breath, then looks at us all. When his eyes catch mine again, I'm not sure he's really seeing anything.

Expressionless, he leaves the room, heading who knows where.

Once he is gone, our diminished group look at each other. I perch on a sofa near where Freddie had been sitting. There's a sense of shock in the room. We're all exhausted, but I don't really want to be on my own right this second. No one makes a move to leave.

Hanneghan asks Cara if she wants more tea, but she says nothing. Kidz gestures to a tray held by one of the hotel staff, and he tops up our waters, our hot sweet tea. Josh leans his head back against the sofa and closes his eyes.

Lukas whispers, 'Are you OK?'

'Before today, I'd never seen a dead body,' I say quietly. 'I mean, a great-uncle in an open coffin once, but nothing like today. It just doesn't compute.'

He nods.

'It's the worst thing. Particularly if it's brutal,' he says. He stares down at the ornate rug.

I don't think to ask him then, what he has seen, or what he knows about brutal death, and how it looks.

'Do you know what happened?' Lukas asks. 'Do any of you know?'

I look at him. His profile familiar from thousands of magazine covers. It's still strange, seeing him in the flesh.

'What do you mean?' I say. Hanneghan looks at us. Pablo too.

'I heard she choked. I think it was Pablo who said it – there was food in her mouth. That's crazy, right? If she had just stayed at the camp, we could have helped her.'

Pablo nods. 'That's what I heard.'

I think this through. The shock of seeing her sprawled out in the sand had obliterated everything else in my mind. I hadn't really processed the whole thing.

Lukas says, more quietly, 'You don't think it was anything else? I was back near the picnic, so I didn't see anything, but it's all… well, I mean…'

'What?' I look at him in shock. 'What else do you think could have happened?'

He shrugs.

I make up my mind quickly. I need to tell Josh what I heard on the plane. Could this have anything to do with that? It's too twisty, too rotten to try to think it through alone.

And if what I heard is true and to blame for this, then someone else, a man, is also due to die.

'I don't really understand exactly what happened,' Hanneghan says. He gestures to a member of staff who brings drinks stronger than tea, but I notice Hanneghan remains on water. 'Look, let's go over what we saw. We'll need to give statements when the police arrive. I think Cara and I should speak to them with Freddie as we were the first two people to reach Marianne. I expect they'll want to do that tonight – or I suppose – this morning. It might take them a few hours to get here. I think it makes sense to try to sort out what happened.

'Yes, we should,' I say. The whole thing is a blur. I want someone to take charge of this and make it seem more manageable. Not like a terrible dream. And of course it's Hanneghan who steps forward to help us.

Josh nods too but looks reluctant to contribute. I haven't heard him speak since he came back.

Kidz grabs some paper. She likes staying busy. 'Shall I just jot down where we all went when the group broke up?'

'Well, I suppose you're all looking at me,' Cara says. She's been a bit dazed since we found Marianne. Now that she speaks, she sounds defensive. 'Marianne came to make sure I was OK. I wish… I would have said if I'd seen her choking! It's not my fault. I know…'

Cara looks at where Freddie had left the room, then turns back to the rest of us. 'I was upset. Marianne came to find me. Once I'd calmed down and it got late, she headed back to check on the cars. She said they wouldn't be long. I wasn't ready to face anyone.' She looks at the door again. 'I said I'd just stay where I was, and Marianne said she'd come and get me when the cars had arrived. I hadn't realised how far away from the camp I'd gone until I was alone. Marianne had brought a lamp. But even with it, I was nervous. Then I heard a noise. It sounded like someone was in pain, or a grunt. Maybe surprise. I suppose…' She looks at us. 'I suppose that was her?'

No one speaks for a moment. Hanneghan nods. 'I guess it must have been. Though can you make much noise if you choke?' He speaks quietly, as though to himself, and I'm not sure most people hear. 'We heard a scream from the picnic.'

'The scream was me,' Cara says, quietly.

'When you found the body?' Kidz asks.

Cara looks down. 'I followed the noise. It was so dark I wasn't sure where I was going. The lamp wasn't great.' She continues in a daze. 'I was afraid. I lost sight of the camp. I realised I'd come too far. I started running in the direction I thought Marianne had gone. Then I found…' She shakes her head. 'Anyway, then you came, and I realised… I realised that… she was dead. I'd found her, but she was already dead.' Now she cries again, and I feel tears prick at my eyes. My throat is tight.

It's so late – everyone is jumpy. Unease weaves itself around us all like smoke – tightens our chests, obscures the truth. Kidz looks at Pablo. We all look at each other.

I suppose one of us could be lying. With what I heard on the plane, it's very likely. I just don't know who.

'There was something in her mouth,' Hanneghan says. 'So she must have choked. I can't even remember what it was. But the police will find it. Let's not make this worse. It's a very sad accident.'

'*Another* sad accident,' Pablo says. 'None of you think this is strange, that Augusto dies by accident, then Marianne?' His voice is raised and Cara lets out a sob as he speaks.

I remember talking to him out in the desert. I didn't see him again until after Marianne was found.

'Freddie said he stayed near the rug too,' Hanneghan says,

seeming to deliberately ignore Pablo. 'But we were all coming and going. Maybe one of us will remember something more tomorrow, after sleep.'

I look around the group, but no one offers anything else.

Lukas takes his turn and says, 'I was with Kidz, looking at some of the shots on camera. We saw Hanneghan. Then I joined in the read-through.'

Hanneghan nods.

'And you, Phoebe?' Kidz says.

'I was with Josh. We did the read through too.'

'OK,' Kidz says, looking exhausted. 'We're not going to get anywhere tonight. The police will go over our statements in the morning. Marianne choked, so I can't imagine there will be too many questions. I know the last twenty-four hours have been difficult but this was a devastating accident, and we'll all miss her.'

Cara stands, tears wet on her cheeks. 'To Marianne.' She holds aloft the whiskey glass, and we all lift ours to meet it.

'To Marianne.'

As I raise my glass, I feel sick. I don't think this stops here.

16

My room smells of cinnamon when I finally climb into bed. It's almost 4 a.m. I down a glass of water and lie back against the pillows.

I close my eyes in the safety of my room. The police will arrive soon with questions. They'll take statements. They might have already spoken to Freddie, Hanneghan and Cara. The accident yesterday, now Marianne. This means a lot of scrutiny for someone pretending to be someone else. On top of everything that's happened, I worry that I'll be found out. What would the police think of me pretending to be someone else when two people have died?

I let myself sink into dreams of sand and blood, gazelles and planes – and at some point I dream of faces changing, melting under the sun, skin dripping. I wake with a start.

I'm soaked in sweat and my muscles ache. Light spills into the room and I realise someone is knocking at the door. It's 9 a.m.; I check my phone, expecting to find a message from Phoebe, needing to see one, but there's nothing. Where is she? It can't just be my phone. The screen is cracked and the Wi-Fi is slow, but it's still working. I have no idea why she isn't replying.

Felix has left a voicemail. God, he messaged me yesterday.

I put it on speaker as I climb out of bed and shout, 'Just a minute,' to whoever is at the door.

His familiar voice spills into the room, charged and dramatic. *'Oh my god, Ellie, if you're not answering then maybe... Maybe it is you. Look, if you do get this, please let me know you're OK. I can't get in touch with Phoebe either. I need to know... please. Love you.'*

What is up with him? I check my watch but I'm sure it's too late to call him back. It must be the middle of the night. I'll do it later. He's always been dramatic. It's too confusing a message for me to get my head around right now. Not after last night. Felix is caught up in a new drama and Phoebe has gone AWOL, but today will need my full attention.

Another knock on the door, louder this time.

'Hello?' I say, as I pull the door open.

'Phoebe, hi. Are you OK?' Josh stands outside, white as a sheet with dark rings round his eyes. Just as handsome, but he looks like shit.

'Come in.' I call for coffee and I curl up on the velvet sofa, sinking deep into the cushions. I tuck my legs under me and wrap my arms round my knees. I'm washed out. Nothing about yesterday seems real.

'How's the shoulder?' I ask, seeing him wince as he sits slowly. 'I didn't really get to ask you last night. How was it, after Kidz and I left?'

He touches his shoulder reflexively. He doesn't look like he's slept. 'It was awful. Freddie didn't say a word. He just sat next to Marianne's body, holding her hand.' He shakes his head in disbelief.

I wrap my arms tighter around myself as last night's death creeps into the room.

'Freddie must be going through hell. How do you go forward

from something like this?' I'd struggled so much after I'd lost Dad. Mum always tells me that I've never been the same since. Grief can take over.

'I can't believe she's dead. I mean, Marianne! Why do stars always seem untouchable – like their lives are governed by different rules?' Josh shakes his head again.

'Did you sleep at all?' I ask as I hear another knock at the door, and I cross the room to open it, smile and say thank you.

I bring the coffee over, with the basket of breakfast goodies and four different types of milk.

'Camel milk!' I lift it and take a sip, pleased to have a distraction. 'Oh God, it's delicious!'

'Sleep was touch and go. My shoulder.' He shrugs. 'No doubt I'll collapse into oblivion at some point.'

There's never going to be a good time to tell him about the plane, but I'd made up my mind to tell him last night. After everything that's happened, I need help. I can't keep this to myself any longer.

'Josh,' I say. 'Remember when I was ill on the plane...' And I tell him what I'd heard: the plan to kill, the fact that it will happen very soon, whether it was even real.

'Oh. My. God.' He shakes his head, stares at me.

I give him a minute for it to sink in, and I refill our cups. The coffee is thick and bitter, and it hits the mark. I feel life flooding back into my veins, and my brain powers up, shaking off the fog of my too-short sleep.

'If I didn't imagine it, then we have to do something about it. I had thought I was over-dramatising things, like it must have been someone running lines, but after yesterday...' I shake my head.

'But maybe that's it? Maybe Marianne was the intended victim?' He looks thoughtful.

I bite my lip. I've thought about this. 'No, they said "he", a number of times. It's a man. The two people talking were either a man or a woman, or two men... I don't know. And anyway, Marianne died choking – at least that's what it looks like.'

Josh picks up one of the pastries and I copy him. They taste of honey and pistachios, and of being far from home, and it's both sweet and a touch of salt.

'So, what's your plan?' He looks at me. 'I mean, you haven't said anything to anyone else yet?'

'No.' I chew a little more. 'First off, I didn't know if it was real, if I hadn't dreamt it. Then I thought I'd made such an idiot of myself on the plane, they wouldn't believe me anyway.'

'Did you hear what Hanneghan said last night... *do you make a noise if you choke*... and he's right. Would you have the air for that? It's most likely she made a noise if she was being attacked, no? Cara said she went to find Marianne because she heard her make a sound – like in pain, she said. Or a grunt. I think the scream we heard came from Cara, which was later. Someone from our group could have sneaked out in the dark and come back. Pablo wasn't running lines with us, remember. And we were all disappearing to refill drinks and get snacks. One of us could have killed her. The dark covers everything.'

Josh looks at me, thoughtful. 'But it looked like she choked. I suppose it wouldn't be hard to kill her then push food to the back of her mouth to disguise the cause of death. But who would do that?'

'It could have been an accident someone was trying to cover up. A fight or an argument that went too far? Or maybe she heard something she shouldn't have done?'

Josh fills up both our coffee cups. 'Or maybe she is one of the people who was planning the murder, and the other one got scared, and didn't trust her? Maybe she dies first, and then the intended male victim. Maybe he'll die today?'

'It's crazy we're even having this discussion! But still, we need to keep our eyes open. I thought Hanneghan seemed the most likely target. Everyone appears to have a grudge against him: Pablo is angry about how his arrival has completely changed the key roles, he's Cara's ex, and with the script demands, it's pressure on Freddie. There also seems to be a lot of anger towards Freddie. I think maybe we should watch them both. If we see something concrete, then we could tell the police. But we don't want to jeopardise our chance with this film… we'd need to be sure.'

Josh nods slowly. 'Right. Let's start there. Pablo said to me he'd been at the picnic rug, but I don't remember him there for a lot of it. He said he was going to have a go with Kidz's camera at one point and went off to take photos with that.'

'I saw Lukas with that later. It's impossible to know exactly where everyone was. There was a lot of booze. It was dark.'

Josh shrugs. 'I was so tired and groggy with all those painkillers.'

'I suppose the police will be able to tell us more when they look at the body. Marianne will surely have an autopsy.'

Josh nods. 'But maybe not soon enough. Look, if someone is planning a murder, then they'll do it quickly.

I'm aware that on one hand I'm trusting Josh and believing he is who he says he is. On the other hand, I'm not who I've said I am. It's a double standard that I'll just need to feel guilty about. I'm not telling anyone the full truth. I don't trust Josh *that* much. I stand up. 'Let's go to breakfast. I'll throw on some clothes. If someone is behind all of this, they'll be on tenterhooks. We need to go and watch them.'

17

The breakfast room is the same room that dinner was served in last night. Still large and airy, but with a different colour palette this morning. The light throws less shade in the room, making it much brighter and the dark purple and black highlights gleam. The huge windows, which look out onto the pool, the other side of the hotel and the background of the desert, remind me how far away we are from everything.

The buffet tables to the side offer up a feast: fruit, cereals, pastries, coffee pots in brass and silver. There's a cluster of tables at the far side of the room, taken up by our party. There's no one else in the restaurant – we're the only guests. So I take some food and head over to sit with Lukas. Kidz sits with Pablo, Cara with Josh, and Freddie sits alone as I see Hanneghan enter.

'Hey, Phoebe.' Lukas nods at me as I sit down.

Josh is sitting further up near Cara as we'd agreed to go in separately to talk to as many people as possible.

Hanneghan talks to a waiter at the buffet table. I half watch him as I speak to Lukas.

'How was it, after I left?' I ask Lukas, quietly, and he looks down at his food.

'It wasn't good,' he says, then he glances over at Freddie. 'I can't imagine how he's managing to sit here. He must be in hell right now.' He speaks softly, and I see Freddie at the far table. Cara is on the adjacent table.

'Do you have any idea what might have happened?' I say to Lukas, as quietly as possible. I rip open a pastry.

'Not really.' He looks at me with interest. 'Do you?'

I shake my head. 'But I have been thinking about it. If someone heard there was a group of rich Hollywood people in the desert, they might have tried to rob her. Do you think someone else could have been out in the desert last night?'

'I have no idea, but it's preferable to thinking it was something to do with one of us,' Lukas says, more sharply than I've heard him speak so far, picking up his smoothie and taking a drink. 'Man. I just hate this.' He sighs. 'It's hard to just sit here and eat like nothing has happened. But I doubt anyone wants to be alone right now. I know I don't. I went for a swim before breakfast, just to get out of my room. I can't sleep. My mom died when I was young, a car crash – I was there. It was...' He stops for a second. 'All deaths make me think of her. Even if I don't really know any of these people, it's better to be with them than be alone.'

'Oh, I'm sorry.' I feel for him. He looks so young. I wonder if I should just back off and leave this. But no, Josh and I have decided to try to work out if something's going on.

He gives me a quick smile, then reaches for some bread in front of him. 'Anyway, have you heard Freddie's crazy plans? We're supposed to carry on. To stick to the schedule. He says the best way to honour Marianne is to finish the film.'

I shoot a look back at Freddie.

'He's said that?' I ask quietly.

'Kidz told me,' Lukas says. 'She was here a few minutes ago – she's doing the rounds at breakfast, filling us all in. I don't think

Freddie slept much and he's more focused than ever. Apparently, he needs her death to mean something. That's what Kidz is saying, anyway.'

'Bloody hell,' I say. 'After last night I doubt anyone will want to head back out there. I guess the police will need to finish first.'

Freddie downs a cup of coffee and heads out. He bumps into Cara's chair as he goes, and offers up a quick apology.

Once he's gone, Cara half sobs, then she leaves quickly, knocking a glass on the table over as she goes, and it rolls off the edge, shattering on the hard wood floors, but she doesn't stop.

'What's up with Cara?' Pablo says to the room as he crosses to the buffet. She had almost knocked him over too in her rush to exit. There's a shadow of stubble around his jaw this morning. 'I saw you and Freddie holed up together in the lounge earlier, leaning over the script.' He directs this at Hanneghan who sits quietly at his table.

Hanneghan holds his gaze but says nothing.

'More script changes I'm not privy to?' Pablo's tone is bitter. 'Freddie hasn't spoken to me all morning.'

'His wife has just died, and he's put everything he's got into this film. Give him a break,' Hanneghan says, standing. 'Thank you for breakfast.' Hanneghan smiles at a nearby waiter. 'It was delicious.'

Walking away, Hanneghan doesn't look back at Pablo, who shouts, 'And what if I've banked it all on this film too?'

Hanneghan doesn't turn around, and Pablo slumps down in his chair. He shifts from anger to despondency in a blink. I almost feel sorry for him.

But Lukas mutters, 'Sad ass.'

I consider Pablo and what his potential involvement in this madness could be. Pablo wants exposure and a leading role. He won't get that if Freddie dies. The film would die with him. I doubt

Pablo would want Marianne dead either. I don't even consider Hanneghan – he could never do something like this – but Freddie and Cara are interesting. There's tension there.

I look around the tables. Josh is on his own and I catch his eye and nod to Cara, to let him know I'll follow her.

'I'll check on Cara,' I say to Lukas.

He gives me a quick look. 'Don't get too involved, Phoebe. Don't forget your role in this. I'm just warning you – bigger fish will let you fry first.'

18

I jog past the tapestries and through the light reception area, past the fountain and along the corridor that leads to the large pool suites where Freddie and Cara are staying.

These rooms are bigger, with doors to the pool. I remember from the list Kidz gave me that Cara's room is on the same corridor as Freddie and Marianne's, so I head that way.

But as I pass Freddie's room, I hear Cara's voice and come to a dead stop. Their voices are raised. I listen carefully.

'I need to leave! I don't think I can do another minute here. What else is going to happen? Marianne is dead, Freddie! You can't make me stay!'

I lean my head against the door.

Freddie now. 'Cara, the police are on their way. You can't leave. I know what you mean – I have no idea what's going on but—'

'Oh, Freddie. What will happen if they find out about us?'

Us? Cara and Freddie? Do they mean what I think they mean? But Cara hates Freddie?

I hold my breath, trying to hear more. But they must have moved elsewhere in the room.

The pool door. I bet I can see more from there. Are they the couple from the plane?

I leave via the door further down the corridor and run round to the front. It's easy to find Freddie's room from the other side – their arguing is loud enough. I see the pool door is open a crack.

I run to the side and peer through the window. There are drapes down over the glass doors, but between the curtains, I can make out the two of them. They're in the main reception area of the hotel suite.

The sheer luxury of the room is more than I've ever dreamt of. I can't imagine staying in a room grander than mine, but they clearly exist. It's the other life. The life I've always wondered about.

He reaches out to touch her arm and she pulls away.

'Cara!' He sounds frustrated.

'Fuck off, Freddie! Are you not listening?' She strides out of the first room of the suite, and I realise they've gone into the dining area, which leads to the bathroom.

What is happening with Freddie? His wife and business partner have just died and yet he's still hanging on to this film by his fingernails. But if Kidz is right, then he's in all sorts of financial trouble.

So we've been told to carry on. And the whole time there's been something between him and Cara?

I make a quick decision. This film is my chance. I need to find out what is going on. If Cara is on the brink of pulling out, or another death takes place, then it's all over for me. I haven't done what I needed to do. Not yet. I need to stay hidden.

I open the door to the room a crack more, and I pull it closed behind me. I slip into the room, heart racing, and run to the open doorway through which Cara and Freddie had gone, where a tall dark wood cupboard stands to the right.

I'm about to peer round it, when I hear footsteps and a running tap being turned off.

I panic – I can't get back to the door to the pool in time.

My hands are damp, and I hear, almost in the room, Freddie say, 'Cara, darling, please hear me out.'

I have no choice. I climb into the cupboard, and pull the door closed. There is a slat design in one of the doors. If I stay very still, I can see into the room.

I have to hope they're too engrossed in their conversation to notice me.

'Fuck off, Freddie! I've told you. I'm leaving. I'm not doing this anymore! Marianne is dead! It's like you don't even realise!'

'Oh, Cara, of course I realise. I was married to her for fifteen years! How can you even say that?' Now Freddie is shouting, and instead of pleading with her, he kicks the coffee table, on which papers were spread, and it upturns. Coffee cups fall, and there is a loud crash.

Freddie falls to the sofa, head in hands, and begins sobbing.

I take a sharp breath, but luckily there is so much chaos in the room, neither of them notice.

'For Christ's sake,' his voice is quieter now, 'she was my wife!'

Cara seems caught off guard. She hovers for a second, then she seems to relent. She goes and sits next to Freddie and puts her arm around him.

As though a switch has been flicked, the anger in her face vanishes. I see her arm has dropped round his shoulders, and she slips her fingers into his hair. Then she lifts his chin with her other hand, and pulls his face close to hers. She holds it for a second, then she kisses him, hard and long on the lips.

A goodbye kiss. I recognise that. I've seen that before.

'Of course,' she says quietly, breaking away. 'Of course you're upset. I'm sorry. I'm sorry about Marianne, but we have to end this now. It's over, Freddie. You have to accept that. I know you don't want to lose both of us in the same twenty-four hours, but it was over before last night really. The pressure of this production has been too much. And now Hanneghan is here...' Her voice trails away.

They sit like that for a few seconds, which feels like half an hour to me. Then Freddie lifts his head. His face, still with the grey pallor he'd had at breakfast, also now has red spots in his cheeks. His eyes are bright as he looks at Cara, his profile not unattractive. And his power in Hollywood is unquestioned. There's something in his look now – longing, grief. Something appealing. Endearing. Also repellent. Power, but hunger too.

Cara must recognise it. She pulls back. 'I have to go,' she says. 'I have no choice. I'll call a car and leave this afternoon.'

He shakes his head, and he whispers, leaning closer to her. 'No, Cara. I've lost her, and it's a fucking wrench. She was part of my life for so long. A business partner, for the last few years. You know, as much as I do, she hasn't been a wife to me for some time.' He leans his head in and touches his forehead to hers. 'We were like two fucking armies, trying to take each other down. Smiling for the press and then warring behind closed doors. I was going to leave, then this film lost its funding. Please don't say I have to lose you, because I've lost her.' He almost growls the last part.

She's already told him it's over. He's not ready to take it. I've seen men like that before. I feel my blood run a little colder. Is it my imagination, or does she flinch?

I cannot breathe.

She says nothing, and I watch as Freddie slips his hand around the back of her neck, and his fingers move up into her hair.

'Cara, darling. Grief for her doesn't touch the passion...' On this last word, his voice falters, and his chest swells. 'To touch you, to hold you. I can't lose you.'

My instinct is to run out and scream at him to stop, because she's just made it clear that it's over, but I wonder maybe if there's more to this.

Are they behind everything? Did they both kill her? Had I got it wrong, and the people on the plane were planning to kill a woman, not a man? My heartrate is rapid, my breath becomes short. Maybe it had been murder, and now Cara is panicking.

Cara's voice is quiet. 'There's no going back. You pushed it too far last night. I know we were going to pretend not to get along. But you embarrassed me, Freddie. You laid my life out for people to see. You've changed the script to have me turn to Hanneghan. I only asked him to take the role because of the spotlight it would turn on the film. I'm getting old. In Hollywood thirty-three is practically a hundred. Hanneghan gets all the roles, even in his fifties – women fawn all over him, still. But not me. My roles are drying up. I'm not going to be a leading lady for much longer. So I'm vulnerable, and you exploited that last night. When you talked about my heartbreak, you embarrassed me. I looked stupid. I looked weak. You really hurt me, Freddie.'

'Cara. Forgive me.' Freddie now climbs from the sofa, and kneels before her. He leans his head towards her stomach, and lifts the camisole she wears, to just below her bra. I see the lace peep from the bottom, and my jaw falls open. I steady myself on the inside of the cupboard and I am shocked. Marianne is barely dead. Surely, even just out of respect… I mean. His wife?

And why the fuck am I here?

My thoughts fall fragmented as I watch him kiss her, curving his fingers round her back. She wears a pale thin yellow summer skirt hanging to just above her knee.

I *cannot* be here for this.

I look at Cara's face, trying to think of an escape route. She pulls herself further up on the couch, away from his hands.

'I need to leave, Freddie. Imagine what they'll say, if our affair came to light? Imagine how they'd turn on me, crucify me – us? Your wife only just dead. We'd be destroyed. I'm done.'

She goes to stand, and Freddie pulls her back down roughly. He runs his hands up her back, and pulls her further down on the sofa, pushing her legs apart.

'Tell me this feels wrong.'

Cara makes a sound of protest, pulling at her skirt. Then, 'No, Freddie,' more firmly.

I can't watch this.

The memory of hands on me. Me trying to protest. I freeze. I want to scream out to tell him to stop. I want to do it for her, for me.

I want to be anywhere else. Why did I hide here? My cheeks burn.

Closing my eyes and hiding from this is what I want to do. But I can't. I need to stay present, for Cara – just in case. He's not stopping, and she's saying no. She's said no. She's saying it again.

So soon after Marianne, and while Marianne was alive, presumably – Freddie is more than a shit. He's the very worst. For a second, I hope he's the one someone intends to kill. I'd wring his neck right now if I could.

His hands are tight on her legs, and he buries his head up beneath the cotton of her skirt.

'No!' Cara shouts, and I'm on the point of launching out of the cupboard, when, like an act of God, I hear a knock on the door. And Kidz's voice calls into the room.

'Freddie? Are you there? Can I have word?'

'Five minutes!' Freddie shouts.

Cara leaps up, taking her chance, rearranging her clothes, and she looks angry, flushed. There are tears at the corners of her eyes. 'Imagine if she'd found us,' she hisses.

Freddie shakes his head. 'She won't. I won't let that happen. I'll protect you. I'll protect the film. We'll all be fine. And I meant what I said, Cara.' He touches her on the mouth with his thumb. 'I'm here just for you. I don't ask for anything in return. You said you lived in a sexless marriage for years with Hanneghan when he was a drunk. You've told me so few men are any good at giving – I know you're sick of it all. Well, not with me. I'm here for you. And I'll finish this later. Three more days. Just stay.'

Cara pulls back. 'You're not listening to me! Fuck you, Freddie. The more you talk the more I think it could have been you. Did you kill her, so you could have everything you've ever wanted? You piece of shit.'

He rears back as though slapped.

I hold my breath as she turns away, still tugging at her skirt. Freddie's face darkens as he watches her slip out of the pool door. Then he swears and leaves via the main door, slamming it behind him.

I count to fifty, then I run.

19

Josh stares me, then shakes his head. 'But I thought Cara didn't like Freddie? Last night if looks could kill he'd be a dead man.'

'She doesn't much like him now.' I flop on the couch in his room. 'But no, last night was all an act. I'm not sure how far Freddie was going to push it this morning, but he didn't seem happy for her to break it off.' I shudder at the memory. 'I'm just pleased they were interrupted.'

'Where does that leave us?' Josh sits back on the sofa opposite me.

'People are usually killed because of love or money, aren't they? If they're having an affair... Killing the old wife to make way for a new one is fairly classic.'

Josh's brow furrows. 'Both of them together?'

I shake my head slowly. 'I don't think so. Cara asked Freddie if he'd killed her.'

'Shit.' Josh stares. 'Do you think he did?'

'I have no idea.' I lift my hands to my face. 'I don't know what to think.' I hear my accent slip a little – the stress is making it tough to maintain – and I swallow hard. I can't ever really relax. I speak again, nailing it. 'It won't look good for her, if the affair is discovered now Marianne is dead – I mean, maybe Marianne did find out? It could be suicide. Maybe she found out about the affair and killed herself?' Even as I say this, I don't believe it.

Josh frowns. 'I guess it's a matter for the police. But that would be better for us, in a way, or if it was an accident. As selfish as that sounds. If Freddie is taken into custody, then the film is over.'

The sun is hot now as it glares through the windows. It lights up the full room, and Josh looks so tired.

We're both in this together. We want to solve this. But maybe more to keep the film on track and prevent our shot at stardom from being derailed. My motives aren't pure.

I feel responsible for this. If I'd flagged what I'd heard on the plane earlier, could it have changed things?

The phone rings, and I pick it up. It's Kidz. I listen to her for a minute as she outlines the coming afternoon.

'We're needed downstairs in half an hour,' I mouth at Josh, then say, 'Thanks for letting me know,' to Kidz. I place the receiver back in its cradle and look out through the arched windows. The sky in the far distance blanches white under the sun, and the horizon shimmers.

'What is it? The police?'

'We're going sand surfing and fat biking,' I say. 'Kidz said after five, when it's not so hot. What is it, almost three now?'

'What? After yesterday? Freddie is crazy.' Josh rolls his eyes.

I stand, stretching, suddenly tired – the idea of heading back to the desert doesn't fill me with any pleasure.

'It's in the script, apparently, and Freddie wants to run through the activity to get us used to it. Seems he's true to his word and we're carrying on. To be honest, I feel better getting stuck in. It doesn't feel very real at the moment – it's like we're all on hold until the rest of the crew gets here. Kidz said they're due first thing tomorrow. So not long to go.' I rub at my eyes, remembering how dry they'd been last night.

'This is crazy.' Josh leans his head back against the cushions and closes his eyes. 'Surely it's too hot to head into the desert?'

I look at him. I feel for him, in so much discomfort and having to carry on and smile through it all for the role. Freddie has set some kind of impossible standard of commitment to work. It's so old school.

'Kidz said they've set up a big tent for shade, and we're not doing it for long. I doubt you'll have to do any of the activity. Look, I'll meet you downstairs? I'm going for a nap. She also said the police will be here to speak to the rest of us soon. They spoke to Freddie, Hanneghan and Cara earlier, and I think are looking at where she died. I suppose they'll be looking at Marianne, too.' I'm exhausted.

Suddenly the burden of pretending to be someone else, when everything is falling apart, is exhausting. I need to plan how I'll cope with the police. With two deaths, what will it do to the trust of everyone here if they find out I've been lying about who I really am? I need a moment to myself.

'Hey, Phoebe. You OK?' Hearing him call me that only reminds me of how much I'm lying to him and everyone else.

'See you downstairs,' I manage, hearing a touch of English enter my voice again, and I worry I'm going to give it all away if I don't have five minutes on my own. I need something to ground me. I need to call the real Phoebe. I can't believe I still haven't heard from her.

I close the door behind me and stop still. My cracked phone turns on, thank God, and I get through but the phone rings out. 'Hey, you've got Phoebe Thomas, you're welcome to leave a message.'

20

'Fuck, this is hot!' Pablo climbs up the dune behind me.

The sun shines down hard and reflects back up from the sand with no less intensity as I drag my board up the side of the steep peak. I trip and fall, my hands burning as they touch down. I push myself quickly back up.

I wear shorts, t-shirt and a hat, but I'm roasting. The sun is relentless. It's almost ten degrees cooler than it had been two hours ago, but still, it's like nothing I've known before.

Nevertheless, I run the last few paces back to the top of the dune.

There's a huge tent behind us, set up with sofas, water and thick outdoor rugs, deep red and intricately patterned. Waiters from the hotel have accompanied us out with huge fans, which blow both air and water over you in a cooling mist, for when it's all too much out here. There's water, tea, juice, fruit, nuts. It feels a world away from last night.

'Race you!' I shout as Pablo meets me at the top.

He looks younger in this moment, and I remember he's only in his early thirties, maybe even younger. The alcohol and his frowning has been making him look older. He's wearing shorts and a t-shirt too, and I see why he's been cast as a possible leading man. He's strong, great bone structure, and you'd definitely turn to take a second look if you passed him on the street. With bushy eyebrows and dark brown eyes, and skin a deep olive colour, the screen loves him. I'd read some in-depth interview with him after Sundance. His childhood was tough – he'd talked about his family not having very much, of losing his brother to a hit and run. And Lukas lost someone in a similar way. Maybe grief gave them drive. I suppose you'd have to have a lot of ambition and grit to get from the backstreets of Venezuela to Hollywood.

'Race me? I'll be at the bottom in a flash. Just see if you can keep up!' He grins.

It turns out sand surfing is a blast.

It's harder than snowboarding. Not quite as fast, and you can't make the turns as quickly. It's like a snow day with so much fresh powder you bury your legs up to your knees once you're off the board.

We climb onto the boards, level, and I count down from three. When I shout, 'One!', Pablo whoops, and we push off, flying fast; the long climb more than worth it. The air feels cooler when it comes at you in a rush, and all the worry and heaviness from last night lifts. I've always loved speed, and adrenaline bites like a drug.

I can't believe this is my job.

I've been up and down a few times, and I'm getting the hang of turning.

Pablo, however, is an ace. He turns his board to curve close to me, and I feel heady as I throw my weight forward to try to gain on him downhill.

But he's clearly got some technical expertise way ahead of mine. As we race to the bottom, the speed picks up so much that I wobble, and I try to put in a turn, throwing my weight, but I can't save myself. As Pablo whoops again, flying past me, I tumble off and roll down the last stretch of the dune.

'You OK?' he calls up to where I land, and I spring back up from my hands, throwing in a backflip from my school gymnastic days, just to show off.

He claps, raising his hands above his head; then he shouts, '*Vamos*, Phoebe!' gesturing up the dune again.

I know I'm too tired, and I haven't drunk enough water today, but the rush of it is too much of a pull, my aching limbs, the terror and stress of the last couple of days forgotten. I'm also conscious that some one-on-one time with Pablo gives me a chance to see the real him – and to work out if he was who I heard on the plane. I grab my board and we go again, two, then three more times.

Even he is exhausted on the last run, and he points to his throat, sticking his tongue out. 'Water. Need water,' he says, in a fake croak, laughing, and we head up the other side of the sand dune to where the tent is pitched.

The others had gone fat biking and desert jeep riding. It's good to feel some progress in terms of the film, that this is a rehearsal of sorts. The production feels as though it's hanging by a thread with everything that's happened. But we could be filming for real tomorrow afternoon and despite everything, that's exciting. I'll get to act. And with Hanneghan too.

Kidz is in position with the camera, and she makes the OK sign with her fingers as we approach.

'Got some great shots! You two look like pros!' she calls. 'We might not need the stunt doubles we've got arriving with the rest of the crew! Social media will eat these up.'

Pablo raises his hand to me for a high five, and I hit it hard. He's not what I thought he was. Whatever anger he was carrying last night and this morning, has vanished. He's a lot of fun.

We enter the shade of the tent and the coolness is a relief. I flop down onto one of the low sofas laid out in a big horseshoe. A waiter places a glass of water down for me, and I drink it thirstily, gulping, and when it spills out of my mouth, wetting my top, the sudden cold is like a gift. I sit cross-legged and tilt my head towards a fan, pulling off my hat.

'How was it?' Kidz asks. She sits across from me and looks up from the screen of a camera, which she's been staring at.

'It's the best!' I say. 'You have to try it.'

'I was out fat biking – down the other side of the dune. Enough for one day. Man, that is hard work. You want to try it? Have a go next and I'll come and get some shots. It's basically cycling in the sand, but with huge wheels so you can cover more ground. Cara's out there now with Freddie and Josh.' She grimaces at me, lowering her voice. 'There's still some tension in the air.'

I nod, thinking of Cara this morning, of Freddie pushing her legs apart. The show they've put on for us the last few days has been quite convincing. How long has it been going on for? However long, it seems to be over now. Cara was anything but happy earlier. I wonder if she really will leave.

'Oh, those two, they never quite *seem* to be getting along, do they?' Pablo flops down next to me, and I shoot him a look.

'What do you mean?' I try to keep my tone casual, while digging for what he knows.

'Mean? I mean nothing! She's always shrugging him off, hey.' He parts his hands, lifting his palms as though pushing away the thought, and picks up his water, slugging it down. But he doesn't look me in the eye, and he starts humming as he leans back.

His good mood now seems a little more suspicious.

'Do you have any idea what might have happened to Marianne?' I ask, trying to keep my tone light.

'Marianne?' Pablo looks at me in what seems like genuine surprise. 'Well, she died. It's very sad. What else do you mean?'

'Oh nothing, just that the police are due here soon to ask some questions. I wonder if they might think there was something else to it.'

'I have no idea. *De nada*,' Pablo says, downing another glass of water. 'All I know is Freddie is a shit, but he's a great director. We all put up with his bullshit because we know his reputation. Marianne made it easier to work with him.' He smiles, glancing down. 'She was the real deal.'

'How is everyone?' Hanneghan says as he enters the tent.

My heart speeds up. I feel my face flush, and I stare down at the bottle of water I hold. I'm still not used to seeing him. I force myself to smile, look up and say, 'Were you fat biking?'

He nods, smiling at me. I hold his gaze though my cheeks burn again. Out of my periphery I feel Pablo look at me, and he snorts.

Hanneghan grabs some water and sits at the head of the horseshoe shape. 'Christ, it's hard work. I'm pleased I'm not doing it for real when we film.' He turns to Kidz as he says, 'I've told Freddie I'll do my lines, and then you can take some shots as I head down a dune. But any shots of me riding up, it will have to be the stunt double. My fifty-year-old knees are insisting that I shouldn't try to cycle over the sand with those fat tyres.'

'The sand surfing is great!' I say, with too much enthusiasm, my voice too loud. I cringe inwardly, wishing I could play it cooler around him.

He nods, politely, smiling at me, but he doesn't say anything else. Frustration is the worst. This is not how I saw these few days going. I was supposed to bond a little, get to know him. He was supposed to find me entertaining, funny. He was supposed to be in awe of my acting skills. Why can't I pull this off?

Pablo raises his eyebrows at me. When Hanneghan goes to look at some shots Kidz wants him to see, he makes a heart shape with his fingers and flutters his eyelashes.

'In love with Hanneghan, are we? Good luck with that. You and the rest of tinsel town,' he whispers. Then he laughs and picks up a plate of food.

I sit stone cold, even though he's joking.

But it must be obvious.

I've always loved Hanneghan.

I'm getting this wrong. Hanneghan isn't noticing me, and others are noticing me look at Hanneghan.

I glance at him, in case he heard, and I only breathe again when I see his head bent intently over Kidz's screen.

'Here,' Pablo offers the plate out to me, 'sorry, have some food. I shouldn't mock. I get it. I remember my first film set. All these faces – all the names. And I remember how it feels. Here, have cake. I've been a dick.'

He pronounces 'dick' a bit like 'deek'; he partly hams up his accent to make me laugh. And it works.

'I was the same, at the start. I met my ex-wife on the set of my first film. My brother had just died – I was so driven, ready for success. Marrying her moved me to Hollywood and there's no question doors opened. But the bright lights...' He shrugs. 'The marriage was a mistake. She wasn't who she was projected to be. All that Hollywood glamour is a sham. I was too angry to see it. Neither of us behaved well. She left me, and I did nothing to stop her.' He looks down at his plate, a brief flash of something crossing his face. Then he avoids eye contact as he goes to get more food.

I watch him with a hollow feeling in the pit of my stomach. Fame can twist people. Ambition can push the limits of the most reasonable of us. I had always assumed Pablo had used his first wife as a stepping stone to success. It seems I was wrong. And here I am, pretending I'm someone I'm not.

Josh comes in, red in the face and sweating. He flops next to me. 'I went dune riding in the Land Rover. Now that was fun!'

I pass him water. 'Stay hydrated.'

It's comforting to have him near me. Josh is like my safe space.

'Are we heading back to the hotel soon?' Hanneghan stands. 'I'm tired. Anyone want to come with?'

'Me!' I jump up, not looking at Pablo. 'I'd love to head back.'

Finally. Alone with Hanneghan.

21

The ride back to the hotel isn't a long one, and I open conversation with Hanneghan almost as the doors close. I want to make a connection, but also work out how he fits into all of this. Despite how amazing this evening has been, Josh and I have decided to investigate, and I can't let the side down.

'I can't believe Marianne is dead,' I say.

He nods. 'So sad. I've known her for years. And Freddie. We all worked together years ago, in Venezuela. *Tourist* was a surprise hit. It knocked it out of the park at Cannes.'

He looks out of the window, crossing his legs. His eyes are narrow and his hands fidget. I wonder what he's thinking.

There have been so many mentions of Venezuela.

'Pablo was there too?' I ask.

'Yes, we were all there – Pablo, Cara, Marianne, Freddie, me.' He grins. 'I even met Augusto there. *Tourist* was Pablo's first film and Freddie and Marianne were working on one of their first films together. Cara and I were still married.' His voice has taken on a wistful quality. Their relationship, if anything, hums away – I've caught them both looking at each other. Both seem protective – defensive. But it's clearly painful. I wonder if what Freddie had said to Cara was true – that they'd split because of something other than falling out of love. Maybe Hanneghan had been a drunk. He seems sober now. Maybe spending this time together has brought them closer. It would tie in with Cara ending whatever she'd had going on with Freddie. It's interesting.

I turn the top of the water bottle and think about how to play this. As well as getting close to Hanneghan, I want to push for a reaction to Freddie, to work out how all these relationships fit together. What Hanneghan thinks about how Freddie has responded to Marianne's death.

There had been a line and a photo on Page 6, a New York magazine: *Are Cara and Hanneghan getting back together?* Because I'd caught them looking at each other once or twice, I figure Cara is as good as any a place to touch a nerve. And he's just mentioned her, so it seems like a natural turn in the conversation. I go too far, though. 'Cara and Freddie seem very close.'

His head spins now. 'Really? They don't seem to be getting along at all. In fact, I heard her say she was going to order a car to try to leave later.'

I hate myself as I speak, wishing I commanded his attention without gossip and without pulling on whatever emotional strings he still has for Cara, but he is looking at me intently, and it's what I've craved.

'I walked past his room this morning, after breakfast. They were both leaving. And the way they were adjusting their clothes...' I wince inwardly. I've mashed up the details, but the main truth is in there, and I watch his eyes turn to small pin pricks. He purses his lips, then he leans his head back, and closes his eyes.

For a second, it's like it was all for nothing, but he looks at me again. 'That man is disgusting. His wife is only just dead.' The venom in his voice is almost tangible. Then his face softens. 'But Cara…' He looks out of the window.

He speaks to the desert, not looking at me. 'You know I've heard he slept around – way before this. Even though Marianne saved him. She pulled him out of obscurity. Freddie was barely heard of back then. He struggled to get funding for *Tourist*. Then, magically, he falls in love with Marianne Asquith, a hugely successful producer. He trails after her, reels her in, and then bam. He's Freddie Asquith-Smith, not Fred Smith, and all hail. *Tourist* takes off, produced by Marianne, and he's suddenly a legend.' He shakes his head, his hands fidgeting again. 'Asshole. Everyone raved about how feminist it was for him to take her name too. But, actually, it was just fucking theft.'

He looks at me, his eyebrows raised. 'You know she was being stalked? My money's on an ex-lover of Freddie's. He promised some woman the world then whipped it away. We're all victims of his. They said the investigation into the stalker was closed. Marianne told me when we arrived. But what if whoever it was followed us out here?'

I have no idea what to say. But now Hanneghan is on a roll, he carries on.

'I mean, I know it's not like I'm some angel riding in on a white horse.' He shrugs. 'Cara had every right—' He stops, probably realising he's saying too much to someone he barely knows. He looks back out of the window, the tight frown lines reflected lightly in the glass.

Feeling like the sun's gone out, I push again. I want him to keep talking.

In for a penny, I stir the pot. I thicken it good and proper. I'm not here for the side lines. 'I heard Freddie say you had your demons – that you liked a drink. I thought you might want to know that he's been talking about you.'

He spins and stares at me, his face red with rage. 'He said that to you? He implied I was an alcoholic?' He's practically spitting.

I lean back a little – I've gone too far, but I'm buzzing from the intense way he's looking at me. 'Not to me. No, I just overheard it. I'm sorry. I shouldn't have said—'

'Fucking hell. This week. I didn't even want to do the bloody film. If Cara hadn't asked me, then I wouldn't be here.' His eyes soften. 'She said she needed this one.' He says the last part more to himself.

I know what she means. We all need this film.

We're almost back at the hotel, and I want to spin this moment longer. I came for this. To be close to him. The next step I hadn't given much thought to. I'd figured I'd know once I was here. What I hadn't counted on is my hands trembling, or that there would be butterflies trapped so tight in my chest that there's no room for anything else.

I don't want to make him too angry. I need this film to go ahead so that I can have more moments like this with him. I try to smooth things a little.

'I've been looking forward to working with you all.' I don't say him specifically, even though that's what I mean. 'This is my big break. I hope it goes ahead, despite everything. I suppose it will be easier when the rest of the crew arrive tomorrow.'

He recovers himself a little. 'Look, I'm sorry for getting so angry. You're right. It's your big break, I'm guessing you've not done much before?' he says, smiling a little. 'You need the film too. Cara, Pablo, Josh – even me. I don't want to let Cara down. We all want this to work, and if that means making nice with Freddie, then we will.' He nods like the deal is done. 'With Marianne gone, it will be harder. She was the peacemaker. We'll all have to do our best to cope with Freddie now, if we want this to work. Like the man says, if we're carrying on, we need to do Marianne proud.'

'Yes, Hanneghan. We will,' I manage. And it's all I can do not to cry. We have made a connection. Of sorts.

22

It's late when I find Josh. With everyone back, fatigue has settled in. The day has been long. People ate quickly then vanished to their rooms after dinner. But Hanneghan had said something that stuck. I needed to speak to Josh.

'Hello?' he says as he opens his bedroom door.

'Freddie directed Pablo's first film, *Tourist*. They do know each other – they've worked together before.' I stride in. 'Not only him, but Hanneghan and Cara were there too. If Freddie, Cara, Hanneghan, Pablo and Augusto were all on the same set years ago, there might be something to it. I've checked and we can stream it at the hotel. Want to watch?'

'Sure thing, Nancy Drew,' Josh says, and he pours us both a large glass of wine. 'Film night it is. Want some popcorn? I'll treat you from my fancy hotel fridge. On me. Nothing's too good for my wife.'

I pull a face at him. 'You mean on the company, right?'

We sit on the deep sofa facing the huge flatscreen TV. This lounge is bigger than Mum's flat.

The screen lights up with Hanneghan then Cara's name. 'What is it about Venezuela? So many connections to this week,' I say, taking a big sip of wine. It's comfortable being this close to

Josh. I've missed the closeness of a good friend even in these few days since I've left New York. I gesture to his phone. 'Can I use yours for some googling?'

He nods. 'Yeah, I was thinking the same. Pablo mentioned that Augusto Dittus was a cop there, right? Then he met Hanneghan. That's when he started working for him. Now that they're all on the same film again, it feels like something's coming to a head.' Josh rewinds the movie to the frame where it lists the year the film came out. 'Yep, ten years ago. That's about right.'

Articles flash up on Josh's phone. I scroll through the headlines, reading them out:

New role for Hanneghan
Trouble in Paradise for Hollywood's Golden Couple?
Member of Crew Killed on Location
New Star Emerges
Freddie Asquith-Smith Pulls a Blinder
Who Is Pablo Lastra?

'What about the member of crew killed on location? Was that anything to do with this lot?'

'Nope.' I shake my head as I skim the article. 'A woman died, but she was part of the catering team. Nothing to do with the actors or directors.'

'And the trouble in paradise article, what's that about?' he asks.

'Well, rumours of Cara and Hanneghan having problems. But that's nothing we don't already know. I don't know why that would suddenly have such an impact now. The Pablo stuff is interesting though.'

My mind is whirling, something jars. 'Was it a grief scene that shot Pablo to fame? Didn't he stand out from the extras, so they made his part bigger?'

'Yes, I think so. Why? What are you thinking?'

I lean in. 'Fast forward – go to his big scene.'

The action speeds up. 'Stop!'

Josh presses pause. 'Here?'

We watch the screen. The lead couple are having an argument in a street. The characters are two rich people on a make-or-break holiday, and the man has got them lost. Hanneghan plays the male and I focus in on his features. Younger than he is now, and I study his cheekbones, the lines on his face, comparing them. Cara is the female lead. She wears a fancy quilted bag on her shoulder – the kind with a chain. Out of nowhere, a kid, all of about ten years old, appears and grabs it, then runs like lightning down the street.

'This was the scene Pablo is in,' Josh says. He rewinds. 'He chases this kid. I've seen this a few times before.'

I'm spellbound. The cinematography is beautiful. I can feel the sticky heat of the Venezuelan street radiate from the screen, the colours of sunset like a pink and purple explosion in the background. The lead couple gesture in anger, and then there's a close-up of the boy's face. Pablo is about to step in to chase him, playing the cop.

The camera slows for a second, focusing on the boy and telling his story through detail. He looks vulnerable. He doesn't wear shoes, and he's thin. Make-up has made him dirty, and his clothes are ripped. He sees Cara's bag, and his eyes light up. Then he runs, clutching his hands into fists as he sets off.

I hold my breath. I want him to have it. We all want him to have it.

He grabs it, and Cara, in character, spins, screaming in rage as he makes off down the street.

'Stop him!' she shouts.

There's a steely expression on Pablo's face. The same steel I'd seen this week. Like some part of him has been damaged. But he's playing a part, I remind myself. He's just acting.

Pablo chases him, running, a movie-star run. The camera picks him up like he's made for the screen.

'Watch,' I breathe as Josh sits up. 'Watch this.'

'Chase him!' Cara roars her lines. 'I'll reward you!' Even shouting she is beautiful: poise, grace. Her eyes flash.

The focus shifts to the boy, who is almost out of view. I think he's made it. He thinks he's made it. He turns slowly, and just catches sight of the other three, who are disappearing fast behind him as his naked, tiny feet push him ever further away. Without looking, he runs into the road.

Bam.

The boy falls into the dust; the bag falls to the ground. Blood seeps slowly in a pool, almost touching the edges of the soft leather.

'Here's Pablo,' Josh says.

Pablo lifts the body in his arms, the bag forgotten, and he weeps. A close-up of his face. I want to touch the screen.

I pause for a moment, in awe of what I've seen, then read from an article I'd found online. 'This story quotes him as saying he was originally a background extra, in a police uniform, but then the director had picked him out because of his looks, and asked him to chase the boy. The scene just played out – Pablo went for it, and they kept filming. They expanded his role. He was launched.'

Audiences had wept. Pablo had been nominated for a Newcomers Award.

'Pablo's brother died around then,' I say.

Josh looks confused. 'What, you think…'

'It says here the grief came to him so easily because of his brother. Look at him.'

We look back to the screen. Josh rewinds the action and presses freeze frame on his face. 'He's not acting that. He's lived it.'

Josh stares at me. 'You think there's a connection between then and now? That Pablo was talking on the plane?'

'I can't put my finger on why, but I think something must have happened on that film shoot. Something that's festered. Something that someone needs to pay for.'

23

I'm exhausted. I stand, stretching out. 'I'll head to bed.'

Josh looks thoughtful and stands too.

I think we're done, but the night hasn't finished spilling surprises yet.

I say, 'I wonder how his brother died. You think there was a stolen bag involved? You think—'

'A bag. There you go again.'

'What?'

'A bag. You said the kid stole a bag.'

'Yeah,' I gesture at the screen. 'We just watched it.'

'Nah, we didn't. We didn't watch him steal a bag. We watched him steal a purse. And earlier, at the accident, and again tonight... your accent.'

My stomach drops. I open my mouth but can't think fast enough. I smile, trying to brazen it out. I shake my head as though I don't know what he's talking about.

'So, it is really Phoebe, right?' he says, casually, his light drawl keeping the tone of his words light.

My heart races like a train. 'What do you mean?'

'Well. Every now and again there's been something off, and I couldn't put my finger on it. But your accent slipped to

English this afternoon and I realised that's what's been bothering me. When I got back from the desert today, I read the IMBD biography of Phoebe Thomas carefully. A good old American girl, by all accounts.'

I look up at him, trying to gauge his reaction and guess his next step. But he isn't looking at my face, and he doesn't seem angry – he seems...

'I *am* American,' I say, trying to sound casual, as though I'm confirming something blindingly obvious. Something so trivial it's barely worth saying at all.

'Phoebe Thomas,' he says, and he stares at me, watching me. The way he says the name turns me cold.

I look back at him carefully.

He says nothing for a few seconds. It's like a face off. Then he lifts his chin a fraction, and looks at me quizzically. 'It's not really Phoebe at all, is it?'

I stand and walk towards the door. 'Look, Josh. It's late. Why don't we both get some sleep.' I move slowly – not running, not looking scared.

I find my phone, pick it up casually.

He follows me. As I get to the door, he says, 'I'd prefer it if you just told me the truth, you know. You can only imagine some of the things running through my head right now.'

'What do you mean? I don't know what you're talking about,' I say, going for the bluff.

'Yes, you do. You're not Phoebe Thomas. Whatever your name is – I have no idea – but the American accent that was so great at the start. In the car, after the accident, so many things felt off. I know it's not an everyday situation, but I've been going over it and over it. I realised this afternoon that your accent was one of the things about the accident that was throwing me. Your voice. When you got stressed, you slipped up. Your accent changed.'

'My mom—'

'Your mom is from London, yeah, you said. But seriously, Phoebe Thomas grew up in the US. I checked. And surely in times of stress your accent would revert to the usual one. You're English, no matter what you say. And some of the things you say occasionally – *toilet*, not bathroom; *bag*, not purse. You mentioned *hospital*, not *the hospital* the other day. I'm from England and moved to the US in my teens. I know the language – both of them. And actually, you don't.'

We stand there. Is this all he has? Can I ride it out? My mind is splashing around trying to work out a route, when he says, 'And you look like her, but if you *really* look, then you're not the same.'

'What?' I feel sick.

'Well, neither of you have active social media. Strange in itself, but I guess if there's some cover up going on, then disabling that is the first thing to do.'

We had both paused all social media when we agreed to swap.

I'm going to throw up. 'The Wi-Fi is crap here.' But even to me this sounds feeble.

'But I searched for publicity shots – everything we do is online now, right? And I found some for Phoebe Thomas, and it's close enough, but it's not you. I looked at everything I could find. I bet if we pulled the polaroid they took at the costume fitting, we'd be able to see. If we looked close enough – closer than anyone would ever do for a cursory glance at the costume records. The headshot looks good enough, I'd guess. But what if we went to Kidz and found the sheet with them on, and we *really* looked. I've been watching you all evening, wondering if I was imagining it all. But I'm right, aren't I?'

My hands close in fists.

'My big question is where is Phoebe Thomas right now? Because no one turns down their first role. No one.' He leans closer. 'Have you done something to her? Are you the one behind all of this?' He waves his hand outwards. Marianne, Augusto, dead in the dark.

'No!' *Shit. What is he thinking?* 'Christ, no! It's not like that at all! I'm Phoebe's friend – she was ill. She was terrified her agent would drop her if she pulled out last minute. We were flat sharing. We look the same. It was her idea!' I'm half shouting now, desperate for him to believe me. By assuming her identity, I have made him suspicious of more than me just pretending to be someone else.

My God, the police! What will they think? I'll have to be honest with them, fess up to everything. I feel sick at all the implications. This was such a stupid idea.

I look back to Josh – he still doesn't look convinced.

'Can we start with your real name?'

I pull out my phone. 'Look – these are the messages to Phoebe!' I tap on our chat and scroll through. I show him a few photos I've sent. I show him the ones from the first day, where she wishes me luck. I hope to God he doesn't comment on the lack of messages in the last few days. 'Here, photos of us. She's my best friend.' I flip though the photos from the summer. My phone stays lit for about ten seconds, then dies again in my hands.

Panic burns in my throat. 'You have to believe me! Please, Josh. I was trying to be a good friend. I mean, I know it's in my interest to be here. It's a brilliant opportunity. It's not an entirely selfless act.' I shake my head. Then I look at him and speak carefully. 'And I've enjoyed spending time with you. I might have taken her name, but I've been me. Our friendship – that wasn't a lie. I haven't tried to deceive you.' I lean forward, and stare into his bright blue eyes. I speak carefully. 'Please, Josh. You have to believe me. I haven't been playing you – or anyone else. I'm as in the dark about Marianne as you are. The stuff I've told you about my past roles – that's all me. I came here when Phoebe couldn't, but not for any devious reason.' I hold my breath for a second, watching him. His face is expressionless.

I wait. I daren't move. If he doesn't believe me, then I've got no idea what to do. Everyone will doubt me – before Marianne died, they'd be angry about being lied to. Now, they'd be suspicious to the point of me being in real trouble. Now everything's changed.

'Josh?' I hear the plea in my voice.

He sits down, both hands lifting in a shrug. 'OK. Those messages seem real enough. So, where is she?'

'Well, currently in New York…' I trail off.

'If they're forced to delay because of an investigation, and your friend is feeling better, will you still pretend to be her? Or will you step aside?' He's looking at me with interest now and he asks the question I've tried not to think about.

'I don't know.' I'm being honest with Josh. I want him to know he can trust me. 'I guess I'll have to. She won the part initially. It was never mine.' But I realise this is a lie. I don't think I can now. Not now I *really* think about it.

'It's yours now,' he says. 'All those shots of sandboarding, the camel ride. All the early scope. Plus, our chemistry.'

He half grins, but the joke seems forced. I can tell he's trying hard, like he wants to believe me. This is promising.

I swallow before I speak, and I hope the worst has passed. I'm physically shaking with relief that he seems to believe me. This is the one thing I've been dreading.

'I need to get through the next few days and see what happens. Everyone else arrives tomorrow. Then, assuming the police decide whatever happened was an accident, the filming can resume. It won't be an issue.'

'So, what's your real name? You still haven't told me.' Josh cocks his head.

'Ellie. Ellie Miller. Nice to meet you. Good to make your acquaintance.' In full English, I stick my hand out at him in an attempt at humour and he laughs, but it peters out.

I've got some work to do to convince him. I take a breath. 'Please, don't tell anyone.'

He looks at me for a moment. 'OK. I won't. But that's it, right? No more lies?'

'Scouts honour,' I say. He looks tired. There's nothing else I can do. I'll have to hope he believes me. I prepare to make a slow walk back to my room. The police are here tomorrow. I need to pray he believes me or I'll be in deep shit.

'Night, Josh,' I say.

'Night, *Ellie*. Nah, forget that. I'll stick to Phoebe.' He grins, weakly, but at least it's there.

Once I've closed my door and I'm really on my own, I try calling Phoebe again.

Nothing.

I restart my phone, plugging it in which seems to help and send her another text.

My phone dies halfway through. The screen goes dark. And I stare at the blackness.

I didn't try so hard to get where I am now, to have it all fall at the last minute.

The marble and gilt surrounds of the fancy room are cool and still. The perfume and rose water in the bathroom luxurious.

But this isn't what it's about. It's about Hanneghan. It's all been about him. Hot tears prick my eyes as I think about everything it took to get here.

I told Josh there were no more lies, but that in itself is a lie. I just hope he doesn't find out the rest.

Because Phoebe wasn't really ill. And this wasn't her idea.

This has been my idea from the start.

TWELVE WEEKS EARLIER

London

24

It really began on the over-heated Northern Line, halfway through a stickered sandwich from Sainsburys that had only minutes left before it turned to absolute cardboard.

I'd dived into one of the small stores in the West End, starving, but skint. I was nursing the bruise of having just been turned down for another theatre part. It wasn't even a paying role, but it's all about the exposure. If exposure really paid, I'd be a millionaire. And not eating cardboard sandwiches.

Next to the takeaway food, there was a magazine, with the cover shouting about a new film being shot. The latest sex scandal meant one of the leading stars was stepping down.

I couldn't even afford magazines, but I bought it. There was something... a gut feeling.

I read it sat on a ripped nylon seat on the tube, a discarded packet of crisps on the next chair. There's nothing glamorous about discounted dry chicken sandwiches and a tube carriage with no air-con in the early summer, nothing to make the moment memorable, nothing fitting. But I read about the cast. Then I went home and researched. I spent hours trawling IMBD. Then social media.

I found one. A possible way in. A woman about my age. A

very small part on the film. Starting a course in a few weeks in New York. I stared at her face in disbelief.

I didn't sleep that night. By the time I had all the details, and I'd filled in the form, it was almost dawn.

The plan didn't get off to a good start: *Unfortunately, our summer courses are all fully booked.*

But there was a waiting list, and as with many things you manifest, if you really push for it, the universe will make space for you.

I had to shift at least half a stone to make this work, so I went hard on the diet.

I told Mum, booked a ticket and got on a plane.

I arrived a week before the course. There were things to do.

EARLIER THAT SUMMER

New York

25

JFK isn't the holy grail of glamour I had thought it might be. When the pilot had said, *We'll be landing in JFK in thirty minutes* I thought I might explode with the glitzy dreams of youth.

But it's just an airport, and not even a particularly nice one.

I'd never been to the US before. Mum has never taken me. She preferred Europe, Asia. She's been to the US before, and it wasn't a great time in her life.

'Be careful,' was all she'd said, when I told her I was going.

I take the train into Manhattan, and when I walk out of Penn Station, and see signs for Madison Square Garden, I catch my breath.

It's already hot. Sticky and humid. My hair feels damp, and I wear cheap sunglasses I picked up in Camden market.

I'm really here.

I've booked into a hostel for a few days, which comes to about £50 a night. I dump my bag, then I put on my best dress – a mix of sexy summer and smart, and check myself in the mirror. I have long blonde hair, poker straight. I've been starving myself for almost two weeks now, and I'm looking thinner.

In this dress, in the sunglasses, I'm ready.

Can I go through with this? Do I dare?

I stare at myself. For all the things I've done so far in life, of which I'm not proud, I'm about to go lower than I've ever gone before. But needs must. I mean, if you have right on your side, can you be wrong?

You can do this, I whisper, seeing a ghost of my eight-year-old self. I see the tears on her face. My face.

I head to the JuJu Bar. My best guess at where to find him. I order a drink, pull out my phone, and check the area.

Nothing yet.

Nervous, I scroll through the screen shots I've taken from his social media account.

Back in NYC! Date stamped two weeks ago.

Three weeks back at the top of the world! A photo of a view taken from a skyscraper office, location tag: law firm on Wall Street.

Monday night drinks with buddies! Good to see these faces again! Tagged location: The JuJu Bar.

It's Monday night. I can only hope. The bar is just off Wall Street. I'm praying the Monday nights drinks are a regular thing.

I scope again, checking the profile picture against the men I see in the bar. Not here yet.

After an hour of lingering over my drink, a group of men walk in, dressed in suits.

My stomach is tight. I play with my drink. It's a pale red, and I've barely touched it. I shift it slightly on its cardboard coaster. I look out at the street. I swing my hair over my shoulder. I check my phone.

I see him. He's here, with the group. They're all loud and

laughing. One saunters to the bar with the air of someone carrying money he wants people to watch him spend.

It isn't him, but I can't help but look at him. I use the reflection in the mirror behind the bar, in the bottles lined up and ready for Monday night drinks. His face twists in thick glass from a gin bottle, green and hollow.

Once the drinks are heading to the table, I wait.

I drink the pale red cocktail in front of me, and I order another.

The one I'm waiting for has dark brown hair. It's wavy and thick like hers. He's tanned as though it's the end of the summer rather than the start, but I know he's been working in the Middle East. His social media is littered with brunches in five-star hotels, dragon boat racing, tall buildings and weekends in the desert.

He moves, finally. His round.

I lift my drink and pull out my phone, climb down from the bar stool and walk towards him, head down.

We bump into each other. He actually sidesteps, but I manage to throw my drink down my front anyway. My thin white dress – pale pink now, soaking through.

'Shit!' I say loudly. 'Oh, I'm so sorry, did I get any on you? I was looking at my phone!'

'It's my fault,' he says, smiling, white teeth and brown eyes. 'I tried to get out of your way but I didn't try hard enough. You've lost all your drink – can I get you another?'

'Oh, I was leaving. My friend is having car trouble and she can't make it. We were meeting...' I let it trail away and I look at my glass. 'I've been waiting for a while, and I was looking forward to a drink. I got an acting role today!'

'Oh congratulations! My sister's an actor,' he says, proudly. 'Come on, it's my round. You get to choose a drink. You're welcome to join us – although I know it's probably far from ideal, hanging out with a group of lawyers.'

I laugh. 'I wouldn't want to intrude.'

We walk to the bar. I flick my blonde hair over my shoulder; I smile at him as I talk. 'Is your sister working right now?'

'She's got a job at the end of the summer. She's being cagey about it, but she's coming to New York in a few days. We're from a small town near Boston. I won't get to see her, though. I'm on a plane in forty-eight hours. But I'm loaning her my apartment. And what about you? You're British – do you live here?'

'I just finished an audition. I'm heading back to London soon after the role is over. It's a tiny one and I paid through the nose to get here. It's just a commercial. The director is one of my old tutors.' I hold his gaze for a second. I've rehearsed my story. It's all lies. 'I was hoping to catch up with my friend while I'm here, but I'll have to try again tomorrow.'

The drinks are in front of us now, and he hasn't started back to his friends.

'I'll stay here – I don't want to get in your way,' I say, crossing one leg over the other, and silently praying he goes for it. 'I may as well enjoy being out in Manhattan while I get the chance.'

He lifts the tray of drinks, then pauses. 'Look. I'll take these over, then do you fancy a drink out by the river? On me. At least you'll get to see a bit of the city. What a waste if you only came here for work and no play.'

He colours slightly. 'I'm Matt, by the way.'

'Emma,' I say and hold out my hand. 'Good to meet you, Matt. I'll wait right here.'

We're a bottle in and we're deep in his family holiday memories. He tells me about a boat trip out near Cape Cod.

'So, who's the better sailor – you or your sister?' I say, grinning, and topping up his drink.

He laughs. 'Of course I'll say me! But if I'm honest, probably her. She's a natural. She saved me once. The boom knocked me clean off and she spent a good fifteen minutes fishing me out. I couldn't climb back onboard!'

I grin. 'And who has the better music taste?'

'Well me, obviously! I'm a sucker for rock. She's more of a pop fan. She likes country and western too. Sorry, I feel like all I'm doing is talking about me!'

'It's interesting! And you picked such a great spot.' I gesture out to the water. We're sat on a roof bar in Battery Park, and there are enough fairy lights hanging to power the city. It's beautiful. The night is still warm, and as we're talking, *California Girls* by Katy Perry starts playing over the sound system.

'I bet your sister liked this one!' I say, nodding to the music. 'I can't get enough of Katy Perry!' Though I'm not really a fan. I've heard this song so many times my head might explode.

'So much! Like, on repeat, all summer that year!' He sits back, studying me. 'You know, you look a bit similar to her. I mean – very different. Different hair, different style. But there's something around the eyes. And bone structure.'

We talk about favourite films, first heartbreaks, we talk about dreams. I keep him talking and soak it all in.

At some point he leans in to kiss me, whispering, 'Not so much like my sister I can't do this,' and he tastes of beer, salted chips and I feel a buzz of excitement. It gets late late. We share a cab, and I'm about to head in with him when I thank him nicely for a lovely evening. I take his number. I don't go inside and his face falls. But now I know where he lives, and where she'll be staying.

26

Three days later and two days before the course is due to start, I track Phoebe down. I know where her brother's apartment is, and I know that's where she's headed. I wear my huge sunglasses again, and I buy a coffee and sit at a café nearby, where I can keep watch.

It takes hours. I'm on my third coffee and my bum is starting to go numb, when I see her. Her IMBD photo must be quite recent. Her hair is dark brown and wavy, like her brother's. She's roughly my height but thinner than I usually am. Not now, though – I reckon we're about the same now.

I watch how she swings her hair. I look at her gait as she heads into the apartment.

She's wearing a dress. I normally go for jeans and t-shirts. She has big silver hoop earrings, and two other smaller hoops in her left ear. She wears heels and an ankle bracelet.

I have one earbud in, listening to the playlist I'd made: some country and western songs her brother had mentioned, the whole back catalogue of Katy Perry. I do my homework, carefully.

The afternoon fades into the evening and pigeons land nearby, picking up crumbs. I eat cake at my table. I order a smoothie.

'You decided to move in?' jokes the waiter.

I smile at him, indicate my laptop. 'It's a great writing spot.'

I pack up quickly when I see her head out again, and I follow her down the street. She heads to a store on the corner, and I follow her in. I practise her swinging stride, moving my hips a little more than I usually do. When she laughs at something an attendant says, she kind of tips her head to the left a little.

The next time I laugh, I do the same. I try it out in the mirror of the lift as I head down to the basement floor of Target. I saw her take the escalator.

It's all so slight. Barely there adjustments. You can imitate someone in mannerisms with no physical similarity at all. You can recognise people by a laugh, a tilt of the head, a walk. I'm aiming for all of it. Impressionists do it all the time. There's no reason I can't. A twenty-four-hour study and a close grilling of her brother. Plus the physical stuff – as good as I can get. I only really need to convince *her* we're similar. Similar enough anyway. I'd been ecstatic when I saw her picture after reading about the film. I finally get a shot. I have four weeks to get her to trust me and make her think the crazy plan I'll half suggest is the only option.

I catch up with her again around the section with dresses. I watch as she picks them up and half pouts in the mirror each time. I pick up a dress and try out my half pout. I feel silly, but there's no room for that.

She buys some wedge heels and a flippy yellow dress. I buy the same wedge heels, and I buy a similar dress in blue. She trails the make-up section – fuck, I'd almost forgotten make-up – she picks up a lipstick crayon, and I can't quite see which one it is. But I take a few photos from a distance, pretending to check my phone, and I zoom in to find one with a similar shade. Heavy on the eyebrow pencil; I must practise.

On the way out, I buy hoop earrings too, and I'm ready. I have to be. The course starts tomorrow. Now it's just the hair. I made an appointment the day I arrived, and I know what I need to say now. I book myself in to get an additional ear-piercing.

'Are you sure?' the colourist lifts my blonde hair and lets it fall through her fingers. 'Dark brown?'

I pull out my phone. 'This shade, please.' I show her the photos I'd taken earlier of Phoebe, but I'm carefully not to reveal her face. 'I just love this style!'

'Your hair isn't as thick as that. You'll need to dry it with a lot of volume to hold the style. The colour I can do though…' She hums as she trails off in thought, and says a few numbers which mean nothing to me. 'And you want this cut?'

I nod.

My hair is the thing I'll mind the most. But needs must. It won't mean anything without the hair.

I touch it one last time as the colourist grabs some scissors. 'We'll do the cut after, but no point colouring all of this is if you're going shoulder length. Shall I just take some weight off before we start?'

This is it. This is the point of no return. For all the things I'm about to do, cutting my hair is the one that makes me want to cry.

THURSDAY

DAY FIVE

Abu Dhabi

27

'Phoebe, are you awake? We're all heading downstairs.'

I hear Kidz through the door. I roll over and look at my phone – it's 8 a.m.

Turning cold with dread, I remember the conversation with Josh last night. I need to try to find him first thing, and pray that he's still on side. I don't want any doubts creeping in. Not with the police coming today. Not when there's so much more to the story than I told him.

'So early,' I say, pulling the door open to Kidz, wearing only the t-shirt I slept in. 'What's going on?'

'Police are here.' She checks her phone as she speaks. 'I need to get everyone downstairs. They want to talk to us before breakfast. I think they want statements first. They've asked us all to stay at the hotel today. The breakfast room is open so you can eat when you're not needed, and get coffee. You OK?'

I nod. 'Statements from us all, I guess.' I wonder how many questions they may have. I expected the police before now.

'Yes.' She puts her hand on my arm. 'I know it's a lot. If you want any help, or you want anyone in there with you, just say. It's just a formality. Freddie won't let anyone be interviewed without a lawyer – he's been advised. The lawyers arrive later, which could take hours as they're coming from the city. The other plane is landing later too so everyone will arrive once the police are finished. Hopefully we'll get it all wrapped up quickly, then we can *finally* start shooting.'

'Are you OK?' I ask. Kidz's habit of asking fifty questions a day, most of which she doesn't seem to expect an answer to, means I forget to ask how she's coping. She's holding us all together.

She looks surprised and I say, 'You're doing a lot. And Freddie isn't the easiest boss.' There are rings around her eyes that I'm sure weren't there when we started out.

'Oh, I'm fine!' Then her eyes close briefly. 'Between you and me, this is my last job for Freddie. I was contracted, and I couldn't just pull out... reputation and all that. You understand? But I'm free to start something new next, and to be honest, this whole experience can't be over soon enough.'

'OK, well, you can always talk to me.'

She opens her mouth, then closes it again. Whatever she was about to say shut down. Then she offers up a quick smile. 'See you downstairs.'

I take a seat in the dining room as Freddie clears his throat. He glances round the room, and Cara, Lukas and Josh enter. I look at Josh, willing him to smile at me so I can check we're still on the same page after last night.

I sit with Pablo and Lukas. We're down to eight. I can feel Marianne's absence.

'Have you spoken to the police?' Pablo asks, breaking bread onto his plate and slathering it with butter. 'I had a chat with one of them earlier. They asked for my autograph. I advertise a line of aftershave in the UAE and apparently it does very well.' He's smiling.

'I'm giving my statement next,' Lukas says. His brow furrows and he puts down an uneaten piece of toast. He wears baggy yoga-style pants today and a white t-shirt, with a silk headband. He refills his coffee from the tall pot on the table and offers some to me, but doesn't really look at me. 'I wonder if someone *did* see something…' He looks at Pablo.

'What do you mean?' Pablo stares back at him. His smile disappears as his eyebrows knit and his eyes furrow. 'What are you implying, that there was more to Marianne's death? If that's true, and if someone did see something, then one of us might have a lot to worry about right now.'

'Morning,' Freddie speaks to the room. He is paper white and doesn't look as though he's slept much. His cheery tone sounds forced. 'I know you'll all be wanting to get on with filming. The police are here to take statements and conduct interviews later once our lawyers arrive. Today we've been asked to stay at the hotel. Please, enjoy the facilities. There's nothing to worry about. I'm sure we can all get back to filming, and to making a film Marianne would be proud of soon.'

Pablo chews slowly and stares at Lukas.

I look for Josh, trying to catch his eye. He's the only one who knows I'm not who I say I am and the arrival of the police has reminded me that makes me vulnerable.

The police might have found something to suggest Marianne's death wasn't an accident. After what I saw yesterday, Cara has every reason to have had a hand in it. As does Freddie.

Looking at Cara now, she's laughing weakly at something Josh has said, and she looks exhausted – probably much like the rest of us. But tiredness and exhaustion are no guarantee of innocence. They could be the opposite. Seconds later, her smile vanishes and is replaced with something more like blankness. She suddenly looks like she has everything to lose.

Lukas pushes his chair away and heads out. Our table has been silent for the last few minutes, but now Pablo leans closer to me. I see he's staring at Freddie. 'Look, it's just occurred to me, I know something, and if we find out today Marianne's death wasn't an accident...' He stops, and I realise how much we all question whether it was really an accident. He looks at me, leaning in and speaking more quietly. 'I found out Cara and Freddie are having an affair.'

'No,' I whisper. I decide to act surprised.

'They both know I know. I've promised not to tell anyone – not even the police. I thought it was only fair out of loyalty to Freddie.'

I remember Kidz saying something about another rewrite with a change of direction for Pablo in the script, and I realise it's not cash Pablo will want, but prominence in the film. The concern on his face deepens further.

'I mean, it's not like I think...' But then he stops talking and purses his lips a little, staring down at his coffee. 'Well, for reasons of personal safety, I just thought someone else should know. It shouldn't be *only* me, just in case.'

Before I can say anything, I hear my name called.

'Let's speak later,' I say to him, and I see an officer stood at the side of the room. As I head towards him, I glance back. Pablo is staring at Freddie.

I can't think about Pablo now. I've got to pass myself off as someone else, in a potential murder investigation. And I need to hope that Josh doesn't let slip what he knows. I feel sick as I follow the officer.

If I'm really any good at acting, this will be my biggest test yet.

28

I'm brought into a room to speak to the same officers who interviewed me after Augusto's death.

Once again, one smiles more than the other, and he greets me with familiarity, and asks how I'm doing.

'Strange, that we are speaking again so soon,' he says, delivering the statement as though it's a question and I nod.

'We're all devastated by Marianne's death. So tragic,' I say, trying to read his face. I have no idea if they've examined her body. They might already know if it was an accident or not.

Not giving anything away, he just nods.

He asks about the evening and I try to give as much information as possible about where I was, and about what I remembered.

'You attempted to give her CPR?' he asks, making notes although the tape is already recording.

'Yes, and Elijah Hanneghan did. He gave her mouth to mouth and I tried to work on her heart.'

He nods. The room is quiet for a moment.

'How well do you know Cara Strauss?' he asks.

His face is inscrutable.

'I met her when we flew here.' There must be something behind this question.

Now is my chance to tell him. Now is the time to say what I think I'd heard on the plane. I half open my mouth.

Courage fails me – I just can't have any more focus on me. I chicken out, and I smile as innocently as I can as I say, 'Why do you ask about Cara?'

'Oh, I'm a fan.' His face is as much a mask as mine.

Something's coming.

I wonder what they know.

EARLIER THAT SUMMER

New York

29

The morning of the course registration I'm up bright and early. The room in the hostel is sun-lit before 5 a.m. – the curtains offer little shade. I pack all my bags and I'm out quickly, taking everything with me as I head over to the school. It's a long trek with all of my things, but that's OK. I need to look tired when I get there.

I wear the wedge heels and the blue Target dress. I have hoops in, and I haul my bags over the cracks in the street, lengthening my stride and swinging my hips a little.

I register at a table outside where I smile as broadly as I can when I'm asked for my name. I hook my hair over my right ear, and when the guy taking names makes a joke, I dip my head a little before I laugh.

I pick up my timetable. There's a coffee and croissant stand and I'm starving so I head over there. It doesn't happen straight away. I need to be patient.

By now, all the new students wear name stickers. I chat to a few. We stand in a circle on the lawn, and there's a kind of nervous laughter, along with some people stamping big personalities into the group like a larger name tag.

I wait. I drink more coffee.

I wait some more.

'Hey, great dress!' A male voice behind me is loud. I check left and right, but no, he's staring at me.

I commit.

'Hey, I'm Ellie!' I catch my hair, which has fallen forward, and I lift and tuck it behind my ear. 'You like?' I dust it down with my hands. 'I had no idea what to wear. I've literally just got off the plane and come straight here, but what do you wear to the drama class of your dreams?'

'You're from England!' His face lights up. 'Oh my god I love your accent! I'm Felix. You're on the drama class too?'

'There are other classes?'

'Yes – there's like music, dance, and something else.' He shrugs. 'But the four-week drama class is where it's at!'

He slips his arm through mine like we've been friends for years. 'Come on, I've met a few others. We're having coffee over on the grass. Come join.'

I pull my suitcase in the other hand, and wheel it behind me, walking tall on my wedges, my stride long, throwing my weight to each leg as I go. When Felix tells me a joke, I dip my head before I lift it higher to laugh.

Sitting on the grass, Felix introduces me to about five other students, all roughly the same age. One or two are younger, and they look at me without much interest. I see their eyes flick over me, finding nothing to latch on to. I hate these bored babies. Why is it ageing beyond a certain point only erases you? Now I'm over twenty-two, I've started to feel like I'm past it, which is madness. In the world of acting, age works differently for women than men. It's like dog years: one for a man, seven for a woman. I don't want it to be too late. It can't be too late.

I pitch into the conversation quickly. I need to establish myself.

Her self. I need to be clear to everyone from the off so that when she arrives, I'm the original, she's the copy.

Halfway through a story I've got the attention of all them, even the bored babies, all of eighteen, it turns out. I recount the horrors of a long-haul economy flight. Everyone gets this.

'No way, so he was breathing into your actual ear?' Felix pulls a face. 'Were you, like, sick?'

'I didn't know what to do! I was squished between the sleeping breather, who is practically hugging me, and then on the other side of me, some kid grabs my earring and pulls hard, saying, 'Pretty'.'

'No way!' This comes from one of the bored babies who rolls her eyes. 'They should have a separate section on planes for kids!'

'So, what did you do? You couldn't sit there for another four hours?' This is Felix.

'I made eye contact with one of the air stewards. I'd been having a conversation earlier with them about Katy Perry – I just love her – and I made a desperate face, and they moved me to a seat in Business.'

'No way!'

'Can you believe it?' I shrug a little, copy the laugh. 'I've never done anything except walk through the expensive seats before. So I made the most of it. I got free drinks, made my bed go flat...' I'm still telling the fabricated story, making sure I have their attention, when it happens.

'Stop, Ellie! Stop!' Felix jumps to his feet.

'What's going on?' I tense. It's too early for me to be found out. Too early for me to be called a fraud, surely. But maybe I'm too easy to read. Maybe they're all laughing at me, wondering why they're talking to someone who is clearly playing a part, trying to play them. Playing it all wrong.

'Wait. Do you know her? Is she your twin?' Felix is pointing over to someone getting a coffee.

They wear the same dress as me, only in yellow. The same wedges. Same hair – cut and colour. I see them laugh from here. The laugh I've been rehearsing for twelve straight hours.

'Her? Why, do you think she looks the same as me?' I keep my voice as neutral as possible. I force myself to sound surprised, relaxed. 'That's a great dress she's wearing.'

'Oh my god!' The bored babies are both standing up too. And the one who'd spoken earlier speaks again. 'Ellie, isn't it? Ellie, it's like looking at you! She's identical. I mean, look at her!'

She turns, and it must be strange, looking over at a group of people, already best friends in the way of the sudden intimacy you get when travelling, or arriving miles from home for a course where you know no one. A group of people who are all staring at you, like you're something to be studied, to be surprised by. And one of them looks as close to you as she can get, without climbing into your skin and looking out your eyes.

Felix is already waving. 'Hey!'

Phoebe walks over. Her hips swing in her long stride, her wedges giving her height.

'Hey,' Felix says again. 'Come meet our friend Ellie!'

I'm so thankful I got here first. I would have gone to pieces if I'd had to be the one who was being measured. As it is, I'm the control, I'm the original model. No eyes on me – they're all on her. She's the extra. I've slipped in under the radar of being unremarkable. The remarkable thing is not that Phoebe is Phoebe, but that someone else is also Phoebe. That there are two of us, from two different countries, two different worlds, standing metres apart and apparently almost entirely the same.

Even I'm freaked out.

'There are two of you! Please tell me you're related, or I will lose my mind,' Felix says, eyes wide, staring from one to the other. From her to me.

And she and I do the same. I look at her. She looks at me. I make sure I mirror her shock. I rake my eyes from her feet up to her face in the same way she does me. I tuck my hair behind my ear again, a fraction of a second before she does. My stomach is tight like it's A levels all over again. But the time I've spent watching her pays off, the hours in the café, trailing her in New York. The clothes, the hair, the shoes, the make-up.

'No way,' she breathes, eyes wide.

'Tell me you love Katy Perry,' I say. 'If you love Katy Perry too then I know we're twins from another mother.'

'Katy Perry is my absolute favourite,' she says, and she sounds almost scared. She looks at the rest of the group. 'Am I being pranked?' She looks behind her for cameras. 'Is this like what that Ashton Kutcher programme used to do?'

I remember I'd be freaked out too, if I hadn't planned it all, and I step back a little. 'I think I might faint,' I say.

Felix imitates my accent, sounding more like the royal family than I ever do. '*She might faint* – oh this is just spooky! Get her a chair. Get them both a chair. The identikits!'

30

Like I'm riding a rollercoaster, my stomach is in freefall as I walk beside Phoebe. The circumstances have drawn an invisible line between the two of us. I just hope it's tight enough.

At first the group clustered round us, asking questions, exclaiming over the craziness of it. When Felix suggests we all go and get lunch somewhere once registration is finished, Phoebe and I walk side by side as we drift into the busy streets. There's no way to walk as a group on the sidewalk, so it's just her and me, alone in the crowd.

I have to make this work. It can't be weird.

But it's so weird.

'How long have you been acting?' I start with the easy things. The things we all have in common.

'Since I was small.' She smiles, not at me, at a memory. I look at her side-on as we pause at the road, waiting for the lights to change. 'I was about eight when I made my family watch all these shows.'

'Ha! Me too. Only it was just me and Mum. But Sunday afternoons were all about the shows, always wearing Mum's make-up too.'

'Same!' This time she smiles at me. 'I'm sorry, I just can't get used to it. Like, even our hair's the same.'

I touch my new hair.

'Have you been here long?' she asks, tilting her head a little with the question. I remember this for later.

'I arrived this morning! I've never been to New York before. I've always wanted to come, but my mum hates it, so we never visited.'

'No way! What, you came straight from the plane?'

I nod, gesturing to the bag I pull. 'I'm properly tired. I took a night flight as it was cheaper. I'm staying at a youth hostel, but I haven't checked in yet.'

She raises her eyebrows and says nothing.

'Here we are! Cheap and loads of it. Come eat,' Felix calls, standing outside a Korean BBQ. 'You'll love it here. I know the manager, so we'll get some extras.'

'Do you know everyone, Felix?' I ask as he beams at me.

'I certainly do. And for the identikits, I'm getting star treatment.' He touches me on the arm as I pass him, dropping his voice. 'I've decided you two are my favourites. We're going to be best friends this summer. You just watch.'

The table is round but not wide, and we cram in. True to his word, Felix disappears off to embrace the manager, and soon plates arrive: charred vegetables, BBQ meats, bowls of noodles, beer. Time ticks on as we eat, voices rising in laughter as the beer disappears. Despite my nerves, I'm having the time of my life.

I try to let Phoebe come to me. We sit next to each other, but I make sure I talk to everyone. I recount stories of England when people ask me questions about it, and I exaggerate all the details. They ask about the Queen's funeral – I say I camped out. The queue – I tell them I queued for eight hours. Neither of these things is true but I know they want me to be the most English of

English. Like you want Santa Claus at Christmas, and the Pope in Rome.

'Do you drink tea, like all the time?' one of the bored babies asks.

'It's my favourite drink,' I say, nodding.

Then I sit back and whisper to Phoebe, 'I can't stand the stuff.'

I'm rewarded with a smile, and slowly it becomes us and them. When they ask if I've ever met Hugh Grant, I say, *I bumped into him once on Oxford Street*, but I offer up a wink to Phoebe who laughs into her plate of food.

When the afternoon feels like it's run its course, and I've used some of the things her brother mentioned – I've told Phoebe about my love of boats, to be met with a shake of the head and: *But I love boats – how is it we're so similar?*

Then I pretend to call the hostel. I say, in a surprised voice, 'Oh, they've over booked for tonight!'

Phoebe had been talking and she turns back to me. 'What, they've given your bed away?'

I nod, and let my shoulders sag. 'They say there's space at the one much further downtown. I guess I'll have to drag my bag there.' I stare at my phone. I wait.

I know for a fact they have space tonight. I checked just in case I didn't manage to pull off an invite from Phoebe.

But she doesn't let me down. There are a few beats, and I say nothing. Then she says, 'You know what, I'm staying at my brother's place. There's a sofa in there. You can come and sleep on it tonight if you like, until the hostel nearby has space.'

'Really?' I bite my lip. 'You're sure? I wouldn't want to be in the way.'

Felix must have overheard, because he says loudly to the table, 'This is too much! Now the identikits are roomies!'

A cheer goes up from the table, and I laugh, grimacing at

Phoebe. 'God, I'm so sorry. I guess we'll have to put up with some of this.'

She touches my hand, and offers up a smile. 'There are worse things. It's never good to be alone in New York. Let me help with your bag and we'll head home.'

Abu Dhabi

31

Showering in my room after a quick swim in the pool with Lukas, I think about Phoebe again. Something strange is going on. I have no idea why she's ignoring me, but that must be why I haven't heard from her yet. With everything else going on, I'd stopped worrying about it but now it's heavy in my chest. Despite the cracked screen my phone is more or less working, and she's like my sister. There's no way she'd ignore me for this long unless something was wrong. Surely she doesn't... know.

I wrap myself up in a towel and sit cross-legged on the bed, staring at my phone.

Still nothing. Maybe it is the signal. But I'm sure the messages I'd sent to Mum are going through.

Wi-Fi is patchy though. Freddie had given a blanket rule we must maintain social media silence. Maybe he's asked the hotel to move to a slower Wi-Fi signal to do this – it only seems to last for minutes. Maybe it's just always worse in the desert.

Fifteen unanswered messages to Phoebe. It feels as though I've gone from living inside her skin for the summer – to nothing.

Felix might know something, and I haven't replied to him yet after his crazy voicemail. I'd completely forgotten about it. I send him an upbeat message. We'd decided not to tell any of the group we were swapping places so he will assume she's over here. I doubt he's seen her but he might know something.

I tap out a message:

Hey! How's the big NY? Missing my K-Town karaoke! Sorry to be late replying – crazy busy!

And I follow with some emojis.
The response is so quick I've barely blinked.

Oh my god. Thank god. I've been broken hearted. I thought it was you! Oh my god! xoxo

What?

What do you mean?

I tap out, and wait.
His reply is swift.

We thought you were dead!!! A girl with your name was hit by a bus two days ago. Like your actual name. She was working in that singing diner off Broadway. I thought it was you! The group heard about it from someone working there – how mad. You're back in London, yes??

I go cold inside. I feel sick. Something like doom presses down on me and all the air in my lungs vanishes in a flash. I can barely swallow. I'd told no one about the diner apart from Phoebe, as I wasn't planning on being there. Swapping the jobs had always been part of the plan. I'd lined up the job so that I'd have a real option to offer her in the swap.

This girl who died. She had my name?

My fingers shake as I type. Nothing makes sense. My head is fuzzy.

She was killed. She was run over. I'm so sorry, Ells. I'm literally crying right now with relief. Someone from the diner identified the body, but they obviously screwed up. My heart was broken. Oh, thank God you're okay!

I drop the phone.
What?
Phoebe can't be dead. Of course she can't.
No.
What have I done?

32

There are moments when it seems the world has stopped spinning. Of course it has. It can't have carried on. Seismic moments, so huge an earthquake must have shaken the ground.

I am rocked.

Phoebe can't be dead. It's not possible.

I re-read Felix's message.

There's no reason for Felix to lie. It's not a joke – it's not remotely funny. And Phoebe hasn't been replying to my messages.

I cry. I scream into a pillow on my bed.

My hands start shaking and I get a glass of water.

Time passes and I'm not sure how long I've been in my room. I can't remember when I got here. The morning seems years ago.

I dial reception and ask for an outside line for a mobile number in New York, and I phone Felix.

'Oh darling,' he says, his voice so familiar. 'Thank God!'

'The poor girl,' I say, and search for details. It can't be Phoebe. It can't.

'Have you heard from Phoebe?' I say, my throat raw.

'No – she'll be sunning it up in Abu Dhabi, surely! I doubt we'll hear from her for a bit. Her head will be well and truly turned.'

'The girl had my name? It makes no sense.'

'Oh, I wouldn't worry – as long as it's not you. I mean, I'm not heartless, I wish the poor thing hadn't died. She was run over by a bus so it can't have been pretty. They're waiting for a formal ID. If I didn't know someone who worked there, I wouldn't have heard. For a moment I thought you might have got a job there and not gone back to London. Imagine!'

I drop the phone. I can't speak to him. None of them knew I'd got the job, because it was Phoebe who was going to take it, not me.

If Phoebe had come here, then she wouldn't be dead.

What happens now – will they try to contact Mum, thinking it's me?

How will I explain to Phoebe's family... how do you say...

I sit on the bed. I cross my legs and hug the pillow.

'Ellie! *Ellie!*'

I'd forgotten to cancel the call. Felix is shouting for me.

Picking up the phone, I take a breath. 'Sorry, it really hit me. It feels like it could have been me.' What I'm saying makes no sense, but it doesn't matter. Felix barely listens anyway.

'Of course! Look, I'm due in London in a few days for some family thing. Let's meet. I was going to call you. It's just been kinda crazy for the last few days.'

I panic. I can't tell him I took Phoebe's place. Not now. I'll have to face it at some point. When news of her death reaches her agent, they'll obviously contact someone about the film. It will throw up all sorts of questions. I'll be blown apart – there'll be no defence. And all the questions the police ask will be amplified. Why did I lie? Why was I masquerading as someone else? What else have I lied about?

There are two dead bodies here and Josh already knows I'm not who I say I am.

And I can't bear the idea of never seeing Phoebe again.

'Want to give me your London address?'

'Oh, look, normally of course I'd love to see you! But I'm actually away.' I close my eyes and try to come up with something plausible. I start babbling. 'My aunt in Devon has had a stroke. So we've headed down there.'

I don't have an aunt in Devon.

'Oh darling, it's all happening to you. When are you back?'

'Erm, not sure. Mum is with her now.' God, I hate myself.

'OK, well, let's stay in touch. I'm so glad you're OK. Love you.'

'Love you,' I say.

I thank God that was the last thing I said to Phoebe.

I feel like screaming, running as far as I can, or getting drunk. I down a shot from one of the crystal decanters at the side of the room and I climb into bed. I need to wait for this to pass.

Everything's spinning out of control.

Breathing quickly, I feel hot then cold. My fingers tingle and my skin itches.

There are a few times in my life when I've felt like everything's been blown apart. The first time was when I lost Dad. Mum told me. The idea I'd never see him again was too big to get my head round. I spent weeks, months, crying. Imagining a world where he'd walk through the door and we'd play happy families.

It was such a big moment, it was almost like it blotted out other moments before that. Memories of him have hazed. He used to take me out – balloons and the zoo. It's like an image I've stolen from all the movies I've watched. The merry go round; a giraffe with a bandaged leg I cried about. I've clung to the few memories like they're sheathed in gold.

Mum has been so worried about me, since we lost Dad, but I don't talk to her about it. I've searched through photo albums to try and remind myself, but it's so hard for Mum and the old ones in there are few and far between. She doesn't like speaking about him. It's like he barely existed. We live alongside each other in an agreed silence. I don't mention him to protect her – she lost him too. She never ever mentions him. I've never taken up the therapy she's tried to push on me.

I know Mum worries I've never really got over it. Loss at any point is tough. Loss when you're eight years old is like a body blow.

Mum had sat me down and told me one day that she was so very sorry, but he was never coming back. Then she'd hugged me. It wasn't as though I'd had a particularly normal family life. He'd only ever visited a few times. But to know you will never see your dad again, that it's final, can twist you up. I know in many ways it defined me. It's why I'm here.

That was about the time when Hanneghan's first big film took off. As did my poster obsessions, and the repeated watching of all his films. There's always comfort at the movies. There's nothing else like it. Taking you out of yourself, and transplanting you into the life in front of you, golden and in technicolour.

It became a real obsession. Hanneghan became a real obsession.

I came here to get close to him. My ambition to be part of this world of make believe is all to see Hanneghan. Every world Hanneghan has created took me away from who I was, and defined who I want to be. It's why I'm here.

I must stay here and protect him – at all costs – if he's a target. Another shot.

I visualise. I'll only get through the next few days if I can believe Phoebe's alive. I think of her in the diner, getting coffee. Her arms hugging me tight, the sound of her laugh. The way she'd scrunched up one side of her face when putting on mascara, pouting after lipstick. She lost sunglasses on a daily basis.

Phoebe. If I abandon the plan it would make her death meaningless. I need to stick with everything. Like we're doing the film for Marianne. I can make it count.

Almost trance-like, I stay like that until I have the strength to get out of bed.

I'm good at talking myself into a frame of mind. I think, *There's just no way Phoebe is dead* until I almost believe it.

The room feels too cold. I step outside onto the balcony and stare at the pool, the bar, the desert. *What have I done?*

I give myself a good shake. *Phoebe is alive. I'll see her again quite soon.*

Phoebe is alive and working in a diner. I have to believe that to move forward. Otherwise…

33

Time is pressing.

I head downstairs. Pablo's tableau – on his knees, the boy in his arms, the expression on his face – is at the forefront of my mind when I hear him, kicking off royally in reception.

'*Cojones*! Fucking ridiculous! You try to kill me!'

The huge gold vases and marble floors throw his voice around, striking it off the walls.

I can't see his expression, but he leans on the reception counter and the manager has a look on his face that seems to have taken up residence. A man holding fast under fire.

In his anger Pablo sounds more Spanish than I've heard him so far. He slams his hand down on the reception desk as I enter, and Kidz comes running. We exchange a look but she shrugs. *No idea.*

The pressure of the last few days has been building. I'm not surprised it's starting to seep out. It feels like everyone's beginning to boil. The interminable wait for filming to begin and for the truth of what happened to Marianne, is a lot.

'You know I'm fucking allergic! No Brazil nuts!'

'Hey, Pablo. Everything OK?' I ask.

His dark hair is messed up and he is flushed. His lips look a little swollen. Bee stung and sore.

He looks at me quickly, then back to the manager who stares at a computer screen, harassed. The manager has become a little more wide-eyed with each day we've been here.

'They delivered a salad with chopped Brazil nuts! I ordered room service, told them to wheel it in, while I finished getting changed after a swim. Brazil nuts! What are they trying to do to me? I've taken my EpiPen, but look!'

He holds his arm up to reveal his skin covered in hives. And now I look at him again, there's a faint rash on his face too.

'How much is it to ask that they remember the only thing I'm allergic to!'

It had been mentioned on the plane, and I'd heard Pablo talking about it on the first night. We'd all heard.

The manager looks up from the screen he's checking. 'It was definitely not on the order, sir. I'm so sorry. I don't know how it happened. We have a warning on your room about the nuts.'

'Now! Find out what the fuck happened!' Pablo roars. He spins to Kidz, and softer this time, but pleading, 'Can you find out?'

He's genuinely shaken. His voice veers from upset to anger and back again. There's a tremor in there, just for a second, before he roars again at the manager.

'Someone has tried to *kill* me!'

'Can you call an ambulance?' Kidz says, turning to the manager. She passes her hand over her face before she speaks, and I notice she's looking washed out.

Pablo shakes his head. 'The swelling's going down. I'm OK. I didn't eat any. I spat out the mouthful of food. It wasn't enough to do any real harm. But I'm fucking upset. Even with them out of the room, I'll leave it an hour or two before I head back in.'

'We'll arrange a new room for you immediately, sir. I'll have all your things moved.' The manager is swift and efficient. 'I'll

198

speak to the staff. It must be a mix up. We've ensured that Brazil nuts have not been on any menu, but there may still be some in the kitchen. I can't apologise enough. But you will not go back into that room, and I'll speak to the kitchen. We'll have them all removed from the premises this afternoon.'

How do nuts get into a salad sent to the room of the one person who is allergic to them?

'Let's go and sit in the lounge,' I say.

'I'll have coffee brought in.' Kidz talks gently.

I take Pablo's arm. 'Let's go.'

'Madam, did you find what you were looking for?' The manager directs this at me. I have no idea what he's talking about, but I want to follow Pablo, so I decide to ask him later. He must have mixed me up with someone else and I give a half nod.

'What's going on?' Pablo mutters. 'If I hadn't realised before I'd taken the EpiPen, I could have passed out. It could have been...' He shakes his head.

We enter the lounge and a waiter rushes over with coffee and tiny cakes – they've done this each time there's been a crisis. I wonder if they keep an emergency trolley prepared now. There's water on the table and I pour three large glasses.

Pablo drinks a glass straight down and I can see him making a concerted effort to calm down.

'Why would someone do that?' Kidz says. She shakes her head.

'It doesn't sound like a mistake,' I say. I worry that I might upset Pablo further, but he doesn't seem to be listening anyway. It feels ridiculous to try to carry on pretending that nothing weird or scary is happening right now.

When he says, 'Like I said. Someone tried to kill me,' I wonder if he could be right. I'd written off his earlier accusation as anger, drama in the moment. But actually, it would be one way to kill someone. Is he the target, and not Hanneghan?

Kidz looks worried, and says, 'Look, I better tell Freddie about this.'

'The police,' Pablo says. 'If someone tried to kill me, so soon after the death of Marianne, then I want the police told. Not Freddie. Are they still here?'

'I'm not sure.' Kidz stands. 'I think they spoke to Freddie about half an hour ago and left. I can always call them.'

After Kidz disappears, he glances around him and lowers his voice. 'The thing I told you, about their affair. I told the police.'

'You did?' I say, my voice squeaking a little.

He nods, then he stares down at the table. 'I just thought I should. It was going round and round in my head that maybe Freddie had something to do with Marianne's death – or Cara. I can't have that on my conscience. That might have something to do with what happened to me. If Freddie doesn't know I've already told them, maybe he tried to kill me to stop me saying anything? Or the nuts were a way of warning me not to. Either way, that makes sense.'

We look at each other, and I don't know whether I agree with Pablo or whether it sounds crazy.

But the hotel walls are closing in a little more, luxurious to claustrophobic, in the blink of an eye.

34

Footsteps sound behind us and I expect to see Freddie returning with Kidz, but instead Lukas walks in, along with Cara.

Cara's hair is up and back in a messy bun. She wears work-out leggings and is make-up free. There's a touch of the ethereal to her; she looks so pale she's almost transparent. Like all the blood is slowly draining out of her from a small leak, a slow puncture. Each time I see her she's worse. I know how much she'd wanted to leave, but the police had asked us all to stay here, and I wonder if it's slowly crushing her.

Lukas must think the same, because he slips his hand under her arm and says, 'Here, sit down, Cara. I'll get you some water.'

He indicates to the sofa opposite Pablo, then sits next to her. I'm in the armchair and we're all positioned round the large glass coffee table. He takes some cake on a plate and pushes it into her hands. He glances at us. He looks worried.

The plate hovers above Cara's knee, then she stands, to reach and put it back down on the table. She hasn't even looked at it.

Still standing, she lifts her hands up as though to retie the bun, but finds it in place and she lowers her arms slowly, looking unsteady.

'Cara?' I ask, speaking gently. 'You OK?'

She looks at me, then round at us all. She seems surprised, startled, as though caught in headlights.

'The police have just asked me to be ready for an interview first thing tomorrow. They said if I leave the hotel in advance they'll arrest me. They were on their way out, but they made a point of finding me before they left.'

'What?' I'm surprised. 'They just called you over?'

She nods, and her hands go to her hair again, then she sits. 'In the reception area. So anyone could hear.'

'They're interviewing us all tomorrow,' Lukas says. 'Kidz told me.'

I nod. 'They're just waiting for the lawyers to arrive. I don't think them wanting to speak to you means anything. They're bound to have questions for all of us.'

She shakes her head. 'They were horrible. Really short. Different to how they'd been before. I think they were trying to scare me. They said as I was the last person to see Marianne alive, they wanted to start with me. And under no circumstances should I think of leaving the hotel.'

'Pah,' Pablo says, gesturing with his hand dismissively. 'All cops are the same. Venezuela, the US, here. I don't trust any of them.'

Pablo's face is looking more normal now. The marks on his arms are paler too.

'I think,' Cara says, 'I think I'm going to rot in jail here. I can feel it.'

'No!' Lukas says, 'It will just be questions. For all of us—'

But she's not listening to him. She interrupts him halfway through what he's saying, her eyes unfocused.

'They think I *killed* her. I can tell. Even when they took the statement – suspicious. I can feel it. I won't be able to leave. I'll die. *Here*. In jail.'

A shout from behind us makes us all turn. 'Pablo, my God, Kidz just told me. Are you OK?' Freddie walks quickly towards us.

Cara must have seen him, because I feel her stand, rather than see it.

Freddie notices her, and as he says, 'Cara?' he leaps forward, urgently.

Wondering why, I turn back.

Cara is mid collapse, folding at the knees. Lukas manages to grab her only just before her head catches the glass of the coffee table.

There's a crash, as Freddie, in his efforts to break her fall, kicks the table. As he shouts, and Lukas calls for me to help him with Cara, coffee spills on the glass, spreading out like thick brown blood, sliding over the side of the table, and spilling to the floor.

'Smelling salts!' Freddie screams, like it's last century.

Kidz instead helps prop Cara up with some cushions and, soon enough, her eyes blink open.

'What happened?' she says.

'Here, water. Take a sip.' Kidz holds a glass to her lips.

'You fainted,' I tell her.

She closes her eyes again. 'The police.'

Freddie has turned pink, and he fidgets. He ignores the water on the table and instead shouts for some service.

'Bring some whiskey, would you?' he says, when a waiter arrives.

Cara pushes herself up off the cushions. 'I'm OK, I'm OK. Sorry I caused a scene.'

I haven't known Cara to mind about causing a scene – so

far on the trip she seems to have enjoyed them. But she's a pale imitation of the person I've watched these last few days. Maybe that was all bluster. Maybe we all dress for the job we want. It's Freddie who's recovered quickly from the grief – Cara seems broken.

Freddie sits down, whiskey in hand. 'Are you sure you're OK?'

She nods, and he seems to remember Pablo in the room. His brow creases a little when he looks at him. 'And someone put nuts in your room?'

Pablo nods, looking from Cara back to Freddie. He doesn't say anything. If the police have focused now on Cara, it could easily be related to what Pablo told them. I have no idea if Freddie knows, but I don't have long to wait to find out. 'They did. It was an accident with the hotel, or maybe someone else put them there deliberately.' He lingers, calm now, on the last word, looking round at us all.

'What does that mean?' Freddie says, then obviously decides to ignore it. Flopping hard on a sofa, eyes still on Cara, he says, 'The police want to talk to me, too. They're coming back first thing tomorrow. Christ. I thought it was going to be fairly straightforward, but it's like something's changed. They were so kind when they first arrived. When I said goodbye to them a few minutes ago they were much more official.'

'Did they say you'd got over the death of your wife very quickly?' Pablo is sneering.

Freddie looks away from him, his jaw clenched.

'Is there news?' Kidz says, in a soothing tone.

'Maybe something to do with the autopsy?' Freddie looks upset, but also very worried. 'They wouldn't say what.'

I realise behind all his bluster he's nervous. The constant fidgeting hasn't stopped. The whiskey in his glass has vanished. It barely breathed.

'They think I did it. They think I killed Marianne. I know it,' Cara says. 'I was the last person to see her alive.'

'Well, I don't want to let them start until the lawyers are here. They are on their way. There was a hold up their end, but they should be here soon. I don't want to piss the police off.' Freddie rubs at his jaw, distracted.

'And I will tell them about the nuts in my room. That was not an accident,' Pablo says.

I wish Josh was here. I feel like something's going to explode.

'For fuck's sake!' Kidz says. 'What is going on?' She looks round nervously.

'They know.' Cara speaks so quietly, she has to say it again. 'Freddie, they *know*.'

'What?' Freddie goes white. His knuckles are pale in his grip on the whiskey glass. He looks nervously to us, then back to her. '*What?*'

'Someone must have told them,' she says. Although she doesn't say to what she's referring, Freddie seems in no doubt. And I'm sure most of us know. We're all silent, like we're eavesdropping on a private conversation. She doesn't seem to be aware of us anymore. She's been in a daze since she entered the room.

She looks at the floor. 'Everyone will know. Oh my god.'

'But who…' Freddie stares at her, and although they haven't spelled it out, I know what they're talking about, and I can't help it. I look at Pablo.

Freddie catches my look, then his mouth falls open. He stares at Pablo. 'You!' he says, almost to himself. Then he half rises. 'This is all *your* fault? You *told* them? You said you wouldn't!'

Freddie seems to lose all control and hurls himself at Pablo. 'You little shit! You told them about us – as though I would do anything to hurt my wife! As though Cara had it in her to kill Marianne? You fucking piece of shit!'

Pablo is slow to react – still weak, I assume, from the EpiPen. He's pushed off the sofa, and rolls underneath Freddie's fists.

The rest of us don't move. It would be like throwing yourself under a runaway train.

'Pablo!' Kidz screams as Freddie's fist punches hard into his tanned skin and stubbled cheek. The sound of the thwack is loud.

'Me?' Pablo rolls him, wrestling for a second, then overturning him. He finally sits astride Freddie and grabs his hands. Blood drips from a cut on his cheek, falling onto Freddie. 'You really expect me to keep something like that from the police? Did you put those nuts in my room to try to shut me up?'

Trying to get back on top, Freddie kicks and writhes, but Pablo grabs Freddie's throat and holds him down with one hand.

Freddie almost shakes Pablo off. Pablo's face is still bleeding, and I'm surprised at Freddie's strength. Of the two, I would put money on Pablo winning the fight.

I'm not wrong. Pablo's expression goes hard quickly. The same expression I saw in the film. He lifts his right arm high in the air, making a fist, his muscles thick and hard through his shirt, his arm swishing up so quickly I'm sure I can hear it.

Cara screams as his hand comes down, knuckles like stone. The crack into Freddie's cheekbone is sharp. It sounds like it's done some serious damage.

The noise seems to stir the room from shocked silence into action.

'Pablo, *stop*!' I shout, and I run to grab him, but he's intent, and whatever button Freddie has pressed, isn't being released.

'You sleep around on your wife and think I'm to blame for this shitty mess?' Pablo roars, and delivers another hit. He's not reigning blows down. Instead, he's much more focused. He's landed about three now, and Freddie has gone very quiet. I can see his eyes are closed.

'Pablo!' Hanneghan appears from behind me with Josh trailing, and hurls himself at the Venezuelan, wrapping his arms around his chest.

Josh helps and they both try to hold him.

They are no match for his rage, but Lukas joins them by trying to pull Freddie from under Pablo. I help Lukas.

In a few minutes, we're all panting, sweating, and Pablo's eyes are like tiny fires.

Kidz has pulled Freddie up to sit against the base of a sofa. One of his eyes is already swelling, and there is blood coming from his nose.

'He's going to need patching up,' Kidz says, her voice shaking, as she leans in to check his eye. 'What the fuck just happened?'

'I'll tell you what happened. That piece of shit just launched himself at me for telling the police the truth! Who does that if they have nothing to hide?'

Freddie lets out a moan as Kidz touches his cheek.

Pablo turns and spits to the side. 'Don't play the victim. You hit me and think I won't hit you back? You fucking loser!' Anger makes his voice loud and his accent more distinct. 'Your wife is dead – who else wants that, except you? You want the next one, so you kill the first one. And then the nuts!' Pablo struggles against Hanneghan's restraint. Josh holds him back, but I can tell it's pulling at his shoulder. Pablo roars, 'Are you going to bring us down, one by one?'

Cara starts to cry, sobbing loudly, and Lukas looks from one man to the other.

As Josh holds Pablo, Hanneghan holds out his hands. 'Look, if the police are coming tomorrow, we will only make this worse. We need to—'

'You!' Pablo roars, switching his focus to Hanneghan. Whatever control he has maintained over himself this week so far, disappears entirely. He wrenches free from our grasp, and pulls himself up, turning and shouting down into Hanneghan's face. Spit flies from his mouth; it's terrifying, looking at someone so consumed with rage.

'Don't you tell me to calm down, you *cojones*! Don't tell me the police will sort this fucking mess! You're the reason my brother lies dead with his killer unpunished! You employed a psycho and made him legit. Pissed and bleary eyed, stood like some fucking zombie, when Dittus covered up the details of my brother's hit and run for a bribe!'

He's shaking with rage. 'I saw it all from too far away. He was smacked from the road. I only got there to hold him as he died. Dittus arrives at the scene to investigate and takes a backhand from someone and you give him the golden Hollywood seal! Anything he said when he was questioned after my complaint later didn't matter. He seemed untouchable. In his fancy suit and his new connections. Well, I'm *glad* he's dead! I wish it had been me who killed him. I'm only sorry he didn't suffer more. *La concha de tu madre!* I wish you were dead too!'

35

Silence settles in the room. Hanneghan stares at Pablo, as though he'd been slapped.

I watch the two of them, neither speaking. Tension like an elastic band pulled tight vibrates between them.

'Fuck this!' Pablo shouts. Then, hands in fists, he strides from the room and doesn't look back.

Cara lays a hand on Hanneghan's arm. She speaks quietly to him, but firmly. 'Ignore him. You know Dittus wasn't always the best man. You've known that for years. But you're not to blame for his actions. I don't know exactly what he's talking about, but he's clearly upset. I'll talk to him when he's calmed down.'

Surrounded by splashes of blood, spilt coffee and an upended table, Freddie stands and shouts after Pablo, 'Where the fuck do you think you're going? Come back and face me!'

'I'm not sure you want that,' Kidz says quietly, holding a napkin to a cut on Freddie's face, which doesn't seem to want to stop bleeding.

'You all saw that. Assault!' Freddie says.

'Actually,' Hanneghan says, 'it was you who assaulted him. I don't think anyone in their right mind would expect him just to lie down and take it. And if I'm going to do the right thing this time, then you hit him, Freddie. So I'd be careful what you accuse him of.'

Hanneghan stands very still, blanched and dazed.

Cara is by his side quickly. 'You don't believe what he said, do you? You'd never condone lying to the police. Whatever Augusto did to Pablo's brother, it wasn't with your blessing. If you'd known that, you'd never have employed him.'

Hanneghan rubs his brow with his thumb and forefingers, like he's trying to rub something out. 'Cara, you know as well as I do I was as pissed as a fart on that shoot. For the whole year. All the time. I would have had no idea what I was doing. I remember a car crash. We all heard about it. One car was run off the road. Didn't one of our catering staff die?'

'Yes, a woman died in another car, and the original car also hit a younger boy,' I say, remembering the report I'd read the other evening. 'That must have been Pablo's brother.'

Hanneghan stares in disbelief. 'Oh my god! I guess if Augusto was investigating and took a bribe from whoever ran the car off the road, then Pablo would have reason to hate him. And me by extension. Though I took no notice of the details. I wasn't my best-self back then.'

Waiting staff rush in quietly, carrying mops and cloths. I'm sure they've never had guests like this before, but they're swift and efficient.

'Perhaps you would be more comfortable in our other lounge. I've had tea sent there,' says the manager, bowing slightly, as though blood and screaming constituted a perfectly normal afternoon.

'Fuck tea, I need something stronger than that,' Freddie says. 'And get off me.' He pushes Kidz a little, as she's still tending to his cut.

Her face cracks and the drained, tired expression she'd been wearing earlier shifts to one of hurt as she stumbles back. She puts one hand out to the back of a sofa, and another goes to her stomach.

'Leave her alone!' I shout. 'I don't care what else is going on, you don't get to shove Kidz!'

But I soon realise that Kidz can take care of herself.

'Freddie, I'm trying to stop you bleeding everywhere. But I don't need to.' Kidz raises her voice and Freddie looks immediately repentant. Her eyes flash with fire. She's still holding the sofa. I wonder if she's feeling sick.

'God, Kidz, I'm sorry.' Freddie stalls for a second, looking unsure about everything.

'Raising your hand to Kidz?' Hanneghan says, staring at Freddie. 'Doesn't help in your mission to prove you have nothing to do with Marianne's death.'

Josh stares at Freddie, and I wonder if he's about to say something. But Freddie closes his eyes for a second.

'Enough!' Freddie tries to stride out of the room, as Pablo had done, but his face is so swollen now it must be difficult for him to see, and one of his steps catches the edge of the broken coffee table and he flips arse over head, sprawling out on the floor.

'Shit,' he says, almost whimpering as he rights himself, sitting up and touching his leg, gingerly.

No one moves a finger to help him this time. Not even Cara. Instead, Kidz walks past and steps over him.

'Drink?' Lukas says to me and Josh.

I nod, grateful, and turn to Hanneghan to see if he is coming too. Cara has her arms around him, and Hanneghan's shoulders are sagging.

'So many complaints about him, for so many years. He's cleaned up after me for so long, I've felt... powerless. But I should have done something,' I hear him say.

'He had a hold over you,' Cara says, stroking his back. 'But you're sober now. You don't owe anything to anybody.'

'I've got no one else to blame,' Hanneghan says, pulling back. 'No one else. I mean, what if it *is* true? What else was that man capable of?' He shakes his head and leaves, with one last look at Cara.

New York

36

The end of the course is close. In nine days, Phoebe flies off to Abu Dhabi. She was fitted for costumes a month or so ago, before the course started. She wasn't allowed to take a picture, but they had taken polaroids of her, and she managed to take a photo of them when they were stuck up on some board by the AD, who wasn't looking. We stare at them now, sipping iced coffee on a Sunday afternoon.

'I can't believe it,' she says, shaking her head. 'Imagine me, going there, actually filming!'

'It's brilliant,' I say, pulling out two muffins from my bag. I'd been down to get the coffees for us.

'I wish it was both of us,' she says, reaching out and grasping my hand.

'I'm pleased for you, really. One day we'll both have our names up in lights. I know it. Imagine!' I open and close my hands, wiggling my fingers and raising my arms high to indicate flashing lights.

I can't tell her this part is now killing me. There's a lot I want to tell her. But I say nothing. We drink the lattes and admire her costume.

She shakes her head. 'I can't believe it, Ellie.'

I hug her tight. 'This is it! This is the start!'

When Phoebe has gone to bed early with a headache, I clean the flat and wonder if he'll call.

I check on Phoebe at around 10 p.m. but she's out like a light.

I make overnight oats for us to eat before class, and leave them in the fridge, staring at the jam jars and wondering.

How will things turn out?

'God, that headache hasn't gone. I feel so tired.' Phoebe drags herself to the small kitchen and fills a glass of water. 'What's wrong with me?'

'Heat, probably,' I say, handing her breakfast. 'Here, eat this. You'll feel better.'

'You are a queen,' she says, and flops on the sofa, curling her legs up. 'Only a few days of the course left. I hope this damn headache goes.' She touches the side of her head lightly. 'Imagine if I was too ill to go! My agent would kill me. He's the only reason I got the job after he pulled some strings. If I don't turn up, then he'll drop me for sure. You don't get many shots at this.'

'Nah,' I say lightly. 'If it came to it, I'd go in your place. We're twins after all!' I twirl on the spot, holding my oats' spoon and she laughs.

Later that evening, her headache still hasn't gone. She goes to bed early, crying briefly. 'I don't know what's wrong with me! It's so frustrating!'

When she wakes in the morning and finds it hard to get out of bed, she cries again. 'Ellie, what do I do?'

'Go to the doctor,' I say.

'What, and tell him I'm too tired to get out of bed? What can they do?'

'It might be iron or something. Look, I'll pick up some vitamins after class today. Are you coming in later?'

She nods, lying her head back down on the pillow. 'Yes, I'll just have another half an hour in bed.'

Phoebe makes it in around 2 p.m. and she still looks tired.

'OK?' I ask.

'I just can't wake up – I feel like I'm underwater.'

'Hang on, I'll get coffee.'

We sit on the grass after class and she lies flat, with sunglasses covering most of her face.

'What's wrong with the starlet?' Felix says, flopping next to us. He picks up her coffee.

I take it off him. 'No, she needs hers. Drink mine.' I push mine into his hands.

'Sweetheart, you need to pull it together,' he says. 'Stop all this mooching and start packing!'

But that night Phoebe goes to bed early again. 'I just can't stay awake.'

Three days later, Felix donates two tickets to a comedy club to us. 'I'd go but I've got a date, and I think she might need cheering up,' he says to me, nodding at Phoebe. Then he calls out in a louder voice. 'Have fun!'

We sit in the chairs in the comedy club in Chelsea and I watch Phoebe, my stomach twisting in two.

'I just can't shake this tiredness. It's like a weight,' she says.

I hadn't bought any coffee that morning. I hadn't made any oats. I feel so bad for her, but she's been bit brighter this afternoon.

'Come on, just enjoy tonight,' I say.

'You'll have to go for me, if I can't. Say you will. Promise.' She twists her fingers into mine.

'What do you mean?' I'm alive to everything – the heat in the room, the baying group of men at a table nearby, my shoes catching a sticky patch under the table. My voice sounds higher than it should. 'What do you mean, Pheebs?'

'Say you'll go! That you'll be me! I can't do it. I think I'm crumbling under the pressure – it's the only thing it can be. I feel heavy, I'm so tired. Every time I think about my agent dropping me, I start to panic. I can't think straight – my head is like mush.' She runs her fingers through her hair.

It doesn't feel like I thought it would. I thought taking what is mine would be easy – that I was being clever.

'I can't. My passport, your name…' I try to think of reasons.

A woman takes the stage and she begins a routine about being a mother in New York.

'You have to!' Her eyes are wide. 'I'll email my agent. I'll say that Phoebe Thomas is my acting name, but my real name is Ellie Miller.' She grabs my hand, squeezes it hard. 'Please, Ellie,' she says. Her voice cracks a little. 'It the obvious answer. To what we both want.' She pauses. 'Well, what I need. I just can't…'

She doesn't finish. She picks up the drink.

The laughter around us is loud but I zone out. I don't feel elated, I feel empty. It shouldn't be this way. But it's all been so planned. The coffees and oats this week. I've been planning it all since I read that magazine on the Northern Line.

Sleeping pills, a prescription I got from the doctor's months ago. Plus melatonin, and some strong antihistamines. Enough to knock her sideways for a few days. Not enough to do her any harm. Long-term, anyway.

But I couldn't do it today. I saw the way it was going, and I ground to a halt. Today she has the fear. Today she believes what I've been hoping she'd believe.

I've given myself the gift I've always wanted – and I've stolen from her.

I feel sick.

But it's too late.

I can make it up to Phoebe. I *have* to.

I agree to switch.

And here we are.

Abu Dhabi

37

'Hey, how you doing?' Josh finds me at a table where I'd been hiding out. We'd had a drink after the fight and then I'd just needed a bit of space so I'd gone off to read my lines.

'I'm word perfect.' I smile at him and gesture to the script I'm holding.

'I saw you at the pool earlier, after that fight. Did you need to burn off some of the craziness?'

'You must have seen Kidz. She headed past earlier. I thought I better focus on work. It feels like this whole film might collapse, you know what I mean? I wasn't ready for it, so I've been going over my lines. If I believe it will still happen, that will make it so, right?' I grin.

Lukas comes in too. 'Any news?' he asks. 'Do you know if Freddie's apologised?'

Josh heads to the bar where there's a pot of coffee left out for guests. He fills three cups. 'Nothing about that, but I did hear Freddie kicking off about something else. No one can find Hanneghan. Says if he's left the hotel he'll raise the roof. He must have been upset though, after Pablo's accusation. Although I don't really know what he meant by what he said.' He shrugs. 'I can't really believe Freddie would have anything to do with

Marianne's death, right? I mean, Freddie wants to seem as though he can keep his eyes on us all. And he has to stay on the right side of the police. He's kind of mean, but not really a rule breaker.'

I sit upright. The part about Hanneghan sticks in my brain. 'What do you mean, they couldn't find Hanneghan? Where's he supposed to be?'

Josh shakes his head. 'I mean, it took me ages to find you. There are certainly places you could hide away.'

'But why would he want to do that? He's not under suspicion. He tried to save Marianne. You remember, he was with us when we found her.'

Lukas cocks his head a little. 'You think maybe he was involved and lying?'

'Of course not,' I say. I force myself to speak calmly, although my blood is stirring and I can't sit still. 'Look, let's go find out what's going on. I don't know about you two, but I could do with some action instead of sitting round twiddling my thumbs.'

We head to the restaurant. Tea and cake are laid out and Cara is sat on her own looking exhausted.

'Let me speak to Cara. I'll do it on my own,' I say. 'Just hang back for a minute. Maybe go and see if Hanneghan has turned up? The manager of the hotel may know. I'd avoid Freddie right now. If anyone knows where Hanneghan is, I think it's Cara. Let me find out.'

'Remember Cara may be involved too,' Josh says, quietly to me, looking uneasy about leaving me on my own with her. 'Pablo mentioned Freddie and Cara. I can't imagine it really is them, but don't take any chances. I know we're trying to work out what's going on, but it's starting to feel more real now.'

'She looks anything but intimidating. I'll be fine. Meet you in the hotel reception in a bit.'

Cara cuts a fragile figure at a table on her own. She seems oblivious to anything else in the room. Her blonde hair is scraped back into a ponytail, and she drums her fingers on the table, staring out at the desert. I can't believe she has anything to do with this, but I overheard two people on the plane.

The table is laden with tiny pistachio and honey treats, as well as more Western-style cakes. There is coffee and tea. I take a cup of apple tea and pull out a chair at Cara's table. 'Mind if I join you?'

She waves assent. She doesn't look particularly pleased to see me, but I doubt she wants to see anyone. I'd never normally force myself on Cara Strauss, the movie star, but today is different. A victim or an aggressor, but also the person closest to Hanneghan. If anyone might know where he is, it's her.

'How are you feeling?' I ask. She looks paler than before. Her plate has an arrangement of untouched food.

'How would you feel?' She shakes her head, sitting back, leaning against the chair as though the effort of sitting upright is too much.

'I think we all found it hard with the police. I found it awful, retelling it all,' I say, and take a sip of tea. 'I don't think they're designed to put you at ease in this kind of situation. I mean, Marianne probably died from choking and then all this stress is for nothing.' I watch her carefully, seeing if she lets anything slip.

She toys with a piece of cake on her plate, which she's broken up but not really eaten. 'It was awful.' Her voice is quiet and she sounds drained. 'To be honest, I wish I could just leave. I don't even want to do the film anymore. I'd pull out of the whole thing.' She covers her face briefly with her hands. 'But we can't, can we? Not now. We have to wait for Marianne's death to be investigated. Everyone knows I was the last one to see her alive. I can't leave now as it will just make me look even more guilty. I'm trapped.'

I nod. 'Yes, but surely it doesn't make any difference. I mean, we were all out there. Just us. There was no way of saving her. Even if anyone had seen her choking.'

'She didn't choke,' Cara says, very quietly.

'What?' I hold my teacup very still. 'How do you know?'

'One of the officers let it slip. When I was giving a statement, I mentioned her choking, and he said "there is no evidence of choking". I couldn't believe it.' She shakes her head. 'The other officer with him told him to stop, that they weren't interviewing until later. But I think they let it slip on purpose. I think they wanted me to know they knew. I think, because I was the last one with her, they assume I've killed her. But why would I want her to die?'

Still reeling from the news of Marianne, I don't register the last part of her statement straight away. Once it slips in, I can't help it. I look at her as I remember Freddie.

She sees my expression and turns white. 'Just because we had an affair doesn't mean I wanted her dead! Christ, why didn't we just announce it in the press! Why would I go about it this way, here of all places? I will hang for this. They'll convict me, and I'll die here!' She bursts into tears.

I believe her. I don't think it was her on the plane. I put my hand on her arm. 'Do you know where Hanneghan is? I've heard he's missing.'

'Missing? Has something happened to him?' She looks up. 'Not Hanneghan too.'

'The police want to talk to him, but no one's seen him.'

'I don't know...' She breaks off, shakes her head. 'Have they tried his room? I'll go there now.'

'I think they already looked there,' I say. She seems frantic now.

'I'll check again.' She leaves, and I think she partly wants to use Hanneghan as an excuse to get away from me. She doesn't seem like she wants to talk to anyone.

I remember how it felt to pump Marianne's chest: the smell of the night, the scream we'd heard.

If it wasn't choking, it could have been anything. Poison? Strangulation? A blow to the head?

If someone tried to disguise her death then maybe they were panicking. Maybe they were about to be discovered. Maybe Marianne wasn't the intended victim. Maybe whatever happened had been intended for the man I heard being discussed on the plane, and something forced a change of plan.

Whatever happened, a suspected murder changes everything.

38

I find Josh and Lukas waiting for me.

'She doesn't know where he is. I'm going to look for him,' I say. 'You in?'

'You think he might be hurt?' Josh looks at me.

'It's possible. Cara says the police told her Marianne's death wasn't caused by choking,' I say. 'That more or less confirms someone here is a killer. We need to look out for each other from now on.'

Lukas seems unsettled by everything. He looks so young as he says, 'What the fuck?'

'Shit,' Josh says.

We look at each other.

'So, we know where Cara and Freddie are. Where are the others?' I say.

'I haven't seen Pablo. Kidz is in her room,' Josh says.

'So just Hanneghan. We need to find him.' My throat is tight. I can't fail at this. Not after everything.

'Who wants to search where?' I ask, trying to keep calm. 'Did the manager know anything?'

'No,' Josh shakes his head. 'Tell you what. I'll head out to the other rooms, the lodges with pools. Lukas, how about you take the changing rooms at the pool, the garages – any other outside buildings. There's a lot of ground to cover.' Josh looks to Lukas who nods.

'I'll check with Kidz, see if there's an update,' I say.

We split up and I head to Kidz' room. When she opens the door, on the landline, she indicates to a chair, and I just hear the end of the conversation.

'No earlier? Really? You can't get here today?'

She swears as she hangs up. 'Freddie's having a meltdown. The lawyers are saying the earliest they can get here is around lunchtime tomorrow, because they're having some bad weather in the city. But the police are putting a lot of pressure on him. And now Hanneghan has gone missing.' Her eyes close and she takes a long slow breath.

'You OK? I came to ask if you knew where he was. We're going to help find him.'

She nods. 'I'm fine. Almost. Just holding it together. There's no sign of him anywhere. Freddie is with the police now. They really do think it's him and Cara. I don't know what to think. But now Hanneghan's gone missing, they're interested in him too.'

My brain stirs.

Something on the side. A flash of yellow. A scarf. It's lying on the back of a chair near the balcony.

Kidz looks at me, still talking about her workload. 'You don't miss much, I'm sure you understand how all this is panning out.' She sits on the chair at the far side of the room. 'I'm out of my depth here. Freddie was only supposed to be without his army of assistants for twenty-four hours and yet here we are. He assumes everyone else will do everything for him. And the signal is awful. I can only work on landlines. I've been stuck in this room for what feels like days.' She scans the room. 'There are worse places to be, admittedly. But poor Marianne. I knew Freddie was... I can't believe it. Or rather, I *can* believe it, but I don't like it. But there's so much money on the line. I don't want it to all fall apart. I need this paycheque.' She pulls a face. 'I know, I know, I can't believe I'm even saying that after Marianne has died.'

'Or been murdered,' I say. I'm listening, but I can't shake the feeling there's something coming forward in my brain, like a figure coming out of the fog. Where did I see something yellow?

'Don't.' Kidz puts her hands over her face in a gesture similar to Cara's earlier. 'I need some help.' She looks at me hopefully. 'You said you'd find Hanneghan?'

'I'll go look. I'll take Josh and Lukas. Where is Cara?'

'She's gone to lie down. She was just here. She said she didn't find Hanneghan in his room and she needs to sleep. She's a mess. I need to put the crew off for another day or so. There's no point them arriving until this is all sorted. Apparently the wind is getting worse near the city. There's some bad weather coming in – and that means a lot of sand in the air. Sandstorms happen quickly here then there's no driving or flying helicopters. So at least that's one thing that doesn't need sorting.'

She runs her hands through her hair. 'I gave up smoking a few years ago but I could really do with one now.'

'Here, I'll get you a drink.' I pour her a whiskey from the drinks tray and hand it to her. 'It worked for me earlier.'

She thanks me, then puts it down untouched. 'Christ, this will cost a fortune. Do you have any idea how expensive it is to pay a whole crew to sit around and do nothing? The extras were local, at least, so we can get the dates changed…' She looks at me, and grinds to a halt. 'Sorry, I'm doing it again. Marianne's death must come first. And we need to find Hanneghan. I'll sort this, and you look for him? Pablo is licking his wounds somewhere, but he might rally if he knows he's needed. He likes being needed.'

'Of course. Anything else?'

'I don't suppose you know where I might have put a memory card for a camera, do you? Freddie asked to see the shots I took after the camel ride. I think he was hoping there might be something on there that would help us find out what happened to Marianne. Maybe one of the photos caught something that shows what happened. It might help him, he said. I gave him the camera, but he called me, livid, about half an hour later. There was no card in there.'

I frown. 'The camera got damaged, or it fell out?'

'No, I'd been through them the day after. There were some great ones I'd been planning on using for social media, once we were given the OK about posting again. General film promo and also some great layout shots. But it was clean when I got it back. No memory card – I have no idea what happened.'

Staring at her, a thought drifts across my brain.

'You don't think *Freddie* might have wiped them?' I say. 'Maybe he's kicking up a fuss about them being missing to draw attention away from the fact that he's deleted them.'

'Why?' Kidz says, looking confused. Then her expression changes. 'You think some of the photos might have caught him doing something he doesn't want any of us to know?'

The long corridors in the hotel don't feel relaxing anymore. As I take the elevator to the floor with the huge apartments, I jump as the doors slide closed behind me. I catch sight of myself in a mirror. For a second, it's like there are two of me. My brain is melting down.

The thick carpets underfoot muffle the sound of my footsteps, and if someone was following me, I wouldn't hear them.

I check for Freddie. Everything I've learnt suggests that he is the person behind all of this. If I meet him and I'm alone, I'll just run.

The corridors are dark ahead of me, and light up as I walk through them. I feel the walls closing in behind me with each step and I have to force myself not to run.

'Hanneghan?' I bang on his door. 'Hanneghan, are you there? It's Phoebe. Kidz is looking for you.'

Nothing.

I'd seen a trolley further back. Retracing my steps, I see it again. Housekeeping. There's a member of staff coming out of one of the rooms. The crew were supposed to arrive tonight. I guess they're giving everything a final check.

'Hi!' I say as brightly as I can.

The member of staff comes out of the open room. 'I'm so sorry, I left my phone in my friend's room.' I point at Hanneghan's. 'We were rehearsing lines, ready for filming.' I flash a smile. I'm relying on the fact that we're all here to film together, to remind her that I'm no stranger to Hanneghan. She'd never let me in if I was a stranger. 'I don't want to disturb him. He's on an important call with Hollywood right now, downstairs.'

I mentally cross my fingers and pray that if I can really ham up Hollywood and acting, I can dazzle my way in. It seems to be working. She nods slowly.

Once the door is closed behind me, I go through his room. I have no idea what I'm looking for, and as I'm about to give up, I see something on the coffee table.

A note.

'No way! I'm coming.' He heads over to a buggy and grabs a key. 'I'm not staying here!'

'Can we get the keys to a Land Rover?' Josh asks, scanning them. 'I don't much fancy a buggy.'

The door had opened automatically when we'd walked down the ramp. The perimeter gates are locked after dark, and no one can get in or out by the road without coming past the security gate. We'll be OK as we're leaving in the opposite direction, straight across the sand. There's no way customers could steal a buggy and leave the surrounds. You wouldn't make it very far across the desert. There is a row of Land Rovers with the hotel logo on the side, but these are locked, with no keys in sight.

Lukas turns on his dune buggy. 'We're going to have to make do with these.'

'I was on one with Kidz the other night. It seemed easy enough,' I say.

Josh looks at me carefully. 'Remember we don't have to. We can look for Hanneghan. Or we can tell the police about the note. If we tell the police he looks a lot more suspicious, maybe like he's colluding with Cara. But we don't owe him anything.'

'No.' My years of adoration of Hanneghan have given nothing back. Josh is right, I owe him nothing. But everything I've done, I've done to get close to him. 'I can't leave him out there to die.'

Lukas shrugs. 'Maybe we *should* tell the police instead?'

Phoebe – there's a cost to me coming here. To getting close to him. I can't leave him out there, possibly in danger. Not after everything. The police will be here tomorrow. I can't let him become a suspect. Whatever is happening to Hanneghan is happening now. We need to get to him.

'Let's go,' I say, and I pull my cap down tight, pushing on my sunglasses. 'Let's get him. It's almost six. We've got over an hour of good light left. It's enough. If we haven't seen him by then, we call the police.'

I don't look back as we drive out across the sand in the direction of the tents. I don't want to see anyone following us.

Instead, I look forwards, across the sand, where the sun spills the mirage of water into the desert on a fluid horizon, and it burns so hot on my back I'm not sure I can take it. But once the speed picks up, and I'm sure we're far enough from the hotel to have got away unnoticed, I feel a rush. Going faster feels much cooler. The rush of air is like a fan. The scent of the desert is intoxicating.

For a second, I let myself just rest in the moment. I don't think of Phoebe, New York, of Hanneghan, of Marianne or Augusto. Of any of it. I enjoy riding up over the curves of the sand, leaning forward, speeding faster. We power up to ride up the peaks and then we slow on the other side. Sand kicks up from the buggy in front of me, and the taste of it reminds me of my journey to the hotel, rolling upside down in the car. Today needs a better result.

The journey is no more than fifteen minutes, now we know the way. I see the tents loom closer. Hanneghan. Is he out here?

We pull to a stop by the tents, and I swing my leg over the buggy, flexing my fingers from all the gripping.

Once the air has stopped rushing at us, it's hot again. I'm pleased I put so much sun cream on this morning, but I wish I'd worn long sleeves. I don't want to stay out here longer than I have to.

'Let's start with the tents,' I say, and we make our way over, the heat from the sand rising as the sun beats down.

The huge tents are rectangular with one side completely open. Around the inside runs the low-level seating we'd sat on the other day, and a huge rug covers the ground. The low tables that held food and water are now bare. The cover of the tent offers a welcome relief from the burn of the sun.

'Hanneghan?' I shout, looking round. Nothing.

'Maybe he's outside,' Josh says, and disappears through the open side of the tent.

Lukas walks the perimeter of the interior, looking closely.

'What's this?' He picks up a cap from the floor.

I recognise it, but I'm not sure from where.

'Is that Pablo's?'

Lukas looks closely, then shrugs. 'I mean, it could be?' He holds it out. 'Do you think so?'

I can't be sure. I remember him wearing a beanie or cap on the plane; he had a cap like this one on the other day.

Josh enters. 'Nothing outside.'

I think. 'It might not be Pablo who left the note. Maybe it was Freddie or Cara, signing as Pablo to throw everyone off the track?' I look at Josh, aware that Lukas doesn't know what I heard on the plane, but there's no time to go into all that.

Heading round the tent from the opposite direction, I pull all the seating forward, checking behind it. I look under the table; I lift the rug at the edges, not really sure what I'm looking for. I start to think that maybe we're chasing a false lead, and Hanneghan never came here at all. Then I find it.

Hanneghan's phone. I know it's his. It's the same one he dropped the other night on the camel ride. I watched him use it in the car on the way back from sand boarding. It has a bronze cover, with a kind of zigzag design on the back.

'Look.' I hold it aloft.

Lukas stops what he's doing and whistles softly. 'You sure it's his?'

I nod.

'Well, if his phone is here,' Josh looks around, 'where's *he* gone?'

40

'No reception. We know he's been here. What do we do now? Do we tell the police? The hotel?' Lukas says.

'Why don't we scan the area?' I say. Thinking about Hanneghan in some kind of danger makes me feel sick. 'The reasons for not telling the police or the hotel in the first place still stand. Let's do a quick recce, and if we can't find him, then we'll head back and tell them immediately. But let's give him the chance to give the note to the police himself.' Adrenaline courses its way through my veins. I'm not sure if it's at the thought of heading further into the desert again, or the idea Hanneghan is in danger.

'Right.' I pull my phone out and look at the compass. I point as I talk. 'I'll go north, you go south, and Lukas goes west. East leads us back to the hotel, so we'd have seen him already.' I look at them. 'You don't have to. If you want to wait here or even head straight back to the hotel, it's OK.'

Josh shakes his head. 'We're here. We'll do it.'

Lukas nods.

'OK, thank you.' I pause for a moment, realising again how Josh has been beside me since we got on the plane. Even when he found out I was lying. Lukas, too, has come along today not questioning my decisions. I smile at them both, grateful.

I say, 'We need to be careful. Look, none of us have got any signal. We can't be stupid and go too far. If we get lost, then it's just someone else to hunt down. And we don't know how long the charge in these machines will last us.' I glance at the buggies. 'We still need to get back to the hotel to call for help.'

'Agreed, let's not make things even crazier,' Josh says. 'We meet here then we head back to the hotel. If one of us doesn't turn up, then the other two go back to the hotel and raise hell, yes?'

'Agreed,' Lukas says.

I feel a swift and profound sense of gratitude to Josh again as he speaks. He's made the whole of this trip easier. If I ever needed to know whether someone would stand by me, then Josh is the living, breathing proof.

As was Phoebe.

But we are where we are.

41

A trail of sand churns behind the buggies of the other two as they disappear almost out of view in their separate directions. I squint a little, watching them, then give up. It's not long until sunset; time has vanished today. I turn on the buggy, and the engine makes almost no sound, but it shoots forward as I turn the handle. I twist my hand a little to reduce the speed. I haven't had the largest amount of water this afternoon. I need to go carefully. Dehydration out here is a killer.

I need to stay focused on where I'm going, so I can remember how to come back.

My heart is racing and my stomach is in knots. I have a bad feeling about what might have happened to Hanneghan.

I see the hill we climbed the other day. It's high. I turn the buggy handles and I pick up pace. I lean into the hill as the buggy climbs, and I increase the speed more as I near the top. It's high up here. I can see quite far. I head down and up over two more peaks. The sun lowers further.

My eyes are dry and my throat burns. I search left and right. Nothing.

I've been gone for what feels like far longer than is sensible. But I can't give up.

I head over a flatter part of the desert, and this is much easier. I cover ground quickly.

As the sun lowers further, another huge peak rises up before me. It's the last one. I don't have much light left.

Leaning into it, I turn the handles, raising the speed, and although the buggy stutters, it makes it all the way to the top. I scan in the remaining light.

Is that...? There's definitely something. I hold my breath, my pulse quickening.

Sailing down the other side is hard. The buggy holds its position, but towards the bottom, where it's quite steep, the wheels seem to dig into the sand and the buggy kicks up and over.

I fly forward, landing in the hot sand.

I sit up gingerly. I touch my arms and legs – nothing seems broken. I've wrenched the muscles in my back and neck, but I can stand. I take a few steps, testing out walking. All good.

But the buggy is upended, wheels still spinning.

Shit. I don't have much experience of dune buggies, or of driving in sand.

I touch it carefully – it's hot, but the engine is off. I pull at the top, and it rolls to the side a bit, then falls back again. I'm going to need to pull much harder. I wish I'd brought more water. My mouth is dry and my throat is burning.

I pull and pull. One last effort. I pull as hard as I can, and the buggy falls over on its side. It catches my arm on its way down. *Fuck* it hurts. There's no one to hear me cry out except the sand and the sky. Now I just need to pull it up to fully right it. This is much easier, as it's no longer part-buried in sand.

I check my watch. It's almost seven. Getting here and getting the buggy back in position has taken a good chunk of the remaining daylight hours. I need to get on with it.

My hands are shaking a little when I climb back on. The shock of falling and the effort of sorting myself out has been exhausting. I need to go and investigate what I saw. If it's Hanneghan, I can't leave him out here.

I climb more carefully this time. So much so I'm in danger of not giving it enough power, but I give myself a talking to. I didn't come this far to stop now.

Leaning forward, I power up the last of the hill. The sun is much lower in the sky and I scan the sand below me.

There. Something. I navigate carefully down the slope, and I make sure I slow gently as I get to the dip.

I just hope I'm not too late.

42

I slow the buggy to a still, then jump off. It looks like a man. *Fuck.*
It must be him. My heart is racing at super speed. I struggle to
breathe normally. *Please, don't let him be dead.* He cannot be
dead. I can't look at another dead body.

'Hanneghan?' I shout as I reach the mound. Whoever it is,
they're unconscious. He lies in a foetal position, with his head
tilted down and one arm slung over his face. His legs curl up
in the hot sand. He looks like he's been here a few hours. For a
second, I can't move.

I force myself to act. My hands shake as I peel back the arm.
Hanneghan.

'Can you hear me? Hello!' I start talking nonsense like they
teach you on a first aid course. Talk to the injured party. I try
to quash a rising terror. I came so far and did so much, lost so
much, to have it come to nothing.

'Can you hear me? Can you tell me what day it is? Hello?'
I check his airways, I tap his cheeks to wake him. He's still
breathing, but there's no sign of life and his pulse feels slow.

'Hanneghan, can you hear me?'

His lips are sunburnt and swollen. His face is burnt too –
blisters are starting to form. He's wearing long trousers and

a t-shirt, and at least his legs are protected, but his arms look painful. He could have been out here for hours.

'Come on, wake up! Help me get you back to the hotel!' I plead with him as I check him over. Tears have started. He's so heavy – how do I lift him? And if I can get him on the buggy, how do I hold him?

I know it's dangerous to move him, and, ideally, I'd wait for the ambulance. But I'm going to have to trust that the reason he's unconscious is nothing to do with a spinal injury, and everything to do with the sun. It will kill him if he stays out here for much longer.

I hook his arm around my shoulder and pull. My arms, already exhausted from righting the buggy, scream at me to stop. I pull harder.

I manage to get him up on his knees, and as I do so, he falls forward. I see a stain on his back, around his kidney area.

Blood.

Looking down at the sand, underneath the body, there's blood too, already drying. The sand's beginning to swallow it up and conceal the evidence. It's not flowing freely. I don't think he'll bleed out, but I have no idea what kind of internal injuries he's sustained – or how he's sustained them.

I need to get him back. I have to.

'Come on!' I shout, throwing everything I have into lifting him, and finally I get him off his knees. We make it almost to the buggy. I have to drag him an inch, then pause and catch my breath. Then I muster the strength for another inch. After what feels like an age, I lie his body over the seat.

This is impossible.

I cry, wiping my face with the back of my hand. I realise I lost my cap somewhere on the way. Probably when I fell. My skin is raw. As I wipe the tears from my cheeks with hands covered in sand, I realise the sun is losing its heat. All this has taken so long, the sun is dipping quickly.

What will I do if I'm out here in the dark? Josh and Lukas will alert everyone at the hotel. Someone will come looking for me – we agreed. But I can't wait for them. I've seen the sunset fall like a curtain here. You're in the light, then the dark. And there are no streetlights in the desert. I have to get us back.

'Oh, come the fuck on!' I scream as I haul him up and across my knee, with his arms straddling my neck. He's a dead weight and frustration builds, giving me the strength I didn't think I had.

I'm leaning too far back on the buggy, holding Hanneghan with one hand, and I struggle to reach the handles, but I have no choice. I have to do this. The right handle is the one that controls the speed, so I hang onto Hanneghan's body with my left arm, my hand grabbing the waistband of his trousers and his arms leaning across my shoulder.

Through sheer will and contortion, I turn the buggy on, and we travel at almost a snail's pace towards the first steep rise of sand.

I scream as we start climbing, like you'd scream on a rollercoaster. I try to will it up. I can't power the buggy too much, and the wheels dig and spin as we get higher, I feel the buggy slowing.

Please don't slide backwards.

If we tip, I can't start us again. We'll be out here all night.

I turn the handles as much as I dare, speeding the buggy up, and we might make it. We're almost at the crest of the peak.

'Come on!' I shout out into the lowering dark. The sky above is velvet royal blue and I stare upwards, we're almost at the top.

'Fucking come on.' This time I can barely speak, but I know if I don't keep myself psyched I will just stop. I don't have much left. My arms are spent, my hands are shaking. I've got nothing. And this is only the first hill.

I close my eyes as we're almost at the peak and the buggy stutters. *Please, please, please.*

Feeling the buggy level out, I open my eyes. We made it. The dip down the other side is impossible to make out clearly. The dark shadows on the sand paint the surface in varying degrees of clarity, and as the buggy begins to tip forward, I go wrong almost immediately.

The buggy's fast. I grab the handle and pull the brake, but a sand mound catches the wheels and the back load of the buggy is too heavy. We fall forward, sliding towards the handlebars first. I try and fail to shift my weight further back.

I beg the desert to help me out. But it's not listening. I feel the front of the buggy stall and catch in the sand; and the back flies up. I'm thrown and I whack my head on something as I arc and spin. The world falls away beneath me, and I lose my grip on Hanneghan.

I lose.

We are upended.

I hit the sand and lie still, staring up at the sky. Sand is starting to lift and rise around me. The storm is beginning.

Everything is falling apart. I have to rely on Josh and Lukas to raise the alarm and bring help.

Who is doing all of this? Why was Hanneghan lured out here? It makes sense for it to be Freddie. Maybe Pablo?

And now Hanneghan – the reason I'm here – lies dying. Blackness drifts around me.

It wasn't supposed to be him, I think, as the night crashes in and my nightmares tug at my senses.

I dream of New York. Where it all began. With Lukas.

EARLIER THAT SUMMER

New York

43

We walk to the meatpacking district. The night is predictably hot, and I carry my heels in my bag. We'd left Phoebe's brother's studio smeared in lipstick and nail varnish, but I'd promised to tidy it up in the morning. I'm doing all the cleaning right now – I need to make sure there's no trace of anything.

We meet Felix near the Flatiron building. He spins as we approach, and we offer up a return pirouette.

He'd been more excited than any of us this afternoon when I'd got the message we had our names on the guestlist.

'We're going to Soho House!' I'd yelped as the message had come through and Felix had squealed. Phoebe had opened one eye, lying prostrate on the grass at Madison Square Park. 'We're what now?' she'd said.

'Soho House? The one with the rooftop pool?' Felix had paused to check he'd got it right then collapsed next to me and grabbed my iced coffee.

'I talked someone at the course into getting us on the guestlist. I'm writing their essay for them in exchange, so you *really* owe me. Lukas O'Connor is going, apparently, but no one knows. I put two and two together on Instagram.'

We'd spent hours getting ready.

'Fabulous!' he says.

'Stunning!' I say.

Phoebe links both our arms. 'Come on. The place is hard to spot – there's barely a sign. But I know where it is.'

Some moments, particularly ones when the sun is beginning to lower, on a hot summer's eve with friends, burn themselves into the back of your retina and remain, to be looked at again in sepia, months later, years later.

This was one of those.

It almost made me come to a full stop. To tell the whole truth. To fall on them, part drunk, arm in arm, skin on skin, and to bring them on the inside. To make them part of me, like they felt they were, right then. Like the air we all shared was blood; fragments of this time knitting us together.

A weightless moment. I wish I'd stayed in it. I wish I'd hung on.

'Here!' Phoebe announces, and we all grin.

'Soho fucking House, baby!' Felix says, and winks. 'Let's go!'

There are fairy lights and cocktails everywhere. People lounge in the pool and others drape themselves over the striped sun loungers like it's ten in the morning and not in the evening, and the bar and restaurant area throng with bodies, positioned like a moving installation – angles and gestures held consciously unselfconsciously, displaying their best side, the most attractive, the most engaging.

Music is loud, and the beats rise through my feet. The dark of the night is more intense when looking up from the lit rooftop, and I feel like I'm in the only place on earth that matters.

'Hustle!' Felix says, approaching with three cocktails. He hands them to us. 'Right, I'm thinking we might all end up heading off separately tonight. If so, then code procedure applies, message the group, give out addresses and then we meet for brunch tomorrow, usual place.'

We clink glasses, and Phoebe and I share a smile. Felix lived a life of hook-ups in a way I didn't even understand. This was par for the course on a night out with him.

I dance as the music picks up pace, and I look around. I'm here for one reason only. The reason I'd offered to write three essays for the girl who knows Lukas's manager and had some English Lit module to finish. The tip-off I had that he'd be turning up.

I've heard he's on the film Phoebe has a part in. The part I'm planning to steal. It's just a rumour, but if he's going, then I've got another in. If there's someone on the film who knows me as Phoebe already, then that makes convincing others much easier. Particularly if the someone is Lukas O'Connor.

I just need five minutes to make an impression.

I'm mid-sentence with someone about the course I'm doing like it's in the past tense, like I've already moved on to bigger and brighter things, when I see him.

Lukas O'Connor is heading away from the pool, towards the lifts. I notice him not because of his features, but more because the crowd parts a little for him, like royalty is passing, and he wears a baggy t-shirt and leather headband I'd seen him snapped in on some social media post earlier that morning. I've been following him closely since I heard the rumours.

For a second, I dry up, and it's lucky the woman I'm talking to is more than happy to fill the gaps in my conversation with her success stories. I wait a second for a lull, then I excuse myself to head to the bathroom. I pass Phoebe who is talking to a very attractive man and likely to be entertained for the next few hours.

Except I don't go to the bathroom. I make for the lift, and luckily Lukas has been pulled into a casual goodbye embrace with someone he may or may not know, and I manage to get to the elevator seconds before him, seemingly leaving at the same time.

I press the button, as I sense him stand behind me, and I don't turn around. I wait until the lift doors part, then I enter, offering up a nod as he walks in.

He nods back, and we stand in silence as the lift begins its glide downwards.

I've no idea how to pull this off. I don't even know what I want from this. I need to seize it, make it work.

I drop my bag. I can't think of anything else. It falls to the floor with a bang, and my phone slides out. I pray I haven't damaged it, but I wait a beat.

Lukas bends down and picks it up, then hands it to me, half turning. 'Is it OK?' He gestures to the phone.

I make a point of staring at the phone and not Lukas, and make as if to tap it and light it up, but I don't quite make contact, and it remains dark.

'Fuck,' I say. 'Looks like I've really whacked it.' I slip into my American accent and sigh, rolling my eyes, then offer a half laugh. 'Klutz!'

He smiles. 'Well, hope it's OK.'

He's turned away and I need something else. 'Oh shit, I can't get an Uber now. I'll have to walk home. And in these heels, too.'

He turns again, glancing down at my shoes. I can see it's an effort for him. He really doesn't want anything to do with me beyond the elevator, but after a second, he offers. 'Look, my car is waiting downstairs. I can drop you, if it's not far?'

'Oh really? Are you sure?'

'Yeah, sure,' he says.

With the brightest smile I can manage, I say, 'Phoebe.'

'Lukas,' he replies, and the lift stops and the door slides open.

There's very little time now, so I launch in with a huge twist to the truth. 'Hey, I thought I recognised you. Is it true you're going to be in Freddie and Marianne's shoot? I'm in it, too. Flying out to Abu Dhabi at the end of month. It's so exciting you're on board now.'

He offers me the first real smile and I realise I've got him. 'No way! Yes – top secret. It's not officially announced yet, but I signed a few weeks ago. You can't keep anything secret. How crazy we'll be working together. I'm only in the Abu Dhabi scenes, though. They're short, yeah?'

I nod, careful with my accent. 'Me too. But oh my god, the hotel!'

At this he shrugs, and I guess fancy hotels are where he spends most of his time when on tour. But he looks unsure for a second. 'I'm a bit nervous – I mean, I'm sure you're a pro so you know what you're doing, but I've never acted. Crazy right?'

'You'll be brilliant. You're a natural on camera. You've been on screen in so many interviews, music videos.' It's not the same thing, but I can see he's listening.

A car waits nearby when we get outside, and someone climbs out and opens the back door. Lukas gets in with a nod, and I follow.

The air is cold in the car after the heat of the street, and Lukas asks for my address, then carries on chatting. 'I think it's the calibre of actors I'm up against, you know? Like Cara Strauss. I've seen her in films for years – what if I can't do it and it's...' He trails off, and I assume he's remembered he has no idea who he's talking to.

'I'll have your back,' I say, making it up as I go along. 'If you want to run your scenes with me, I'll happily do it. As often as you like.'

'You would?' he says, and looks so pleased I feel bad.

'Of course! You got your script yet?'

He shakes his head.

'If it makes you feel any better, I'm exactly the same – I've seen all of Elijah Hanneghan's films,' I say, managing to squeeze his name into the conversation. 'I've heard he might be signing too. But I suppose you know.'

Something darker crosses Lukas's face. The briefest of shadows. 'I've heard the rumours.'

He shuts down. The chattiness of a moment ago grinds to a halt.

As casually as I can, I say, 'Look, you want to grab a quick drink? It seems mad we'll be working together.'

He hesitates, then glances to the driver. 'Yeah, sure. Quick one.' He says the name of some bar to his driver, and we're driven to the back door of a bar from where we're ushered to a booth. Drinks arrive, and the beat of the music is persistent: loud, but not so loud I can't hear what Lukas says next. People looked at us when we came in. The bar staff are very attentive. But this place feels discreet – no one has come over for a selfie.

'You don't seem too pleased Hanneghan's involved?'

'I knew Hanneghan was on board. It's just a sticking point.'

I wonder where this is going.

I lift my glass and take a swallow. I'd gestured at some green cocktail on the list, and it's a little bitter, but I drink half. 'You don't get on with Hanneghan?' I say, pushing a little.

'Not Hanneghan. His driver,' he says, his brown eyes holding my gaze for a second. No smiling. I feel like if I reached out between us, I could touch whatever it is that hangs in the air.

I don't move. The driver.

It floods back, like it always does: the smell of him; his rough hands. Me stood on a street near Leicester Square, sobbing.

The pressure on my skin where his fingers rested, the taste

of him. I say nothing, swallowing hard. What else has Augusto Dittus done?

Luckily, Lukas fills in the gap. 'Forget I said anything.'

But, of course, I don't. I need to know what's behind Lukas's reaction. Tequila shots later, we stagger into the apartment he tells me his label have rented for him.

'So, what's the story,' I say. I have a hard time staying on track. The tequila is hot in my veins. 'With the driver?'

'Oh. That fucker.' He slumps on a bar stool in the biggest kitchen I've ever been in. The lights of Manhattan spread out beneath us. 'The bodyguard. You know he's always there, with Hanneghan. At every fucking premiere. Always.'

I listen to the fridge hum, the car horns outside. I feel as though someone has ripped away a layer of skin. I had not expected the evening to go this way but now we're here.

'I don't know why I'm telling you. Probably because I'm drunk. And this guy... I should warn you about him if you're going to be near him.' He waves his beer bottle around the kitchen, his face set. 'All this. It's all new. I was cutting tracks in my bedroom three years ago. Playing in a band with some dudes from school. Nothing like this. I worked in a kitchen – training to be a chef.' He looks down again. 'My mom was a chef.'

We sit in silence for a moment.

He stares down at his bottle, pushing the label up with his thumb. 'When I hit it big, people changed around me.' He looks up, bites his lip. 'I don't have many people I can trust. And I'm taking a chance telling you. But I'll need a friend over there, and you need to know to stay away from this guy. I don't know how I'll do it – seeing him, hanging around the set.'

I nod again, trying to offer some encouragement. He's almost there.

'He was there when my mom was killed. I was eleven years old.'

'Lukas, I'm so sorry!'

He stands and gets two more beers out of the huge fridge, flicking the tops off and slamming them down.

'Mom was cooking for the crew on a filmset. She did that sometimes – her friend ran a catering company and she liked travel. She worked there for a few weeks then Dad and I visited. I'd never been to Venezuela.' He stops, takes a swallow of beer, then starts again. 'We were in a car late at night. It was blindsided. Mom swerved to avoid it as it crossed into the road ahead of us. We spun off the road. We survived, but her side… It was hopeless. She died on impact. I sat with her, waiting for the ambulance. A young boy, a bystander, was also killed when the other car swerved. The other driver didn't even stop. The police chased him down later.'

He looks out of the window at the outline of the city. The room is silent. I hear a car alarm from somewhere, a horn. I guess what's coming next.

'Augusto Dittus was the officer. He was the one who looked into the other car. The rumour was it was some big shot and Augusto took a backhander to let it slide. Augusto left his job soon after, and became Hanneghan's driver and bodyguard. He stopped Hanneghan getting mugged outside of the film set – his involvement with the crash meant he met all of the right people. It was the fucking loser's route to fortune, and he grabbed at it with both hands. I wouldn't be surprised if he staged the mugging.'

He stops.

'Did he find the other driver?'

'He said he found the car. Ditched by the side of the road and burnt out. It was stolen from the movie set. No names. Well –' his hands close in fists '– if there had been any trace of who took it, it went *missing*.'

'Oh, Lukas,' I say, as softly as I can. 'I'm so sorry.'

'I watched the inquest. All lies. So many lies. Nothing could be proved and there was no evidence. Dittus has a lot to answer for. Anyway, I've decided I can't turn down this opportunity. But I hate him. I hate him so much.'

The silence sits gently. I look back out of the windows, over New York. It's time for me to tell. Not all the truth – but some of it.

'He attacked me when I was fourteen,' I say, quietly.

'What?' Lukas looks up. The misery on his face drops away and he looks shocked. 'Like what, hit you or something?'

'I went to get Hanneghan's autograph when I was fourteen. He was at a premiere in London. I dressed to look much older to try and get near him, and when they were all in the theatre watching the film, I saw Dittus. I tried to get his attention – I was easy pickings. I hate myself now. I couldn't have been more eager. I made doe-eyes at him and tried flirting. It felt so strange but… I've been a fan of Hanneghan's for so long. I thought it was a good idea. I asked if he might be able to get Hanneghan to come over and meet me after the film.' I take a breath. 'He took me round the back. Asked me to get in his car. All of these things I did. Even when he started kissing me, I thought I was still in control. I thought I could say stop. It was when his hands went places I started getting scared. Then when I did say stop, he said the least he deserved was a blow job. He tried… I fought him off, ran away.' I shudder. The taste of him. 'It was before all the Me Too stuff. I just felt stupid – I still feel stupid. It was less than half an hour. But it's stayed with me.'

I don't say it's defined me, but I know it has. Some part of me is twisted up forever.

I'm shaking. I never talk about it. Ever. Who would have thought this is where this night would end?

'You should say something!' Lukas's hand slams down hard on the granite breakfast bar. 'You should get him prosecuted!'

'For what? There's no evidence. Nothing. It was years ago. And I can't piss off Hanneghan.' The last part is something I've thought about since I heard about the film. What would I do if Augusto recognised me on set? He has no reason to. I would be shocked if he's thought about me at all in the last twelve years. But I can't be thrown off course.

Lukas sounds angry. 'Bastard! He deserves to face up to what he's done.'

'But all those eyes in a court, staring at me. And I'm sure he'd be let off. There just isn't enough proof for anything else. We all know how "he said she said" ends.'

Lukas gets more beer, and this time also brings over a bottle. 'Tequila.' Lukas pours two large shots. 'Here.'

I take the glass he holds out, and knock it back. It burns its way down, and I feel the start of a tiny fire deep inside.

'I wish we could…' I say.

'What?'

'Get him out the way…'

I can still feel his hands on me. I wonder how many other young girls he's coerced. 'I wish we could hurt him the way he's hurt us. It's what he deserves.'

Lukas stares down. 'You want to try?'

'Actually, doing that, I mean physically attacking him…' I take another shot, as Lukas pours us both one. Am I just drunk? Could I do this? 'I could never kill someone in cold blood,

I don't think. But Karma might come for him. We could arrange an accident? Like fate?'

'Tell me more,' Lukas says.

My head is dizzy with crazy late-night plans that will seem ridiculous come the morning. Seeing him again, around on the film set, will be difficult. Awful. Will Augusto recognise me? What would he do – put out rumours about me so if I said anything about him it would backfire? Would he have a word with Hanneghan, and get me kicked off the set?

I feel sick at the thought.

Lukas fills the glasses again.

The gleam of possibility feels like the beginning of dawn. It's amazing what you can imagine in the night, with alcohol in your blood. I look out at the skyline. A faint light blue is hovering in the sky. Maybe the heavens are on our side.

'I mean. We could arrange an accident. Let fate decide. If he's supposed to live, he lives. If it ends badly, then Karma has spoken. No one's really to blame.'

'Any opportunity that presents itself,' he says. 'That could work. That way we shouldn't be at risk of prison. I'm not going to prison for that man. It's not murder – it's Karma.' He lifts his glass.

We clink glasses, which feels like we've signed a contract, and I feel like throwing up, but the weight that has rested on my shoulders since I was fourteen, lightens.

Abu Dhabi

44

L ying in the desert, dreams spinning in my head, I go over the accident in the car like I'd gone over and over it since we arrived.

Augusto, through complete chance, had been the driver of my car when we'd arrived. That had felt like Karma giving me the first heads-up.

He'd stared hard at me before we'd got in. He'd said *going to cause any trouble*, and I let Josh think it was because I stank of sick. He'd challenged him, telling him he didn't think he should talk to us like that.

But I knew. He'd already recognised me. Time was pressing.

Driving there, only fifteen minutes away from the hotel, Josh had been saying, 'Hey, you think—'

But I drowned him out with my scream, as I leant forward and grabbed Augusto's shoulder. I also managed to wrap my hand around his head for a second, blotting out his view.

'Oh my god a gazelle, coming straight for us!'

I grasped his seat belt clasp, to hang on, and I released it, as I pointed to nothing at all I screamed again, loudly. 'Oh my god!'

He swerved quickly, throwing us all to one side. Josh yelled,

'Shit!' as I'd closed my eyes and hung on as hard as I could. I felt his body lift, as my seatbelt pulled me tight.

The car ended up on two wheels, and swung off the road into the desert.

Augusto died.

Karma had spoken.

Part of me hates myself, and part of me feels a relief like I've never known.

It's over. That part of my life is finally over.

The black night of the desert lies like a blanket as the sand flies up and over my face.

The wind is picking up. Bad weather on its way.

I close my eyes. I've got nothing left.

45

I come to with a head fog. I have no idea what time it is. It's dark. 1 a.m., 3 a.m.? My watch is completely out of battery and my phone is dead. The wind is up, and I wake coughing. It's hard to breathe. I wipe at my face but there is sand in my eyes, my mouth. I take a deep breath but start to choke and cough.

We're out alone in a sandstorm.

I have to do something.

The buggy is on its side, and I can see Hanneghan lying spread out on the slope of the dune. There's a covering of sand over him. It's not bad yet – the sand is quite light. In the dark it is difficult to make out too much, but I remember films I've seen where the sand is so thick you can't see your hand in front of you. If I just leave him lying there, he'll choke to death. I'll choke.

What should I do?

Looking round, there's not much to work with. I push the buggy, already on its side, as much as I can against the direction of the wind. It will provide a barrier of sorts.

Then I lift Hanneghan's arm.

Slowly, pulling inch by inch, I drag him up and under the protection of the buggy as much as I can. The sand is still getting everywhere, and the wind is stronger with each minute.

There's a container on the back of the buggy. I remember Kidz had stored some camera stuff in hers. I pray for anything of use. I fumble with the catch – it's almost impossible to see.

I find a thick blanket. I can feel the stitching on it – one of the embroidered ones used up near the tents. It's a lifeline.

Throwing it up to spread it out, it flies back in my face, whipping against my cheek. Instead, I have to turn with my back to the wind. This time when I flick it open, the rush of air lifts it up and open, and I pull it hard backwards, covering Hanneghan and the buggy, and then I tuck the back end as much under the buggy as I can. I can only hope it doesn't fly away. It's all we've got.

Then I lift the front end of the blanket, which flaps open, looking out over the empty sand, and I tuck it under my feet.

Instantly, the noise of the wind softens a little. It's not a perfect solution, but when I wipe away the sand from my eyes and mouth, they're not immediately covered again.

I shiver. I've done all I can do.

Josh and Lukas know I'm out here. So I just have to wait. There's nothing else for it.

The niggling feeling at the back of my head asks why they haven't found me yet. Had they headed back to the hotel without me? I have to hope so. If Pablo lured Hanneghan here, and has done this to him, has he got to them too?

I feel so alone. I wish I'd never come.

We can't be out here just to die. Would the universe let that happen?

I close my eyes. My body aches and despite the terror I feel at the sound of the wind, unconsciousness races at me like a train. I'm spent. There's also a kind of peace. If I have to lie here with anyone, I'm glad it's Hanneghan.

★

I must have fallen asleep, as I wake at some point, and everything is black.

Desperate, I check my phone – still dead.

I glance behind me at Hanneghan, curled up against the buggy. There's no sound. I don't think he's moved. I should check him, but I can't...

He's dead. He must be dead.

I need to do something. Banging the horn on the buggy, I scream, 'Help! We're still here!'

They left hours ago.

The wind howls like an animal. We'll die of thirst when the sun comes back out. But that only matters if the storm slows, and it doesn't sound like it's going to any time soon. Buried alive in sand. Is that how it all stops?

All those dreams – big screens, movie premieres, big-dollar roles.

Does it all end in the desert, miles from anyone?

It's only been three days since I got on the plane.

Four since I agreed to come.

So much has happened. There's a reason I've done all of this. Why I've been so fixated on Hanneghan. A reason I would burn everything down to get close to him. He's been the missing chunk of my life since I was eight years old. I've planned all of this to finally meet him. If this is all I get, then I'll take it. I stood in line for so many autographs to try to get close to him. I was in Augusto Dittus's line of fire, while waiting for Hanneghan. I've pivoted around him.

I'm finally with him. My father.

FRIDAY

DAY SIX

46

When I wake, there's a hint of light. It must be dawn. I'm cramped and my throat is so dry; my mouth is cracked and bleeding.

I flex my fingers slowly, waking up my body. I lift the corner of the blanket, but sand still rushes everywhere. It's a living nightmare.

Dropping the blanket, even in here, it's like everything has been coated with orange paint. It's in my mouth, in my eyes. I force myself to concentrate on breathing. If I lose it then huge gulps of air will only make it harder to breathe. The air tastes coarse and rough.

It's cold now, or I'm cold. I can't tell which. All the heat has been sucked up. I'm sweating, but I shiver.

I can't give up. But I'm out of options. All the planning, all the hope.

'Help!' I hit the horn again. I don't turn around to look at him. I can't.

Three days trying to save him. All in vain.

'Help!'

Since he left, it's mostly been a blank. All of it. Mum told me Dad had left. He'd wanted to chase his career. In America. He didn't want us anymore, but we'd be fine, she said. She was here. She'd look after us.

I'd cried, and she'd hugged me. For a long time I was scared she'd leave too. I'd wake in the night and creep into her room to check she was still there.

In the dark, my feet padding across the carpet. Not wanting to wake her, worrying I might be the only one in the house.

Night after night.

And it wasn't as though Dad had ever lived with us. Mum had a holiday romance in New York when she'd been young. I'd been the surprise she didn't know she'd wanted.

I barely remember him. The odd visit. Maybe three or four times? Balloons, the zoo. Memories I worry I'd stolen from a Hallmark holiday film. Who knows what's real when you pin your dreams onto a memory.

Then one day Mum sat me down when I'd been asking to see him and said he wouldn't come again. He'd gone to focus on his career. He'd sent a large chunk of money so I could go to the best school, and that she loved me more than enough for the two of them.

Within a year, Hanneghan was everywhere. Every time I turned on the TV. Posters in town outside cinemas.

I knew I would never get close to him, unless I followed in his footsteps. I decided to become an actor. I'd work my way close to him, then imagine how *proud* he'd be of me one day, when I met him on a film set. Imagine…

I didn't want to rub Mum's face in it, so I never told her why I picked the profession I did. I didn't want her to feel she hadn't done enough. But she must have known.

I can't turn around. If he's dead, I don't want to know.

All I can do is wait. I've sacrificed so much for this. Phoebe for one. And what Dittus did to me at the premiere... that had sealed it. It cannot count for nothing.

I'd make it. Despite everything. To spite everything.

Some moments I wasn't sure if I wanted him to fall on me and embrace me as the daughter he'd abandoned, or if I wanted to kill him. I wasn't even sure when I got on the plane.

Either way, success was the only way forward.

Here I am. And I don't want him to die. Since I heard those two people on the plane, all I've wanted is to save him. Just in case it was him they were targeting.

All I've ever really wanted, is Dad back.

47

My head aches and I don't think I've ever been this thirsty. I can't even open my eyes; my lids are glued shut. I've been curled up in this position for I don't know how long, and there's a ringing in my head now, as sharp as a blade.

Nothing makes sense anymore, and I wish I'd called Mum before I set off last night. I wish I'd told her everything. If I die here, and she has to unpick the mess of the body with my name on it in New York, then realise it's not me, she'll break.

And Phoebe's family. To hear she died in the desert, then find the body isn't her, and give them hope. What an end for both of us.

And it's all my fault.

The ringing is louder. Then a buzz.

I haven't checked on Hanneghan. I can't know he's dead, not after everything. I need to believe he can still be saved.

The buzz is louder now. A real hum in the air.

Then a shout.

'Over here!'

Trembling, I tug at the blanket covering the buggy. As it falls, sunlight pours into our space, drenched in sand, and my eyes sting.

'Phoebe!' A figure stands over me. Just a silhouette, but the most welcome thing I've ever seen.

I blink a few times, but I can't see who it is.

They bend, lifting the rest of the blanket and the sun hits me hard. I try to reach out, but even lifting my arm is an impossible task. The wind is still up, but it feels like there's a lull in the storm.

'Phoebe!' Another figure joins the first, and they kneel now. One passes me water, holding it to my lips, bringing me back to life.

One of them puts a cap on my head.

It helps me blink and look out.

'Josh, Kidz,' I say, but it's like a croak.

'Hanneghan's here too!' Kidz shouts.

I'm light-headed as I'm lifted up and into the back of a Land Rover. Kidz sits next to me, passing me more water, and running her hands over my arms and legs. 'Can you feel this? Can you squeeze my hand?'

'Is he alive?' I say, not sure I can bear the answer.

'Yes,' she says, softly. 'He's barely alive, but he's still breathing. I can't believe you've both been out here all night.'

I feel the throb of the engine start, and we begin to move.

I shake my head, and my throat burns as I speak. Josh and Lukas had known I was here. 'What happened? Why didn't you come and get me? All night…'

I can't compute them not looking for me. We'd all come out together. It doesn't make sense.

Kidz presses a wet cloth to my forehead, pouring fresh water onto my hair, and it feels like the best massage I've ever had. I still don't have enough water in me. Now that my throat is working again, I take a can of water from her and drink the whole thing down then reach for another.

We thought you were already back!' Josh says, through the window. 'I'm sorry. Oh my god, I'm so sorry.'

I shake my head. I can't work it out but it's hard to think after everything. 'You left me out there. When I didn't come and meet you – I thought you'd come. I waited. We waited.'

'They really did think you were already back. It's not their fault,' Kidz says. There's something in her voice. I look at her. She looks almost irritated. 'It's not the time, Phoebe, we can discuss this later, but drop the bullshit. You did come back. Plus there was evidence that Hanneghan was safe, that he'd left in a car from the hotel. We had no idea anyone was out here.' She changes the subject. 'Come on, there's time to discuss that. Let's get you safe.' She presses a button and the window closes on Josh.

The car moves quickly. Josh and Hanneghan are in the vehicle behind us.

The windows of the Land Rover are darkening in orange now. The wind must be picking up again.

I sit up front with Kidz, and I feel raw. The bumps on the sand make me flinch. I sip water and Kidz talks quickly.

I'm too tired to protest. The last few days have been bizarre – disconcerting. People talking to me about things I haven't done. Am I going mad?

'Some of the autopsy results came back. The police are at the hotel now. That's why they launched this search – we kept saying you were somewhere at the hotel and we thought that Hanneghan had left in a Land Rover, but no one could find you so they pulled additional officers. I doubt we would have found you in this storm otherwise.'

Cara had told me it hadn't been choking. 'Was it poison, in Marianne's blood?'

Kidz gives me a funny look. 'How did you know it wasn't

choking? Yes, they found something in her bloodwork. The same thing was in Augusto Dittus's blood. They checked him again once Marianne's results were in. She was killed. She died quickly, they think. There was a larger amount showing in her blood. They're doing more tests. It was the fact that it was made to seem accidental which has put the police on red alert. They came back to the hotel late last night to talk to Freddie and Cara. No one's allowed to leave. There are a lot more officers here now. Augusto's alcohol levels were very high, so initially they'd thought he was drunk. But after the results with Marianne, they went back to his body. It's a drug that manifests as alcohol – the test looks the same. Someone had given it to him before the drive. It's fast acting. With or without the accident, he was dead. In fact, Josh says he remembers Augusto slurring his words when he told you there was only fifteen minutes of the journey left. The chances are that his driving response to the gazelle was so extreme because he was already losing consciousness.'

I feel cold and hot, all at the same time. What I'd done hadn't made a difference. I don't know how I feel about that. Part of me had wanted to be responsible for his death. I feel cheated, and also released. But who put the poison in his blood?

Kidz passes me more water. 'Here, you're still looking pale.'

'So the accident didn't kill him?'

'No, apparently not.'

The funny look is back on her face. I'd spent so long trying to cover up the fact I made up the gazelle and released his seatbelt, that it only just occurs to me now, it was Josh and me in the car with Augusto.

'Oh.' A jolt of fear makes me sit up. 'You don't think – they don't think – that it was Josh or me who gave him something?'

As I glance outside, I catch a glimpse of a police car following us.

'Kidz?' I prompt.

That expression is back on her face. She's not quite meeting my eye. 'What is it?' I start shivering now. I'm even colder.

'Look, we need to get your body to start regulating itself. Don't talk. We're back in a few minutes.'

I push the cloth from my head, and try to make her look me in the eye. 'What? What is it? There's something you're not telling me.'

She looks away, picking up some kind of energy gel and ripping it open, holding it out to me.

'They didn't come, because you were already back at the hotel.'

'But I was here! How many times can I say it?'

Kidz is silent for a second. She doesn't look at me. Then she says, quietly, 'You were accounted for. A Land Rover was missing, so we thought Hanneghan must have driven away. There was some CCTV footage of the Land Rover driving in the opposite direction. No one knew you'd come back here. No one knew Hanneghan was here. No one understands. And now you're lying. I don't know why you're lying, but Augusto and Marianne have been killed, Hanneghan is almost dead, and now you're lying. Freddie and Cara are looking like the main suspects, but now there's you. The lying. What else are you hiding?'

48

'The doctor wants to fly you all to the hospital as soon as the storm has passed. It's calmed a bit, but it's still really bad on the road. The IV should help you. It's mainly dehydration he's worried about. Your body temperature seems to be regulating.' Kidz is brisk. She's not unkind but the friendly face I'm used to has been replaced by a more business-like mask.

I lie in my hotel room, and I can see the edge of a police officer's uniform outside my door.

'Kidz, you can't really think I killed Augusto or Marianne.'

Josh had been kind, but every other face I'd seen had smiled, but seemed wary.

'It was Pablo's name on the note, but it must have been Freddie: his affair with Cara; he was rough with her, so he could be violent; he'll inherit and he's short of money, it will solve his funding issues...' The last one I had been thinking about last night. It *must* be him. 'He asked Hanneghan to meet him out near the tents – to leave him for dead in the desert.'

'Look, no one knows what's going on. Pablo was locked in a changing room at the pool. We found him and let him out after Josh and Lukas got back. He didn't lock himself in there, and it wasn't him who lured Hanneghan out to the desert. He maintains someone tried to kill him. Then the three of you go looking for Hanneghan, can't find him. You come back when the storm starts up. Then *you* go back out, and the next day we find you out with him, sheltering under a blanket. What, did you find Hanneghan and both of you decide to head out? Or did you not find him, then head out on your own to look for him again?' Kidz sits on the edge of my bed, her head cocked and waiting for a reply. 'I want to believe you did a good thing, Phoebe.'

'But I *didn't* come back. I was looking with Josh and Lukas, and I found Hanneghan, but we fell off the buggy and I couldn't go any further. I was waiting for them to come and get me. There was no signal.' None of it makes any sense. I want to cry with frustration. 'We said we'd alert the hotel if one of us was missing. They didn't do that!'

Kidz says nothing for a second. 'Phoebe, you were swimming in the pool. It was dark, but there were enough lights; I know what I saw. Josh and Lukas came back as they couldn't find you and the wind was picking up. They came back to get more people to help come and look.' She shakes her head. 'I was so worried about you. Then I saw you swimming in the pool, and I shouted, and you stood up and waved. You called out you just needed to cool down, and you'd come and find me in a bit.'

My head is so thick with confusion – the events of the last twenty-four hours are overwhelming and it's like I'm caught in a twilight zone somewhere.

'But I was in the desert, the whole time.'

Kidz shrugs. 'I don't know why you're lying. It wasn't just me. Pablo saw you too. And Cara. Cara was the one who told me you wouldn't be down for dinner because you had a headache. We were all stressing about where Hanneghan had gone, and then Lukas suggested we check the cars. The hotel saw one was missing. When we checked the CCTV, the car was seen driving out across the desert, but the opposite way from where the tents are. We assumed Hanneghan was leaving. The police sent a car to search for him.'

Cars, CCTV, deserts – it's a jigsaw, the one thing which I know for sure is where I was. 'Look, I *know* I was in the desert. You must have seen someone else, someone who looked like me. There's no other explanation.' A spark of hope flickers in my stomach, followed by fear. If…

'But that makes no sense. Who could look like you that much? There's only us here! Why are you lying?' I can hear anger in Kidz's voice now, and I get it. She's only going to be angrier in a second. But I have to tell her.

I let my accent fall away. It's been second nature these last few days.

'If there's someone here who looks like me, then the only person I can think it would be, is Phoebe Thomas.' I lie my head back against the pillow. It's all over.

'You're Phoebe Thomas,' Kidz says, as though I'm a child. 'Look, I'll get the doctor in to check you again, I think—'

'No.' I close my eyes.

I've lost.

Whatever happens, I've lost. But at least Hanneghan is alive. I didn't lose everything. 'I'm not Phoebe Thomas. I'm Ellie Miller.'

49

'm in deep shit. The deepest kind there is.

Kidz takes a long look at me. Then she steps back. She doesn't say a word, but turns and leaves the room.

The door bangs behind her.

I don't have long.

If Augusto was killed by some kind of poison, then they'll assume it was Josh or me. We were the ones in the car with him. But a few people went to talk to him when we landed. I remember Pablo heading over to him, and he's been vocal about what happened to his brother.

And if Phoebe is alive, but hasn't told me, and hasn't been answering my messages, then I'm in trouble. She must have worked some of it out. Even all of it. I'd guess she'd have felt better hours after I left. I didn't put anything in her food or drink that morning. Once the effects had worn off, she'd be back to feeling like herself that afternoon. When I'd still been in the air.

If she's worked it out... Felix must be in on whatever she's doing. He was clearly playing his part when he implied she'd been killed.

I've checked the news enough times. There are no reports of a woman hit by a bus. No mention of it on the diner's social media page. They thought that up to throw me. They must know what I've done.

What happens next?

How long has she been here? Anyone seeing her would assume it was me. Even the hotel. It wouldn't be strange to have a guest arriving by taxi – they would have assumed I'd been out on a quick desert trip, or even a longer trip. No alarm bells would ring. And the hotel is empty apart from us. All these rooms, so many places to hide. And all she has to do not to be noticed, is not be in the same room as me at the same time. She can order food and drinks from the bar. All of it is charged to the company. Even sleeping – she could easily ask for a different room. Or fall asleep in one of the unused bars, shower at the pool. She could have been here the whole time, for all I know.

It must be her. She must be here. The manager – he'd asked me a question I didn't understand: he'd asked if I'd found what I was looking for when I hadn't been looking for anything. It made no sense. I'd assumed he confused me with someone else – it makes sense now. It's happened a few times.

There's no way Josh and Lukas would leave me out in the desert unless they honestly thought I was back at the hotel. Seeing is believing.

I have a brief window. I have to fix this. I have to find Phoebe. Because she's obviously not dead. The woman under a bus was a harsh move – but I deserved it.

Phoebe is here and has started messing with my head.

How angry she will be, I don't know. But I stole from her – I stole her big opportunity, and I twisted our friendship.

If she's looking for vengeance, if she's angry, then I need to find her and apologise – beg forgiveness and get her to clear this mess. But there's still something else going on here. Whatever happened to Hanneghan wasn't Phoebe. She has no reason to hurt him. And whoever got him into the desert and left him to die is still in the hotel. Whoever killed Marianne and Augusto is still in the hotel. The two voices I heard on the plane.

I'm sure it's Freddie. He must have wanted to get rid of Hanneghan if he saw how Cara felt about him. And Cara, if she was the other voice, had tried to pull out of the pact on the plane. They must have decided to kill both their partners. Maybe there were huge sums involved.

But there was something else. I remember the flicker of something in the back of my mind when I'd been talking to Kidz before we'd left for the desert. The flash of yellow; her yellow scarf. Where had I seen that before?

Of course – when I'd almost gone to Freddie's room by mistake. No one had answered the door, but then I'd seen someone leaving. And the call to cancel the cars to collect us from the desert had come from that room. Is Kidz the one who killed Marianne? But why target Hanneghan – had he seen something that night in the desert? So many moments, ticking over in my brain.

The clock is counting down. They'll all assume it was me. Of course they will. I needed to save Hanneghan, still need to save him, and make amends to Phoebe.

I've now got to save myself.

50

There's no going out the door. I pull out the IV and tape over my arm and dress as quickly as I can. My body is bruised and stiff after these last few days. I have countless cuts and scratches, and I'm still light-headed. But I have no choice. It's all stacked against me.

I pull on shorts and a t-shirt, then I head to the balcony.

The wind is up. Once the balcony door is open, sand and heat push me backwards, and I flail for a second. But I rally. I have no choice. I remember Augusto's hot breath on me and if I can get past that, then I can do this. Even if I didn't kill him, then I fought back at last. It makes no difference what the final cause was. He attacked me and I got my own back.

I can fight my corner now. I don't know who it is – who took Hanneghan into the desert and who killed Marianne – but whoever it is could land me in jail.

Pulling the door closed behind me, I hold my breath, looking at the sand spinning in the air over the pool. The umbrellas and loungers are all gone, either lying flat or stacked up and put away.

For a moment, I freeze. Can I do this?

Of course I can. I give my hair a shake. I dress for the job I want. You can do anything if you can fake it. Even climbing over balconies and discovering murderers.

I'm not too far from the ground, which helps, but I count roughly where Josh is and I start the climb.

No one is outside due to the weather, and even if they were looking outside, it would be difficult to see me. I've tied a damp scarf around my face to stop the worst of the sand clogging up my airways, but it means I can't breathe as deeply as I usually would, and when I put one foot over the balcony ledge my chest becomes tight.

Slowly.

My foot slips and I fall quickly, only just managing to grab the ledge as I go. I swing for a second, my chest aching as I force myself not to breathe too deeply or too quickly.

Pulling myself up until I can swing my leg up and take some weight on my knee, I stop and count to ten in my head.

Going again, I manage to get my foot over the next balcony. They're close to each other rather than adjacent, giving each room a sense of privacy. It makes it much harder to climb, but I manage one, then two.

I'm almost there.

Come the fuck on! My legs pull heavier and heavier. My head aches and my chest feels at breaking point.

Last one.

I take a huge step, straddle on the edge, then jump. My fingernails dig as I grab the edge of the balcony and I force my head forwards, to get the weight right. Once I'm steady, with my feet on the balcony ledge, I count to three and pull myself up and over.

Tipping forward headfirst onto the balcony floor, I swear as my shoulder jars. I can't remember where the injury came from at this point, but I think it was falling from the buggy after our camel ride. Or falling in the desert.

I will not cry. I hold it tight as I stand, my scarf slipping down from my mouth, and sand swarms in like bees.

Please, Josh, be in.

Banging on the windowpane of his balcony door, I can't even call his name. My chest is so tight I could pop.

I bang again. If he's in the restaurant, or the bar, I'm going to have to smash the door. I look around for something to use, but my vision is littered with tiny black dots and I've used up most of my reserves getting this far.

Grabbing the coffee table by the lounger, I try to lift it. But it's marble and brass. It's too heavy.

Falling against the glass, I push my face up and bang with both hands.

Like a mirage, Josh's face appears from the inside. The lights are on in his room and his is the best face I've seen in as long as I can remember.

'Phoebe!' I see his lips move rather than hear his voice, but the wind is loud now, rustling palm trees and clattering anything not pegged down.

He slides the lock, and the doors open.

I fall in with the sand and the weather, and as I trip and lie flat on the ornate rug, a silence and stillness falls in the room as Josh closes the door.

'What the fuck is going on?'

51

'Josh!' I cough out his name, and it takes a moment of slow breathing before I can speak normally. The softness of the rug underneath my battered body is like a mother's hug. But I'm nowhere near done yet.

'What the fuck are you doing? You know you shouldn't be out in the sandstorm. This one is bad – I think they said something about a dust storm as well. I don't know. The point is, what the fuck are you doing outside, and why didn't you use the door?'

He pulls me up by the arm, and the room spins for a second as I blink the sand from my eyes.

'I can't be seen in the hotel. You must know what they're saying.'

'Look, Ellie. English Ellie. I was freaking out when we couldn't find you. When you didn't come back, we waited, but we couldn't see anything and it was getting dark. We decided we needed to go back to the hotel to get help. Then we get back, Kidz tells me you were already there and had gone for a swim! That's messed up.'

His arms are folded and I can see how angry he is.

'I didn't come back.'

He shakes his head. 'What? Yes, you did. I mean, I didn't see you, but Kidz did, and Cara. I was pissed off, so I didn't come looking for you. Then the missing car was discovered, and we assumed Hanneghan had driven away. The police were here by then. It doesn't look great for him – trying to run away. For either of you, to be honest.'

I grab the water jug on his table and lift it, knocking most of it back. I still can't shift the sand from my throat.

'It wasn't me.' I flop onto his sofa. No point wasting my energy when I'm explaining. I'll need that in a minute. 'Look, you remember I told you I'd switched places with my friend?'

He nods, and sits too. His arms unfold and I can see he's really listening.

'I got a message from a friend, which I thought meant that Phoebe had been killed. I was devasted, and kept checking the news, but there was nothing about it anywhere. If everyone thought I was dead, they surely would have contacted someone back at home – my mum. But they didn't. My friend must have made it up. To mess with my head.'

I finish the water in the jug. Almost back to normal. 'The point is, it's her. She's here.'

Josh's eyes dart to the door, then back to me. 'She's here?' He looks hesitant, then carries on. 'The police asked me about Augusto. They said he was poisoned before the accident.'

I keep reliving the release of the seatbelt catch as I'd pressed it, how I'd willed him to fly forward through the windscreen.

'They think I poisoned him,' I say. Not a question, but he nods anyway.

'They don't know anything for sure, but we were the last ones to see him alive. I told them we just sat in the back seat. Neither of us gave him anything to drink. I've told them that.'

Thank God for Josh. 'Thank you.'

'It's the truth. The accident is fuzzy in my head, but you lay on that seat exhausted. Until the accident, you didn't move.'

'But someone did. I saw Pablo go and speak to the driver. I've been focused on Freddie. But really, it could be Pablo. Maybe it *was* him who wrote that note?' I try to remember exactly what I'd seen as we'd got off the plane. I'd been so slow as I felt so shit.

'Yeah. There were a few of them. And Lukas too, I think.' Josh glances at the window, still coated with orange, as he speaks. 'But now they'll know that you were lying the whole time. It won't look good.'

I nod. 'We need to find her. We need to find Phoebe to clear my name.'

I say *we* and hold my breath, and his lack of objection is the sweetest non-sound I've heard all day.

'What's the plan?'

'Pablo is a good place to start. He had reason to hate the driver, and that nut incident – he could have fabricated it? He could have got hold of some, then exposed himself briefly, and used his EpiPen. Is that possible? Maybe he was doing a redirect?'

Josh stands up. 'Shall I go to Pablo's room?'

I pull myself up too, and it feels like each bone cracks as I force myself to stand. 'And we need to check Lukas's room, just in case.' I keep the rest to myself. I've been wrestling with this.

Lukas and I had agreed to arrange an accident. But what if Lukas had taken it one step further? I have no idea how far he would have gone. I remind myself I don't really know him at all. Once we'd agreed on our plan, we had to make it seem like we didn't know each other.

What if he decided an accident wasn't good enough?

'The other thing that's been niggling me is the memory card. Kidz said someone took the memory card from the camera the night Marianne was killed. I remember Pablo had the camera that night. I hate to say it… But Kidz could be involved. I saw her outside Freddie's room the night the cars were cancelled. The call came from that room.'

'Lukas had the camera too, I remember him holding it. But Freddie had it as well? He had reason to kill Marianne. Oh it could be bloody anyone.' Josh grimaces.

'I'll start with Pablo,' I say.

'OK, I'll speak to Lukas.' Josh grabs a hoodie from the end of his bed. 'Here, put this hoodie on. They'll be looking for you.'

52

I push open the door to the stairway and strain to hear any sound at all.

Nothing.

Good to go. I run as lightly as I can down the smooth, marble-tiled stairs, praying I don't slip. I make it to the bottom, and push the door open. This leads to the lifts just off reception. It's the worst place to be spotted. Ducking into doorways if I see someone coming, and listening out for any hint of noise, I make it almost to Pablo's room. He'd been moved to the ground floor the other day. It's near Freddie's, where I hid earlier this week. I only remember this as I hear Freddie's voice, muffled by tapestries and carpet.

There are more police. The odd officer is stood outside a room. I can't get caught.

Fuck. I look left and right. There's no point running back to the reception area – too exposed. There's an alcove, with a large plant, by a window. Luckily, no one will be outside, so I press myself as hard as I can against the glass, and slide to the floor, behind the huge vase.

If he looks then he'll see me. I can only hope.

'…shitfest and the media will…' He gets louder, and then I see his feet walk away. Freddie is walking behind an officer leading him somewhere.

I count to ten and then I run to Pablo's room.

Raising my hand to knock, I see the door is open the tiniest fraction.

Why would he leave it ajar?

'Pablo?' I push the door open, and fuck...

Blood on a pale rug.

Pablo lying unconscious.

'Pablo!' I run and drop beside him, trying to identify where the bleeding is coming from. His wrists are slashed and there's a knife on the rug.

So much blood.

'Pablo!' I shout again, and tap his cheek, trying to wake him. I bend my cheek over his mouth and wait – the faintest of breaths.

What to use? There's a t-shirt discarded over the back of a chair, and I grab it, wrapping it tight round his wrists. I knot it and shout, 'Help!' No time to worry about being discovered now. I need to help Pablo.

But there's no one down this far. I'll need to go and find someone. Freddie's was the only other occupied room and I've just seen him leave. Who is doing this?

I double up on the t-shirt. There's an embroidered linen cloth on the coffee table, and I wrap it round his wrist – tying it tightly for pressure. Then I lift his arm up, propping it onto the sofa. Hopefully that will slow the blood flow.

'I'll go and get help,' I tell Pablo, though he's not listening. I'm not sure he'll ever be able to listen to anyone again.

'Oh my god!' There's a scream from the glass doors which leads to the pool.

I look up. A face I recognise almost as much as my own.

Phoebe's hands fly to her face, and she looks at me in terror.

'What the fuck have you done?'

53

Facing her, almost at the open glass doors, I stand in the room as the swirling sandy air, rushes in.

'Phoebe. I'm sorry... I... I don't know where to start, but I didn't kill him.' I look behind at Pablo on the floor. 'I'm not even sure he's dead. I just found him he—'

'Stay away from me!' Phoebe takes a step back. Her eyes go to the knife on the rug, then to me. I look down at the hoodie Josh lent me. A pale green, but now it's soaked in Pablo's blood. And I have his blood all over my hands.

'Phoebe, it's not—'

'Who the fuck *are* you, Ellie?' Instead of stepping further back she steps towards me.

For a moment we stare at each other, the wind whipping round us, and her eyes are wary. Large and scared. But Phoebe is made of courage and grit.

Then she takes a step forward, lunges low and dives past me.

I spin, not sure what she's doing. Then I see a flash of steel.

She's picked up the knife.

'Phoebe, it wasn't me!' I shout, but it seems to make no difference. We stand poised, neither moving, the knife between us.

I take a step back. She takes a step forward.

Behind her, Pablo lies stretched out on the floor, and I need to save him. I can't deal with this now.

This time she lunges.

As my hands stretch out first to save my face, I see a flash of light, reflected off the blade.

'Stay back!' she shouts, waving the knife.

As I flinch, I trip, and I fall to the floor.

I get up quickly, trying to ward her off. I'm almost outside now.

Shit. 'Look, Phoebe, it's not—'

'Don't you dare!' She braces herself, one foot forward, the other behind. Her hand holding the knife is thrust forward.

'Don't you dare tell me you didn't fucking drug me! I felt so much better the afternoon you left. Miraculously healed! Out of nowhere! And it made no sense.

'I called Felix. He came round and we went through the fridge. There were some overnight oats you'd made me the day before. I'd taken them to my room to eat when you were cleaning, but I'd put them back in the fridge for later. Felix knew someone, and we had them tested...' She stares at me for a second, like she's never seen me before. 'You were always so eager to clean up. I could never understand it – I hate cleaning. But I understand it now.'

'I...' I want to tell her it wasn't me, that I hadn't meant to, that I still loved her. But there's no point. I did it all. And if I did really love her, how could I have? I'm worthless, really, when it comes down to it. I hurt everyone. I'm like a lit torch singeing everything I pass.

'How could you? You were my best friend!'

I've never seen her looking like this – so angry, I believe she'll use the knife. It waves around, catching the light from the ceiling, turning red quickly as it reflects the blood on the rug.

But I know about anger. I know that when you feel so powerless and so angry, you can kill. It's what I'd tried to do to Augusto. I hadn't even managed that.

Tears fall down my face. I've lost. I've really lost.

'No tears. What, you think I'll feel sorry for you? You stole this. All this.' She gestures at the hotel, the luxury. 'My chance and you took it, and you made me think I couldn't do it.'

'I'm so sorry,' I say, and I can't stop the crying.

She takes a step towards me, the knife waving. 'You deserve to burn, Ellie Miller!'

I see the blade coming towards me, and I manage to sidestep. I grab her other arm, and I pull her hard, trying to tip her to the floor. I need to hurry this up – we need to save Pablo.

She screams, pulling me back.

We fall, flying fast towards the doors to the pool. Then we roll. I see the knife flash, and I try to grab her wrist, but then she's on top of me, and she hits my face hard with the back of her hand.

My cheek is like fire, and I push her with everything I've got left.

We roll again. Sand is thick in the air and it's hard to see. I scramble up, and spin left and right. I can see her, but I can't see the knife.

'Come here!' she screams.

Instead, I run.

'Where are you going?' she runs after me, and I hear the whack of something falling. I kick whatever it is, and it sends me spinning. I fall over with a crash.

'You bitch!'

She hits me full force, and we fall together, rolling over the edge of the pool, into the water.

I'm flooded. Water is in my ears, up my nose. Chlorine stings my cuts and scratches and as I kick out to get to the surface, I strike against her.

Phoebe is in here with me. I need to get back to Pablo.

Thrusting my head up into the air, I take a huge gasp. But I'd forgotten about the sand, and my throat immediately tightens; I start coughing.

There's a pressure on my neck. Phoebe emerges next to me, one arm grabbing at my throat. I start to go under.

'No!' I shout. Water splutters out of my nose as I manage to swim up. 'No, stop! We don't have to do this. I'm sorry. I know what I've done is awful, but I had to come. I just had to.'

Her face is up against mine now. The eyes I've studied, the expressions I've copied. This one is new. Rage and fury.

'No fucking way did you!' She hits me again on my cheek, and I give up. I push back, swimming away, enough to hold the side. Then I stop.

'Go on then. If you want to kill me, kill me. I am so sorry. I know I deserve it. I just had to come. All my life I've waited to get close to him.'

'Him? Who?' She's only inches away.

'Hanneghan. Elijah Hanneghan. He's my dad, Phoebe. He left when I was eight, said he was never coming back. But I had to see him again. It's all I've ever wanted.'

54

I can barely lift my arms to the side of the pool, never mind pull myself out.

Phoebe pushes herself up first, then stares at me. 'Oh, for fucks sake,' she says. Then she watches me try to drag myself out.

We sit on the side of the pool, coughing.

'We need to get inside,' I say, my chest tight and pressing. I gesture back to Pablo's room and we get up.

I pull the door closed behind us, and we stand soaking, dripping on the carpet, trying to catch our breath in the sudden silence of stepping out of the storm.

'You must have real issues – you believe Hanneghan is your dad?' She's still angry, but she's not holding the knife anymore. I can't see it anywhere. The sting and the anger between us has quietened. She looks more like the Phoebe I know. The rage of the moment has dimmed. Now things are calmer, I doubt she would really have hurt me. Or maybe she would have hurt me. I doubt she would have killed me.

'I just wanted to try and get close to him. He doesn't know me. I only met him a handful of times before he stopped coming. I've always wondered about him. I've never felt... whole. Since he left...'

She says nothing for a moment.

'I am so upset. I loved you, Ellie. Whatever shit is going on in your head, I loved you.'

'I'm so sorry. It was never about you. I wasn't expecting to find a friend like you. I wasn't expecting any of it. What I've done is unforgiveable. I don't expect you to believe me – but there's no time right now for this. Pablo is needs our help. Can we do this later?'

She coughs.

'Come on, we need to get help. I promise, it wasn't me who hurt him. I was trying to help him.'

She looks doubtful and uneasy, but she nods. It's obvious Pablo needs our help, whatever I've done.

Slowly, like dolls running on empty batteries, we cross to Pablo and kneel beside him. His arm is still up on the sofa but he's very pale.

'I thought you'd stabbed him,' Phoebe says, still hesitant. Still looking at me with suspicion.

'No.' I try to find his pulse. 'I totally understand you might not believe me, but I didn't. Someone tried to kill him the other day, and I wasn't sure if I believed him or if he'd set it up to look like that. But I think we have our answer now.'

I check his pulse. 'He's still alive. Can you run to the front desk? He needs a doctor quickly.'

'Where are you going?'

'There was a memory stick missing, from a camera that Pablo and Lukas had been looking at. And Pablo and Lukas were the two people talking to the driver before he got into the car.' I have a flash of the scene. Lukas heading over with cans of water. Handing them out. There's Kidz too, but she was nowhere near Dittus.

'What does that mean?' Phoebe says, looking from Pablo to me.

'Maybe Pablo snapped something that showed Lukas with Marianne. Maybe it was Lukas who killed her. I just have no idea why.'

'I'll get help,' Phoebe says, her eyes wide now. 'I'll phone the front desk.'

'Yes. I'll go too. Josh might need...' Josh. He was going to see Lukas. My heart aches at the thought of something happening to him. He's been my friend, my protector.

'Josh?'

I smile at her, so close and so far away. 'My other best friend.'

Then I run.

55

'Josh,' I shout, banging on Lukas's door. 'Josh, are you there?'

There's a silence so crushing I can hear my heart beat in this empty corridor.

'Josh!' I bang again. Someone must hear. Someone must come.

The door opens a crack, and I throw my weight up against it. I fall in, rolling on my shoulder. I wince, but I'm up quickly. I have no idea what I'll see.

Lukas.

Thank God there's no Josh.

My heart freezes in my chest as Lukas stares at me with an expression I haven't seen before. He moves his hand – he's holding a knife. It's similar to the one I saw on Pablo's floor, and words die in my throat.

A kitchen knife. There must be a fully stocked chef's range of five-star implements at the hotel. There for the taking.

Even though I've reasoned this out, I don't believe what I'm looking at. Lukas. Young, focused on meditation and peace. Helpful. Even after our conversation in New York. He's been hurt like I've been hurt. I've felt so sorry for him. How could *he* be the one?

'Don't move, Phoebe. Stay right there. I've made it so we can both get away now. Pablo will take the fall. I signed his name on the note for that reason. And it will look like he's taken his own life. Don't worry. It's all under control.'

Barely breathing, I nod slowly.

'You've been to Pablo's, I see.' Lukas looks me up and down. Josh's sweatshirt clings to me; I'm soaking wet from the pool, but it hasn't washed away the blood. I'm drenched in it. 'I hear he cut his wrists. He used a kitchen knife, like this one.' He waves it in the air. 'I wore one of his caps to get it from the kitchen.' He stares at me defiantly. 'CCTV will see him taking it.'

'Pablo.' I remember he had been looking at the camera that night in desert. 'Was there something on the camera, did he see something to do with Marianne?' My words stop and start I'm so nervous about jolting him. Upsetting him. I still barely move a muscle.

'Clever thing, aren't you. But I knew that already. Yes. That night. In the desert.' He looks sad, for a second. 'You know I didn't want this. I wanted Augusto dead. Hanneghan dead. But this has got out of hand.' He morphs from the killer before me, to the man I had tequila with in New York in the early hours of the morning. He looks no more than a child, really.

'And Marianne?'

He wipes at his face, and I realise he's crying. 'She saw me. I had the syringe out, for Hanneghan. I cancelled the cars, pretending to be Marianne. I needed time. Then I was going to leave him. I was going to drag him further out, and leave him to die. Once he was dead, it was up to fate to work it all out. The drug is a good one. It just seems like alcohol poisoning, and it's gone in forty-eight hours. He used to be an alcoholic. I thought if I left some whiskey...'

We stare at each other. 'So, what, Marianne saw you with the syringe?'

He nods. He's stopped crying now. He wipes at his face, angry and sore. 'I had gloves on, ready, and I could see Hanneghan. I was walking towards him when Marianne came out of the dark, and asked me what I was doing, if I was OK. She looked down at the syringe, and I just panicked. I looked at her. She looked at me and the gloves. Again at the syringe. Hanneghan was a little way off. I grabbed her, dragged her backwards with my hand over her mouth until we were out of view, then I pushed it into her instead.'

Fuck.

'I hadn't meant…' He looks at me. 'I don't think I'll get over it. But then it was done. And now I just need to get out of here.'

I can't believe what I'm hearing.

Lukas looks down. 'My dad cried a lot. Afterwards, when Mom was gone. Months and months of silence, being distant. The doctors tried antidepressants. Friends tried to get help. But nothing.

'I know it was Hanneghan in that car. I remember seeing his face, his eyes were closed. He'd passed out behind the wheel. To this day I don't think he has any recollection that he hit us. There was a bump, and his car swerved and carried on. He was almost slumped over the wheel when it happened. I guess the bump woke him up. There was no proof. I said I thought it was him, but Augusto was in charge of the investigation. I told Augusto I thought it had been the movie star. He did nothing. He used it to help himself. He burned the car. Said it had crashed further up. He must have taken Hanneghan to safety.'

He stops, swallows hard. 'When the police arrived, once I'd said goodbye to Mom, I thought there would be some kind of justice. But nothing. When the car was found crashed and then burnt out, Augusto said it had been stolen from the film set. He

304

said he found the car empty. He lied, and our family crumbled. They killed Mom and ruined Dad. All of a sudden, Augusto was Hanneghan's number one bodyguard and driver. Never left his side. He got his ticket to fancy planes and hotels. I don't know how much Hanneghan remembers, or even knew. But he deserves to die. He was so pissed the whole time, he remembers nothing. Hanneghan is the murderer and Augusto allowed him to walk free. Between them, they killed her and skipped justice.'

'Look, we need to tell the police. We can explain about Augusto…'

'Don't fucking move!' Lukas changes from vulnerable to terrifying in a flash.

I freeze again. I stumble around for words. I need him to calm down. 'Who was the other one?'

'Other one?'

'I heard two people on the flight, planning to kill someone. If one was you, then who was the other person?'

Lukas's face breaks into a smile, and he laughs. 'Ha! Yes. I was worried if Hanneghan died you'd suspect me. We'd planned to kill Augusto together, so I needed to throw you off track. I saw you go through to the back of the plane, and I went in, and performed a conversation, as though there were two of us. I knew that would confuse you. You'd never suspect me then. All your talk of Karma and manifesting. I needed to give you something you'd believe in.'

My mouth drops open.

Lukas twists his face and lifts his chin, his voice changing. *'That storm was vile! Mock me, but the universe is saying no!'* He laughs. 'Did you like my performance? Was I convincing? I thought the universe thing was a nice touch. Marianne is known for her superstitious ways. And Kidz kept crossing herself on the flight during the storm. It could have been any of them.' He shrugs. 'It worked. You didn't think it was me. You thought there were another two people planning murder. I mean, *as if*.'

'Now I've covered everything. It will seem like Pablo went off to slash his wrists after trying to kill Hanneghan. I've left the rest of the poison in his room. There're no loose ends.' Lukas talks almost to himself. With his spare hand he rubs his face, frowning. He jiggles the handle of the knife in his hand. He plays with it loosely like it's nothing more than a car key. Then he looks at me. A raise of the eyebrows, and he takes the smallest of steps.

I'm out of options. I scan the room, and I do the only thing I can think of. I press the fire alarm.

56

Piercing and loud, the alarm wails into the room. It's transformative for Lukas. He spins on the spot and lifts his arms high, shouting, 'No! Why the fuck? They'll come and check the room. I'm trying to help us…'

The alarm is relentless. Even if you wanted to ignore it, you couldn't.

I don't want to rush at Lukas and risk forcing him to panic more. Pablo lies bleeding in his room. I know Lukas won't hesitate to kill again. I need to be careful.

Diving at me, Lukas grabs my arm and twists it up behind my back. He pulls the knife up against my throat, then pushes me forward towards the doors to the pool. He's surprisingly strong, and I stumble, but he holds me upright.

He swings me round to the side, then strikes out with his foot, kicking the doors wide open. He takes a huge gulp of a breath, and pushes me out, back into air thick with sand, and I would take my chances out here any day of the week and twice on Sundays if Hanneghan lives. Lukas could be going after him, even now. To finish him off. I make a deal to any god listening: I will be better, kinder, more generous, less obsessive, repentant… The list runs through my head.

We move out, and I can see a few figures, hazy through the sandy air, leaving by the pool doors. I hear shouting.

Lukas pulls me tight, pulling my hair; the blade is sharp on my neck. I feel it nick the skin. Sand is in my throat again. I can't regulate my breathing. I can't do anything. I feel dizzy.

'Come on. We need to get out of here.' Lukas's voice is rough in my ear, and he drags me backwards, pulling me towards the exit for the courtyard that leads to the garages. I stumble, my feet scuffing along the tiles; the sand blankets everything. I hope someone sees me – I'm desperate for them to see me. But the few people I see are running away from the building because of the fire alarm. They're not looking at me, they're looking at the building, to see where the fire is. Staff leave via different doors. There's a cluster of people in the courtyard. I can see a police car parked there, by the hotel entrance. The officer with the kind eyes – I summon him up. I manifest him here, right now.

Then we stop. Lukas pulls an arm away from me and I hear the car door open. The hand with the knife at my neck is still tight, and there are tiny black dots in my vision.

'Get in,' he hisses.

He spins me and pushes me forward. A Land Rover. He shoves me hard, and I bang my knee as I fall into the passenger seat.

He runs to other side, and I take my chance. I lean in to the wheel, and am just about to land on the horn when he jumps in and jabs at my hand with the knife.

I've not been fast enough. He hasn't made it into the driver's seat, but he managed to get the knife in ahead of him, and my first finger is sliced open. Blood flows down my arm and I can see a flash of white through the cut. It's gone deep.

'Think you'll ever play the piano again?' Lukas says. 'Is it one of the special skills all you actors lie about on your resume?'

I grab my finger in the fist of my other hand and close it tight.

I don't recognise this man. The man who cried when he told me about his mother. Who was nervous about the role. He'd only seemed a boy. His actions have changed him. He's changed. Or maybe I never knew him at all.

His glib remarks spark a brief flash of familiarity, and despite everything, it makes me stop and think. Why do I recognise that? And then it comes to me. It's me. Of course, it is. He's covering, he's masking. He's dressing for the job he wants. The real Lukas is in there, caught up in circumstances he feels are out of his control. I see myself there. Am I as bad as him? I'm stuck still for a second – I need to change.

I was almost him. If I'd allowed the rage to consume me. If I had come here to kill Hanneghan. And I thought about it. It's crossed my mind more than once. The anger, the abandonment I've felt. It's formed me. I drugged Phoebe, and I caused the car accident.

This stops now.

I wonder if I'll see Hanneghan again. And Phoebe. She's alive, but she hates me, which I'll take. And Josh. He'll hate me when he knows the full truth.

Resting my head back against the seat, I try to blank out all the pain.

'Where are we going?' I need to get him talking. I can't give up. I'm not ready to die.

'If I'm going to be honest here, I have no fucking clue. We're going away.' Lukas glances at me. 'Pablo must be dead by now. I just need to dump you somewhere they won't find you. I can hire a plane. I can get out of here. I could have taken you with me, but pulling that alarm showed me that I can't trust you. I've got enough money shored up. Hopefully they'll blame it all on Pablo and then I can always make a comeback. I can say Pablo chucked us both out in the desert and left us there – I made it, you didn't.' He's staring at the road again. We're going too fast for this weather. It's difficult to see ahead of the car for more than a metre or so. 'You know I sweet talked my way into this role. I heard Hanneghan was on the cast, so I thought, yeah, man, let's do it. You should have fucking thought about it a bit more – we could have left together.' His brow creases and he looks in the rear mirror, jumpy. It's impossible to see outside as the sand has thickened again.

'Slow down,' I tell him. I don't even know how he's seeing the road at this speed. 'Slow down!'

'What, you think we're going to hit a gazelle?' He laughs, like a bark. 'Grow up, Phoebe. Grow the fuck up. No one is coming to save you. Life doesn't work like that. You're on your own.'

'Lukas, please…' I run out of words. I'm too tired to cry. Blood leaks through my fisted fingers and the world spins. I won't be awake much longer.

There's a brief flash of something on the left.

I feel the car crunch, and Lukas shouts, 'Fuck!' I roll out of the seat, flying at Lukas, who is up against the car window. I hit my head, a good thump.

I go limp. Lukas pushes me off him, and I crumple between the seats. The Land Rover has stopped. He's not looking at me, and he's dropped the knife. He stares through the window, trying to see what we hit.

'What the fuck was that? Was it another car?' Lukas looks left and right quickly, searching through the front windscreen now, and his voice has risen in pitch.

The wind blows hard against us, and the orange is like paint. For a second it parts, and I can make out the edge of something – another car?

'Is it a police car?' I say, as loudly as I can, trying for distraction. I wave out at the sand. 'Look!'

Then I pull the door handle, haul myself up with one last wrench, and fall out of the seat, crashing to the road.

I'll take my chances with the sand. The wind is stronger here, without the protection of the buildings. I'm coughing quickly. But I lean into it, pulling the hoodie up over my nose. And I step forward, bent, trying to get far away.

'No, you fucking don't,' I hear him shout, but the strength of it is lost in the wind.

I take another step. This time I hear a different voice.

'Get your hands off her!'

I stop, stock still. Turning, I see her. Running full pelt at Lukas. He's only an arm's reach behind me, and she launches herself at him. The knife is back in his hand.

'Get off her!'

Phoebe.

It's the momentary distraction that saves us. There's a brief second where Lukas looks at Phoebe, then looks back to me. 'There's two of you?

Throwing her full running weight at him, Phoebe pushes him to the ground. I panic – for me she's only just been resurrected. She can't die now.

'Get back, Phoebe!' I shout. 'He's got a knife!'

On my knees, I crawl towards them. I'm so dizzy I'm not sure I'll make it, but I can see the knife. It's just out of his reach. His hand is padding round on the ground and he's almost on it. Phoebe sits astride him, and she must be with someone because she shouts, 'I've got him!'

Lukas manages to get the knife in his fingers, and as they close on it, I see Phoebe's face as he raises it, her chest wide and open.

Her eyes flash in fear. I hurl myself forward with everything I've got left, and I land on his hand, on the knife. There's a sharp pain in the top of my leg, and then I crash to ground.

We all roll off, Lukas lying an arm's length away, and Phoebe landing near me. My leg aches and stings. Everything spins.

'Ellie!' Phoebe kneels next to me, holding my hand. 'Oh my god, you're bleeding!'

'You came,' I say. 'You came to get me.'

'I did. I haven't forgiven you, and you might be a thieving fuck, but I can't let you die. I chased after you when the alarm sounded. I saw you leave in the car, so I jumped in one.' She grips my hand hard. Another figure appears, hazy in the sand. Maybe Cara? Phoebe says, 'She's been cut. Her leg, at the top.'

'I'm sorry,' I say, but she doesn't hear.

I see Lukas move to my left, the sand above my head.

The feel of Augusto in the car; the memory of Mum telling me Dad wasn't coming again; New York in the summer; the comedy club; the heat; the hope.

I sink again, into the blissful nothingness I'd known on the plane, before I'd landed in the desert, when I was mid-air, mid-identity, mid-journey.

'The helicopters think they can take off now.'

I'm bandaged up, hooked up to an IV. We all cluster in the huge lounge off the reception area. Pablo is on a stretcher, lying flat and barely conscious.

'Will he be OK?' I ask again.

Kidz smiles. 'The doctor thinks so. You saved his life. His pulse is strong.'

Josh sits with me, holding my hand. Passing me water every few minutes. He's still white as a sheet. He'd been called by an officer to answer a few questions and hadn't managed to get to Lukas's room before the fire alarm and he hasn't left my side since I've been back.

The mood is quiet. Shocked. The police have started interviews already. With the weather, the lawyers never came. But once Freddie understood that Marianne had been murdered, it all changed. He changed. He wants answers for his wife's murder. He fusses round us all, trying to smooth away his debris.

Cara sits next to me, offering me drinks and everything with sugar in it. She holds my hand and hasn't let go. Since Lukas has been forced to show his hand, she's off the hook. She'd jumped in the car with Phoebe without hesitation.

'You were so brave, Phob— sorry, Ellie. You were brilliant. What we would have done without you, I don't know. You saved Hanneghan. You saved his life.'

Originally the prime suspect for Marianne's murder, Cara is now in the clear and I've saved her ex-husband, the man it seems she still loves. Her gratitude knows no bounds.

'If there's anything I can ever do for you, you just say. I've chartered a plane for your mum and family. We'll contact them – get them out.' Cara squeezes my hand tight. 'Not on the company, on me.'

Mum. My eyes fill with tears.

'You can get away with identity theft on a film set, as long as you save a few lives and stop the wrong people going to jail.' Kidz winks.

'Who do we want first?' A uniformed medical officer shouts from the doorway.

'This one,' the doctor says, waving him over to where Pablo lies. 'You two on the other one.'

He says this to me and to Hanneghan, who is awake now, and stitched up, but so pale he's fading into the white sofa on which he lies. If only he had told someone about the note. But Lukas had known which buttons to push. By saying they could clear Cara's name, Hanneghan was a sure thing. He still loves her.

'You saved my life,' Hanneghan says as I stand, helped by Cara and Kidz. 'I can't believe it. I was heading out after reading the note then happened to bump into Lukas. He suggested we go out on the buggy. The next thing I remember is waking up here. I don't even remember him stopping the buggy.' He's lifted into a wheelchair. He looks round at us all. 'I'm not going to ignore it, you know. What Pablo said. I'll visit the area and speak to the police. If Augusto covered up something, I'll do my best to put it right. I would never have employed him if I'd known he could be capable of that. If there's a debt to pay, I'll pay it.'

I realise when he says this, that he doesn't know what Lukas was accusing him of. Pablo was angry because Hanneghan employed the man who covered up the hit and run of his brother. No one has any idea what Lukas thinks – that it had been Hanneghan behind the wheel.

Maybe it hadn't even been him. Pablo said there had been a rumour it had been someone famous. It could have been anyone with money. Augusto would have taken a bribe from anyone who could pay it. Who knows what Lukas really saw? The flash of lights in a car. There's every chance Lukas saw Hanneghan with Augusto later and his memory twisted it.

If anyone knows about memory's ability to twist things, it's me. Augusto is dead. His crimes will die with him.

The courtyard outside is still coated in sand, but the air is much clearer.

'You have to drink lots of milk, apparently. That's what the locals do. The manager was telling me,' Cara says, holding my arm. 'It flushes out the sand.'

Before we get on the helicopter, I look round for Phoebe. She's been with the police for some time, going over what happened with Pablo, with Lukas. Lukas had broken pretty quickly once the police had him. I don't know what's on the camera and the missing memory card, but Lukas does, and the photos were incriminating enough for him to try to kill Pablo. He must think there was no point holding out and denying anything.

'Ellie!'

Phoebe. I open my arms, but she stands a little way off. We have a while to go. I just hope we can find the trust again. We're no longer twin-like. The dye in my hair is fading. No make-up.

We look similar now, but the identikits are no more. Not really doppelgangers. No longer two halves of the same coin. Neither of us the evil twin. I can't really expect her to forgive me. Not after everything.

'They're bringing all of us for a check, but we're waiting for the boring ambulances. You get the helicopter ride.' She stares at me. 'I can't forgive you, you know. You broke my heart. But I'm pleased you're not dead.'

I suppose being pleased I'm not dead, is some kind of a start. I'll have to take it.

The helicopter is loud as we fly over miles and miles of desert. Hanneghan and I are strapped in at the back. We're both attached to IVs and there's a medic two seats up in case we need anything.

'Only another fifteen minutes,' the medic shouts, then he turns back to his radio, talking to someone somewhere about what we need, where we are.

I haven't talked to Hanneghan really, nothing beyond a *how are you*. I've not had the strength.

So, I'm surprised when he reaches out and takes my hand.

'Ellie, I'm so grateful to you.'

I nod, not really knowing how to respond to all the gratitude.

'But look, I want to talk to you quickly, before we get to the hospital, and then I don't see you for a few days.'

'OK.' My stomach clenches a little.

'Your friend, Phoebe, came to see me earlier. She said it will be hard for you to bring it up, so she wanted to tell me herself, to ease the way. She seems like a good friend.' He smiles.

Oh my god. Has she…?

'She said you seem to think I'm your father.'

I can't speak. It's like the dust is back in my throat.

Hanneghan squeezes my hand, and turns so he's looking directly at me. 'It's not true, Ellie. I don't know if your mom told you that for some reason, but I don't have any children. I can't have any children.'

My heart is thudding. After all this, how can he lie to me?

'But I remember you!' I practically shout at him, and I feel tears on my cheeks. 'You didn't come a lot, but you came a few times, before you stopped coming at all. I remember you, you took me to the zoo. You bought me a balloon. A red balloon.'

He doesn't look away. He holds my hand tight, but he shakes his head, gently. 'It wasn't me. If you only saw him when you were young, maybe he looked like me?'

My world tilts on its axis. All the longing for him. The queuing at the premiere. The attack. This trip. Stealing from Phoebe. It had all been about getting close to Hanneghan. About finding my dad. Only for nothing. This can't be true. It must have been him. It can't just be that I remember a resemblance.

I pull my hand away from him and turn my face. I can't bear for him to see me cry.

'It's fine,' I say, because what do you say when your heart is breaking.

'Of course it's not fine,' he says. 'I wish it was true, Ellie. You saved us. You're talented, kind, confident, funny, brave, beautiful… I'm always here for you, if you ever need anything. You saved my life. I'm indebted to you. But I'm not your father. I had an accident in my teens. I can't have children. Ask Cara – it was one of the things that drove us apart. It was one of the reasons I drank so much. I drank to push her away, to destroy myself. Now, maybe I see I destroyed others. I can't have any children, but if I did, I'd want them to be exactly like you.'

It makes no sense. He sounds like he's being honest. I wipe

my face and turn back to him. 'But my mum told me you needed to focus on your career, and didn't have time for a family. That's why you wouldn't be coming anymore.'

'Did she tell you it was me?'

I let the sound of the helicopter drown out the busy thoughts in my head. I try to remember. 'Well, no. She never said your name. But she didn't need to. I remembered. She used to get annoyed with all my posters of you, and me talking about you. And I thought that was because she missed you too. So I stopped mentioning your name.'

He nods slowly. 'How old were you?'

'I was eight when you stopped coming.'

He bites his lip. 'The balloons. The red balloon. Was it a sunny day?'

'Yes,' I say, slowly. I'm not sure where he's going with this.

'We saw giraffes. Was there a baby giraffe?'

'With a bandage on its leg,' I say. He remembers. 'I don't understand, you said it wasn't you.'

He takes my hand again. 'Did we go on the merry-go-round, and did I drop my ice cream?'

The whole thing. He remembers the whole memory. That's all of it.

I open my mouth, but words dry up. I feel like I'm about to be hit. My head buzzes. My vision is cloudy.

'That's my first big film, Ellie. I played the dad. And in the film, I tell my daughter I'm going and I might not come back. Then I go to war, and I die. I think you've made it your memory. If you were eight, then it will have been around the same time. It was my first big break. I'm so sorry, Ellie. I wish it wasn't true. But I'm not your father.'

Epilogue

Two Days Later

'Have you told her?'

'She's been in and out of consciousness. She needs rest. We've not wanted to—'

'But you have to tell her! You can't let her go on thinking that…'

The voices fade in and out. Every time someone official comes in my room I say I'm tired. I feign sleep.

The bed is so comfortable. My limbs still ache.

I drift off. Sleep comes easily.

The next time I wake, the voices are louder.

'I'm going in! I'm going to tell her. This is madness! Phoebe has told us what's been happening. She saved so many people. But we can't just leave her there, believing—'

'I understand how you feel, Ms Miller, I do. As Ellie's aunt, you get the final say. She's too old for a guardian, and it's really up to her. But my advice as a mental health practitioner is that we need to take this slowly. Together. There's too much to unravel. The original trauma has obviously not been dealt with, for delusions of this scale – what she tried to do this summer, well, she needs gentle handling. Real care. I would advise against—'

This time there are footsteps. Aunt Robyn comes in and approaches the bed. I won't catch her eye. I keep my lids pressed closed. I just can't. Not again. I'm so sleepy.

'But what do we do?'

The light in the room has changed. It's dark outside.

'Give her time, Ms Miller. Give her time. The attack, her father abandoning her, then her mother's death. Delusional disorder can be triggered by trauma. Her mind is creating a family out of nothing. You need to give her time. You say she's always refused therapy…'

I stop listening. Blood pounds in my ears. Lights flash behind my eyes. I'm so tired I can barely open my mouth to scream.

'…*her mother's death*…' They had said that. They can't be talking about Mum? My mum? They can't.

The edges of my memory lift a little, like a sticker unpeeling.

Sleep. I need sleep.

Three Days Later

'Ellie?'

I open my eyes. Aunt Robyn sits on the edge of my bed. So like Mum my stomach takes a punch and my throat catches.

'Ellie, are you awake?'

There's nothing for it. I can't lie here forever. They'll commit me.

I nod, and try to smile.

'Oh, Ellie.'

Aunt Robyn starts to cry, and I feel her arms around me. I'd clung to Mum all summer. Leaving the country had helped. I could suspend the fact she...

But that night comes back to me. It had been just after Easter. Mum had sat me down and delivered her sternest lecture so far on my need to get some therapy.

'I can see you're not happy, Ellie. I just wish I could help.'

I'd broken down, and I'd told her about Dittus's attack years ago. I hadn't mentioned Hanneghan – the attack was enough. I told her I felt his fingers on me still. That I couldn't forgive myself for being so stupid. So naïve.

I didn't tell her who it was, but I told her what had happened. What he'd tried to do. Even though I'd got away, I was still struggling.

We'd set off to the police station the next day. I'd been so upset, she'd leant over to touch me. She'd looked away from the road just for a second. A tree is all I remember. And then...

Then...

I'd found the magazine on a tube in the aftermath. I had to make it count. I'd been like someone on a mission. To find the man I thought was my father. To convince myself that Mum wasn't really dead. I'd just needed to get away. From London. From my life. From the truth.

'Oh Ellie. Christ. We'll get you some help. The film company has paid. All your medical bills. Plus compensation. You can stay here if you like. We can stay away from home for a while. A holiday. And you can see the doctor who's been looking after you. Do some talking.'

The problem with being able to talk yourself into a version of the truth, is that when you wake up to reality, it's like it's only just happened.

Two Weeks Later

Sitting up in bed, I'm surrounded by a breakfast for the stars. It doesn't taste the same. Nothing tastes the same.

'I still can't believe, all this time, you thought he was your father.' Phoebe sits on the edge of my bed.

I can't think of much to say to her. We talk over the events even though each time it's like I'm picking a scab.

'Robyn said my father is a married man, with a successful business and a family of his own. For all I know, he was the man in the bar who'd offered us a thousand dollars and a bottle of champagne to make out. I'll never know him.' I push pancake with maple syrup into my mouth, to stop myself having to say anything else.

Phoebe drinks a cappuccino from the hospital café. I stare into a void. A father out there I'll never know. A mum buried. Who am I now? Who can I ever be?

Just as the edges of darkness touch me, and I go cold inside, I force my eyes open. I look at the room. Out the window.

The hospitals here are amazing. Abu Dhabi looks stunning from the window.

And Phoebe. She's still here.

It's not easy. It will take work. I doubt she'll ever really forgive me. I'd like to get there again, but everyone I love leaves me or dies. Why would she stay?

At dinner time, Kidz visits.

She talks at lightning speed, so many questions, but I don't need to answer. I just have one to ask.

'How are you feeling?' she says. 'We're all living it up in a five-star hotel right now. All-day brunch on Friday. No more camels, thank God.'

'All-day brunch – unlimited champagne?' I ask.

She laughs and nods.

'But you didn't have any,' I say.

She shakes her head. 'What do you mean?'

'You didn't want to ride on the camel, you threw up in the desert. I haven't seen you drink a drop. You're pregnant, aren't you?' I'm pretty sure, and her face gives her away. Her mouth falls open, but she says nothing for a second.

'You picked it up from all that?' she finally says.

'And a few other things. I saw you coming out of Freddie's room. On that first night. You had a yellow scarf on, covering your head, and I saw it in your room. And his ease at screaming at you – in the way you'd only ever do if you'd been intimate with someone. The hurt on your face. Freddie's the father, isn't he?'

She lets out a long slow whistle. She stares at her hands, then looks out of the window. I can see the huge mosque from here. It's bright white, and it catches the sun. A wide expanse of blue, and huge roads, an ordered city. Not too busy, beautiful.

'I guess out of everyone you've earned the right to the truth.' She smiles. The rapid speech slows. The questions stop. 'It wasn't him I went to see. I still haven't told him. I will do – he has a right to know. We weren't together. He's good-looking – I mean, it's a fact, it's not in question. And his power and his insight into films… There are moments he's so attractive it's like a magnet.'

I nod. I've seen it. He can be compelling. And he can be a shit.

'Just once, and I was unlucky with the timing. One night, and then this.' Her hand goes to her stomach. 'Or lucky, depending on how you see it.'

'If it wasn't Freddie you went to see, then who?' I'm confused. I eat chicken which is soft and cooked in butter. I chew carefully as I wait for a reply. *Eat*, they all say. *Eat*.

'Marianne. I know it's messed up, but I planned to tell her first. She was always so kind to me. It just wasn't fair – not to her. I was pissed when he made his move. And he was Freddie Asquith-Smith. I mean, what do you do? I was flattered. You know what I mean? But the next day... Well, I felt like shit. But I couldn't tell her. I tried, over and over again. I went to see her, but it just wouldn't...' She stops.

Broccoli and some kind of bean sauce. I sip orange juice.

I swallow Kidz' words. Things click. 'You followed her. Went to her house. Called her with your number withheld – you were trying to tell about the baby. So, you were the stalker – that was you?'

Kidz grimaces. 'I called her, but I *had* to hide my number. I chickened out each time. She thought she was getting funny phone calls. And, yes, I went to her house. I wore a cap each time in case Freddie saw me. But each time I left. She thought someone was following her. I hate myself that I caused her the worry. But they never had kids, and I didn't want to blindside her with Freddie's. Who knows if they didn't want them, or couldn't have them. I just wish I'd been stronger. Freddie's announced he's stepping back. The affair with Cara has come to light, and he's taking a hit. A few other one-night stands have come forward. Like me, I suppose. No one likes a cheater, but now Marianne's dead, he's been dropped by most of the money in Hollywood. Also –' she shakes her head '– after what Pablo said, there's been an investigation into the car accident in Venezuela. It seems Freddie might have been the one to sign out the car that ended up in the crash. Nothing for certain yet, but if it was Freddie who was behind the wheel and who paid off Augusto, we won't see his face again.'

Pudding. Chocolate mousse with some raspberry thing on the side. We both eat and I watch the bright of the day drop to the dark of the night. Visiting hours end soon. It's an early dinner.

Before she goes, she leans in and takes my hand. 'I know you must feel like shit. Doing all of that, thinking you were chasing your father, just to lose him all over again. It must hurt.'

Tears spring to my eyes. Shame cuts sharply, quick and deep.

'But when it mattered, you were brilliant, Ellie. You saved us all. You did it. Without you, I don't know where we'd be. Try to focus on healing. Focus on you. Rest those demons.'

Cara visits. She's come out of the whole ordeal well. Freddie has been painted the villain and she is another victim of his promiscuity. The film has been picked up by another producer, with a new director on board to finish the project, in Marianne's memory. A legacy.

'Doppelgangers will sell!' she says, excitedly. 'Or twins – similar, but not the same. We'll put you both in! When you're strong enough. Marianne would have wanted it. You've earned your shot. Call me when you feel up to it. You'll be a star! Both of you.'

Phoebe visits again.

Her brother comes with her, arriving from Oman, and he recognises me straight away. I say sorry to them both.

Each time she comes there's a question, anger, upset. But she's been a few times now. Each time it's a little easier.

I'd called Felix and sobbed down the phone to him. I need to make amends. He'd been harsh and disbelieving. I'll have to work hard with him, but at least we're speaking now.

Just as she's leaving, she says, 'I still can't believe it, Ellie. That you could do that to me. I mean, I get why you did it – I suppose I've always taken my family for granted.' She stops. Then shakes her head like there's sand stuck in her ears. 'I'm so sorry about your mom. Your aunt is great. We've talked a lot. You know, this summer, you meant everything to me.'

Four Weeks Later

The night is dark and on my first night out of hospital, I'm meeting Josh for dinner. We're staying at the same hotel, but he'd insisted on taking me to a different one, on Saadiyat Island, with a beach.

Josh: turn-on-the-street-good looks.

'Sand, but also sea. Let's change things up,' he'd said.

The night is soft on my skin. Abu Dhabi is as beautiful in the dark as it is in the sun. There's music from the hotel behind me, and I sit at a table in the outdoor restaurant, overlooking the water. Lights pick out the odd boat. Citronella hangs in the air.

Josh has been there at each step. I see him at the other side of the restaurant, speaking to the waiter. He looks my way and catches my eye.

He smiles.

This summer. London, New York, Abu Dhabi. Ellie then Phoebe, now Ellie again. Blonde, with my hair a little longer.

And Josh. There's comfort in starting something new with someone who knows the worst parts of you, and still turns up. I don't know what will happen.

Take each day at a time, Robyn tells me. The therapist tells me.

I go to text Mum, then stop.

Truth, like sand, shifting.

Acknowledgements

A HUGE thank you to my agent, Eve White, and also Ludo Cinelli and Steven Evans.

Thanks also to Head of Zeus, Bloomsbury Publishing, for all that they do. Bethan Jones is an editor extraordinaire. The team is amazing: Peyton Stableford, Polly Grice, Jo Liddiard, Nikky Ward, Lydia Forbes, Jessie Price, Dan Groenewald, Rachel Rees and Emily Champion. Also, thanks to Sophie Ransom PR for her work.

A particular thank you to Tim Sullivan for his movie making knowledge. Many thanks to Nadine Matheson for her legal advice.

Thanks are due to Rachael Mason and Helena Thomas for New York research assistance. For Abu Dhabi, camel rides and an actual close brush with a gazelle, thanks to Matt and Jane Beniston.

On a trip to Syria years ago, I was caught in a sandstorm in a desert. I wish I could remember the name of the brilliant guide who got us through it. If you're reading this, then thank you. I was terrified.

I'm indebted to friends who offered editing advice: Kate Simants, Jo Furniss, Heather Critchlow, Ella Berman, Katherine Crowdell and Dominic Nolan. And many thanks to author friends for the company: Erin, Angela, Clare, Niki, Fliss, Lou, Harriet, Liz, Susie, Victoria, Barry-James, Rob and a lifeline of a WhatsApp group.

And thanks to Victoria Quinney for the coffee breaks.

A huge thank you to the best of friends, Aine Foley Magee. Missed every single day.

As always, love to my parents, sister and children. And to Rob.

About the Author

RACHEL WOLF grew up in the north of England and studied at Durham University. Before turning to writing, she worked for a holiday company and travelled widely. Her thrillers take inspiration from some of those travels.

Do you want more glamorous,
escapist thrillers from
Rachel Wolf?

'Agatha Christie meets *Succession*.'
JO FURNISS

'The perfect mix of *Glass Onion* meets *Death on the Nile*.'
SARAH GOODWIN

Available to enjoy now
in paperback, ebook and audio.